# THE STORM INSIDE

a novel by

*Alexis Anne*

*orm Inside* Copyright © 2013 by Alexis Sykes

: 978-0615888958
061588895X

by Alexis Anne
eposit Photos

the United States of America
pril 2016

# BOOKS BY ALEXIS ANNE

The Storm Inside
Reflected in the Rain
When Lightning Strikes
Never Let Go
Tease
Stripped
Tempt
Burn

Undressing Cara
Loving Rebecca
Kissing Owen
Filters

# PRAISE FOR *THE STORM INSIDE* & *TEMPT*

## *The Storm Inside*

"It was one of the best love stories I have read to date. The writing at times was so descriptive you could feel the love, pain, confusion and desperation between the characters."
*-Books Unhinged Book Blog*

"This book starts off with a BANG! Literally!! Their scenes together were so intense and the sex scenes were so hot, my whole body felt on fire." *-Lustful Literature*

"The sex was HOT! Jake melted me with his words."
*-Miscellaneous Thoughts of a Bookaholic*

"I loved the writer's portrayal of what life can throw at young love." *-Brenda's Book Beat*

## *Tempt*

"Very erotic" *–Cosmopolitan.com*

"This has truly been an awesome book and an amazing series." *–Books of Past, Present, and Future*

**To Nate~**

*I love you more than the mind can hide.*

## *Prologue*

$\mathcal{J}$ ake slammed my back into the wall of the shack, the boards of the wall bending and flexing from the impact. For a moment I worried we'd punch a hole right in the side of the building, but then Jake nipped my earlobe at the exact same moment he flexed his hips into mine, and I forgot everything I was thinking.

Everything but him.

I didn't think about the ten years he'd been gone or how much I hated him. All I could feel was his hard body pressed up against mine, his rough hands as they desperately roamed over my skin, and the intensity in his kiss.

We'd always made an explosive combination—that clearly hadn't changed. If anything, the added experience and time apart made what we'd had in the past look sweet and warm. Because this—what we were doing now— was off the charts insane. It was brutal and animalistic in the most fantastic way.

The afternoon thunderstorm was howling outside.

It was my favorite time of day, and Jake knew it. The thing about Florida's summertime storms was that you could *feel* them. When lightning strikes, the air crackles with electricity moving through everything around you. The moment it splits the sky, thunder vibrates so deeply it shakes the earth and every molecule in your body. You feel it everywhere.

Thunderstorms are a full body experience from the light and the vibrations, to the sound of the wind, the pounding of the rain, and the taste of the humidity in the air.

It's like Mother Nature is trying to sweep you away in a symphony of senses. And at the moment I was swept away by both the storm and by Jake. I was completely lost to everything.

It had always been like this with us. Ten years hadn't dulled it at all. If anything, the waiting only made it more intense than ever.

His hand closed around my jaw, turning my head away so that he could nuzzle my neck. As his tongue stroked upward along my skin, the muscles in my belly clenched and I squeezed my legs around him tighter.

"Oh god, Eve . . ." he moaned, pinning my hands to the wall and looking up at me with fire in his eyes as he continued to rock against me. The intensity with which he wanted me only made me crave him more. I ground back against his firm waist even harder.

Words seemed to ruin everything between us, so I wasn't about to start talking now. I just panted, throwing my head back, and pushing against him with my hips to let him know I wanted to continue. There was no doubt in my mind how wet I was, my body was practically begging to have Jake back inside me.

Taking my cue, he released my wrists and slowly, silently, began to undress me, not that it took much. My bikini was held on by four sets of strings.

His eyes hungrily roamed over my naked breasts with a passion that made me shiver with hot desire.

Thunder rattled the roof as Jake stepped back, pulling me toward him with his hand knotted in my hair. The tug on my hair follicles hurt in the most fantastic way. He crushed his lips against mine and I would have cried out in pain if it hadn't felt so good.

The one thing that kept running through my head, the one thing I couldn't ignore any longer, was how badly I wanted this man. Every inch of me wanted to possess him. I felt like a tigress stalking her prey. Jake was mine and no one else's. Always had been, always would be.

The shack was dank and old: there wasn't a surface in the place that seemed clean or inviting, let alone suitable for our naked bodies.

Jake's towel was flung over the back of a folding chair and with a quick flip of his wrist, the towel now covered the seat. I let him pull me onto his lap, my toes just barely reaching the floor on either side of him. His warm and sweaty skin against mine was electric and I gasped. I needed him inside me, *now*.

With one hand on his shoulder and my toes on the ground, I reached down, grasping the full warmth of his cock in my palm, and guided it right inside of my warm, wet, and throbbing body.

Jake gasped at my touch and I sunk my nails into his shoulder as a thousand sensations overwhelmed me, taking my breath away.

And that was just the first inch.

Jake was grinning at me through his own haze of pleasure. Cocky bastard. He was always so damn proud of his dick. But he had every right to be. It was long and thick, pink and perfect. Just the right size, really. Any bigger and it just wouldn't have been fun, but too much smaller . . . Well, where was the fun in that?

His hands grasped my hips, taking control. I may have been the body on top, but Jake was in command, not just coaxing me upward, but actually lifting me with his strong arms, until he was just barely still inside me.

That's when he started to tease me with very quick, short strokes. In and out. Each one making me gasp with pleasure, until he suddenly thrust upward, burying most of himself deep inside. I shuddered and moaned, realizing I could be as loud as I wanted, no one was anywhere near the shack on the water. We were as alone as two people could possibly be.

The air sizzled around us as another bolt of lightning struck incredibly close. I sank as far down onto Jake as I could, pushing hard until I was sure we were locked together. The way we should have always been.

He closed his eyes and let out a hiss, "Oh fuck I'm so deep inside you." Then he buried his face in my shoulder, holding me tight against his body.

I began to rock. Just small movements at first as I got used to him. But then his warm mouth closed over my nipple and all hell broke loose.

I cried out as much with shock and pain as I did for pleasure. And when he used his teeth to gently tug, I cried out again. I went from being wet, to absolutely soaking, and Jake knew it. With one hand on my hip and one cupping my breast, we began to slam into each other. Over and over, the heat building, the sweat covering our skin. I felt Jake in every inch of my body. I could have sworn I felt him in my hair and my toes.

The only problem was that there were so many sensations, so much that felt so good, I couldn't tell which way was up. That was when Jake stopped me. Brought me to a full standstill as his hands ran up the layer of sweat on my arms, over my shoulders, and tangled in my hair. He kissed me hard and the sensation of being still was actually as enjoyable as moving.

"Stand up for me," he murmured, pushing my body upward. I could barely hear him over the rain.

He spun me around, then pulled me back down onto his lap. He slid right back inside as if we hadn't moved at all, but now it felt completely different, moving in the opposite direction, gliding back and forth over the bundle of nerves just inside my body.

I went limp from the pleasure.

So Jake pulled me back against him, letting my head rest on his muscular shoulder, his hands roaming up my stomach to my own shoulders. He hooked his large hands over the top of them and pulled down on my body, forcing us even closer together.

I shuddered.

"Oh, baby, you feel so damn good . . ." he gasped breathlessly into my ear.

I didn't respond. I just closed my eyes and let myself feel everything. His cock buried deep inside me, his chiseled muscles working against me, his warm breath on my ear, and his spicy scent in my nose.

He rocked in and out of me in short movements as his hands glided along my skin in the most reverent way possible. It was like he was worshiping me.

Then he cupped my breasts, bringing my nipples perfectly between his large thumbs and fingers. That's when he started to play—teasing me gently, tugging and thrusting. I was flying high and completely lost to everything but Jake.

I never wanted to stop feeling like this. It had to be the most amazing combination of sensations known to man. I couldn't catch my breath and I didn't want to. I was putty in his hands and he was molding me into a work of art. I was reduced to a slick of hot sweat and incoherent moaning.

The thunder rumbled the shack again and the rain continued to pound on the roof. Just as Jake was pounding inside of me.

Oh yes, this was absolutely my favorite time of day: Fuck Me O'clock.

We went on like that for a while—savoring and pulling every last drop of sensation we could out of our time together. Making up for everything we had lost. Until I was sure my body wasn't capable of any more.

"Come on baby. Give it to me. I want to hear you." Somehow those words were exactly what I needed. It focused me and a fantastic warmth bloomed inside my belly. I started to pulse in the beginning of what felt like the most powerful orgasm I could ever remember feeling. It frightened me. I was positive it was going to hurt more than please. For a split second I even considered asking Jake to stop, but before I could think too much, the pulsing and throbbing took over. It washed out from my center, vibrating and contracting every muscle in my body.

I was so overcome by it I began yelling out incoherently, shouting god knows what, as I came powerfully around Jake, squeezing and savoring him inside me, and his body pressing up against me. I was barely aware of his own barks of pleasure as he followed me into oblivion.

When we were finally done, when we'd wrung every last drop out of our tired and ragged bodies, I collapsed against his shoulder again. All I could see was black. There was nothing left.

We laid like that for a long time, the sweat dripping from our naked bodies as we caught our breath. We stayed there long enough for the rain to slow and the thunder to move off into the distance.

Long enough for my brain to jump-start and realize what had just happened.

I had just made a massive mistake.

# Chapter 1

*One month earlier...*

$\mathcal{I}$ was in shock. There was really no other way to describe how I felt as I climbed out of my car, the end of another long workday, to find Jake standing on my front lawn.

Sixty seconds ago I was blissfully unaware my life was about to be turned upside down. I'd been happily driving home, singing, thinking about dinner, and then, *bam!* A big, fat, unexpected surprise jumped out of the shadows. A man I never expected to see again was standing on my front lawn, waiting for me to get home.

"What the hell are you doing here?" I yelled at him. I didn't care who heard me. Shock was quickly transforming into blind, furious rage.

"I came to talk, if you'll let me," he called back. His voice wasn't angry like mine, just amplified to carry over the distance and the wind.

"So talk," I said shaking my head. This was absurd. Ten years. *Ten years* . . . and he thought he could just appear on my lawn? I let my arms fall to my sides, my blazer and bag each dangling from a hand.

The thunder rumbled and Jake waited for it to pass, shoving his large, gorgeous hands into his pockets.

Old memories of those hands roaming my body flashed through my mind. My stomach, my breasts, caressing my face . . . he loved to touch me any chance I'd give him. Jake was a toucher, he understood the world through his hands.

I started to panic—thoughts like that were dangerous.

"I'm sorry," he called softly.

It made a little piece of me ache deep down inside where I still unconditionally loved that man. I knew part of me was his. No matter what happened or what he did, that piece of me belonged to Jake Spencer.

But the rest was completely heartbroken, even all these years later. "I hate you," I said firmly. I meant it. I hated him. I'd given him everything: my heart, my soul, my life . . . and he'd run away. It didn't matter that Jake was a screwed up kid from a screwed up family. It didn't matter that running away from his life was a sane option. All that mattered was how he left— suddenly and without explanation.

*Ten years.*

You don't leave someone you love—without any communication—for ten years and then suddenly show up on her front doorstep unannounced.

Who does that?

He took a step toward me and I took a step back, right into the side of my car. "Baby, please let me explain everything." He was clearly upset, his brow was furrowed and his green eyes were dark. For the life of me I couldn't get over his transformation. Ten years had done him good. The last time I saw him he was tall and lean—and by lean I mean he needed a good meal or ten. But he had always been strong. Despite his scrawny appearance his body was made of pure muscle, even then.

But now . . . Now he could get a job as a cover model. The wavy dark hair and flashing green eyes were deadly enough, but add in fifty pounds of new muscle and the designer suit he was wearing . . . he was fucking gorgeous. Not to mention he still had that chipped front tooth and crooked smile that promised he was someone who knew his way around.

And then there was the hint of a dimple in his right cheek.

*My dimple.*

At least that was what he used to call it.

Because I was the only one who ever noticed it. It was mine. When we were alone, away from the world and all the troubles that seemed to follow him, Jake smiled all the time. And I could never resist touching it—running my fingers over the soft, smooth skin of his cheek and down into the little dent. He'd smile even bigger and then grab me, kissing me hard. If I was lucky I wouldn't escape from his hold for the next hour, not that I would have tried.

But that was then.

The air sizzled with electricity as the temperature dropped again. The storm front was approaching fast. It was just a matter of time before the rain hit.

"So talk fast, Jake Spencer."

He pulled himself up straight, amplifying just how large and strong he was now. And damn it all, my body responded like a high performance engine ready to hit the racetrack.

"Can we please go inside before we get struck by lightning?"

"Only a handful of people die every year from lightning strikes. I think I'll take my chances."

He arched a speculative eyebrow. Jake was not amused. "Suit yourself, Eve." He took another step toward me and I froze, I had nowhere else to escape to. My back was already pressed up against my car. I felt trapped and caged even though we were in my driveway out in the open. He sighed and rolled his eyes, "What the hell do you think I'm gonna do to you? I just want to talk."

"You know, you keep saying that, but I'm not hearing anything useful."

I think I pissed him off a little with that comment because suddenly his eyes flashed and the muscle in his jaw flexed. "Damn it, Eve," he muttered, running his fingers through that gorgeous hair of his. Part of me wanted to reach out and run my own fingers through it.

I was an idiot. Obviously.

"Give me a damn good reason to listen to you." I really wanted him to say something magical because I wanted to take him inside, sit down and talk like we used to. Pretend a decade hadn't been lost. We would lay at opposite ends of the couch and he'd grab my foot, massaging it with his ridiculously large thumbs while he spoke.

His voice.

Oh, god his voice. It was actually better than I remembered it. Deep and distinctive with this deliciously rough vibration that reverberated through my body when he spoke.

"You know what happened that night," he said softly while looking me in the eye.

It took my breath away. "Yes," I said nodding. I knew he had his reasons for leaving, I just didn't understand why he had to toss me aside like a piece of trash. "You knew how much I loved you, Jake . . ."

He squeezed his eyes shut and clenched his fist, "Baby, I am so sorry I hurt you." His eyes shot back open, "You are the last person I have ever wanted to hurt, Eve. I will never, ever be able to make it up to you."

Damn right he wouldn't. Having the person you love disappear is like dying—and I never wanted to feel that way again.

Somehow he'd moved closer. I think maybe he was inching toward me as he spoke, like I was a wounded animal he might spook if he moved too fast. Hell, maybe that was exactly what I was. Maybe he was doing the right thing. But it didn't matter. Either way I felt more and more panicked the closer he got. My heart was racing and it was getting harder to control my breathing.

"But you did hurt me. Why? Why couldn't you call . . . explain . . . anything?" I asked shaking my head. The panic was getting worse.

He was only inches away now. The wind was really kicking up, tossing my dark hair around and blowing my clothing. I could smell him. It was the same, but different. The old Jake was like an undercurrent to the new one. They mixed and mingled and I had trouble separating the two. They were both intoxicating, weaving their way inside me and bringing back all of those old feelings of desire and need.

That was what it always was with Jake— *need.* I needed him, to be with him and around him. I needed his touch and his reassurance. When he was gone it was like I was empty. When he was with me, I was full. He was my drug and I could never, ever get enough.

He licked his lips and looked away as he spoke, "I was in a total daze. I barely remember Tom cleaning me up and taking me away. Next thing I knew we were in a hotel in D.C. while he got my paperwork together. Then I was in Iraq with him working on his contract." He squeezed his eyes shut and shook his head, "It was months before I had my head on straight enough to really realize where I was and what had happened."

I don't know why I did it, but I reached up and turned his head toward me. I wanted to see his eyes. They were always the most expressive part of Jake. I could see a thousand things he'd never said in those deep depths. The contact of my skin against his was almost too much—it didn't feel real. And when his eyes finally connected with mine again, I couldn't breathe. There was a storm inside Jake: two opposing lives fighting to live in one body. There was the life he couldn't quite leave behind, and the life he had created for himself. Jake was clearly a different person than the boy I'd last met, but inside him there was still that longing and regret. And it was all directed at me.

"Why didn't you call?" I whispered. I was trembling. Maybe it was the adrenaline, maybe it was fear or desire, I had no clue. All I knew was that I was overwhelmed by it all and having Jake so close again was like an overdose.

Those green eyes of his drank all of me in, memorizing me. He searched my face, finally landing on my lips. That was when I realized how hard Jake was breathing. He placed his hands on the car behind me, trapping me where I was, Jake in front and around me, the car pressed up against my back. I had nowhere to go, nowhere to run, and no desire to do either.

His delicious scent, mixed with his expensive cologne, was making me dizzy and warm; but having him so physically close was really the killer. It made me completely paralyzed.

He swallowed, "Eve . . . I wanted to call. I can't tell you how many times I stood there with a phone in my hands." He was breathing even harder now and a real look of pain crossed his handsome face. "Can I please kiss you?"

I wanted to scream, "*Yes! Oh, god yes, please kiss me. Take me right here against the car. I don't care if my neighbors watch.*" But instead I just stood there, staring at him staring at me. He looked like he wanted to devour me.

I wanted to be devoured.

He kissed me.

His soft lips pressed gently against mine and it was as if the entire world just stopped. Time ceased to exist. It was just his lips and mine, a perfectly chaste kiss, and yet he may as well have been inside me. I could feel him everywhere and my body ached for more.

Then he pulled back and pressed his forehead to mine. For a minute we both mourned. It was our one chance to cry and feel everything we'd been keeping back. I needed to feel it with him, I realize that now. He had been my soul mate, my very best friend, and no one else on earth could possibly understand how heartbroken I'd been when he left. This was finally my chance to connect with someone who truly understood my desperation.

And then he broke my heart all over again.

"Baby, you loved me too much. I would have drowned you if I'd stayed."

*I loved him too much?* Was there such a thing?

Could you really love someone *too much*?

"Fuck you, Jake," I whispered hoarsely. He was tall and strong and overwhelming. I needed him away from me, and yet I couldn't bring myself to push him away. I'd finally gotten him back . . .

He shook his head, our foreheads still pressed together. His voice cracked when he spoke, "I knew you were better off without me, so I stayed away. I wanted you to move on and make a good life for yourself. I was no good for you, Eve." He pressed his forehead harder against mine and squeezed his eyes shut, "I didn't want to stay away, darlin', believe me. The only place I've ever wanted be is here, with you."

That set something off inside me. It was like an explosion detonating right at my core. I placed my hands firmly against his chest and pushed as hard as I could. He took a deep breath and stepped back, his head low as he looked down at me. I wanted to scream and punch, but what I really wanted to do was strangle the bastard. "Then why didn't you come home?" The anger was in control and I had absolutely no desire to rein it in. Rage felt pretty damn good. "You don't leave the people you love. We would have figured it out, Jake. We would have."

He shook his head and his eyes hardened, "No. I didn't have the tools to deal with my life. I needed help, *real help*, and that's what I got. I worked my ass off for the last ten years to create a whole new person. As much as you loved me, Eve, you couldn't do that for me. And if I'd tried to do that here, with you, it would have ruined us. I promise you that."

It hurt, really it did. To have someone you loved so much tell you that you weren't enough. And as all that sank in I finally began to wonder . . . why was Jake here? He'd already let ten years pass—what had suddenly changed to bring him home? A feeling of dread quickly crept up inside me. My skin tingled and the hairs on my arm shot up. Or maybe we really were about to get struck by lightning. "Why are you on my lawn, Jake?"

"I'm back," he said simply. But it was so much more complicated than that.

"Back from the dead, back for a vacation . . . what exactly do you mean?"

"I mean I live here now. I have an apartment and a business and my life is back here in Tampa."

I was dumbfounded. Finally, after years of wondering and wishing, Jake had decided to return home . . . and it was the worst news I could think of.

I had finally, *finally*, gotten over him. I had a good life, good friends, and a fantastic career. I was happy. Sure, I wasn't married with a house full of little munchkins. And no, I hadn't fallen in love with anyone else. But I was *happy*.

Jake was misery.

And I knew without a shadow of a doubt having him back in my life would lead to more pain and heartbreak. It was just what we did to each other. We were too much.

Maybe he was right when he said I loved him too

much. Maybe he loved me too much too. The two of us together were self destructive and blind. We blocked out the world and allowed ourselves to be consumed.

I didn't care what he'd done in the last ten years. He was still the man who broke my heart and left me behind to pick up the pieces.

There was absolutely no way I was letting someone like that back into my life. Happiness wasn't something you could find on every street corner. It had taken hard work and I would be damned if I'd let this cocky son of a bitch just show up, say a few magic words, and have me eating out of the palm of his hand again.

"Oh, so I'm good enough for you now?" I bit out the words like they didn't belong in my mouth.

Jake just about burned a whole through me with his stare. His eyes were dark and smoldering with a fire so hot it scared the pants off me. He was rigid, like every muscle in his body was suddenly tensed, and a vein in his neck bulged. "No, *I* am." He said it so softly, so firmly, I could tell it had taken every ounce of strength in his powerful body to say it. "I wasn't good enough for you. You don't hurt the ones you love, and you don't use them to make yourself feel better. That was what I was doing to you, Eve. It wasn't right. Maybe leaving wasn't right either, but it's what happened. Like it or not, I left. But I'm back now, and I'm ready to be the man you deserve."

"Leave." I said it so fast even I didn't believe I'd said it at first. But as my brain and my body caught up with each other I knew I was right. My instincts knew

Jake was a black hole of pain. "This isn't going to happen, Jake. You and I are done. We are the past and I need you to leave. Now."

He studied me, those careful green eyes seeing something because after a moment his entire expression changed and his body relaxed. "All right," he said, cocking his head to the side and looking at me pointedly. "I'm sure I'll be seeing you at some point. Tampa's a small town, darlin'."

"And yet . . . you're going to stay as far away from me as you can." I forced a smile and winked.

Jake chuckled, "We'll see about that."

I pointed at the old orange Ford Bronco parked at my curb. Jake had lovingly restored it in college. He'd taken the top off and replaced it with a removable rag top. The inside was coated in the same liner they used in the beds of pick-up trucks. It was his baby. He'd loved it because it was as rough and durable as he was. And that thought just squeezed my heart more. I knew how much Jake had been forced to overcome. I knew what had happened the night of our college graduation and why Jake had to run. I knew all of this and yet I still couldn't forgive him. "Go."

He nodded and winked at me, his cocky half-grin showing off his chipped front tooth. It all made me melt just as stupidly as it always had. There was just something about Jake that was different from anyone else I'd ever met.

I didn't move a muscle until the Bronco pulled away and he honked the horn.

He was gone again, and that thought would have broken me if I didn't also know without a shadow of a doubt that this was just the beginning. That was not the last time I would be seeing Jake Spencer.

## Chapter 2

*It* had been three weeks since Jake's unannounced visit to my house. I hadn't heard from him since, which I was relieved about, but he was constantly on my mind. That's what happens when old ghosts show up on your doorstep. They bring back old memories, make you relive the past, and wonder about your decisions. I was going over every piece of new information I'd gotten from him, trying to figure out how it fit into the puzzle that was my life.

It had taken a while—my defenses were up at first. I was angry and upset. But then it started to fade and I was able to actually hear the things Jake said on my lawn. Jennie had helped, too. She was my best friend and roommate. She'd helped me tease out the details.

The big ones being he'd had issues. Great big giant ones that really did need time and professional help to solve.

He hadn't wanted to leave me.

He'd wanted to be with me as desperately as I'd wanted him here.

But it didn't change facts or reality. We'd been madly in love once and it ended badly. I knew I didn't want to live through a Jake Spencer broken heart ever again.

There was just one problem. One giant, glaring problem.

In the ten years since Jake had left, I'd never loved anyone else.

I'd dated. It wasn't like I'd just sat around pining for my long lost love like some graying spinster. I'd even gotten pretty serious once. Sebastian Monroe was a fine man who had been good to my family and me. My sisters adored him, he and my dad got along great—even my mom was taken with him. He was tall, dark, and dashing. We were extremely comfortable with each other and I couldn't have asked for a better man in my life. Sebastian was as pure hearted and up-standing as anyone could ask for.

But I could never bring myself to say I loved him.

The stark difference between my feelings for Jake and my feelings for Sebastian lead me to break it off before he proposed. I couldn't live a quiet, stable life. I needed fireworks. I needed my pulse to race every time he walked into the room. I needed my body to groan every time his skin touched mine. I needed his voice to make my heart stop.

Sebastian did none of those things.

As much as I liked him, I didn't love him.

As much as I enjoyed sex with him, it didn't rock my world.

But that was the best I'd come across.

It had only taken Jake moments to do to my body what no one else had managed in ten years. And that thought alone was driving me crazy. I couldn't get it out of my head.

Nothing had changed—not in that department. Ten years and I still had that same visceral response to Jake that I had the first time I met him all those years ago.

My reaction had been so intense and so different I had never forgotten a single moment of our first week together. I'd never been boy crazy, in fact I was worried there was something wrong with me.

Everywhere I looked my friends were frantically losing their minds dating. They had crushes and were losing their virginity, meanwhile all I could see were silly boys I'd rather not touch.

Then Jake walked into my life and everything changed.

I don't know if it was love at first sight (I'm really not sure what the heck that means) but he took my breath away. Everything else fell away and there was only his handsome, smiling face. Then he looked at me and I saw that same shocked look in his eyes. It was an instant connection and we were immediately drawn together like two magnets. He was as blind to the people around us as I was.

We spent nearly every minute of the next week locked together in a quiet conversation that only made sense to us. We talked about everything—it was the strangest thing. Somehow in a single sitting we could move from movies to politics to religion; all while smiling and touching and caressing. And the kissing... I thought kissing was a little bit gross until Jake kissed me. Then I couldn't get enough.

Every moment with my body pressed up against his was ecstasy.

Every moment we were apart was hell.

We'd known each other three days when he pulled back from a long, deep kiss and stared into my eyes. I couldn't breathe when he did that—I could see forever in his eyes. A look of fear flashed across his face, he squinted his eyes just a little bit, and murmured a question. "Are you seeing anyone else?"

Was I seeing anyone else? Did anyone else exist? "No," I whispered.

Jake relaxed and melted against my body beneath his. He swallowed and dipped his head down, tracing an invisible line up the skin of my throat. His breath was warm as he whispered in my ear, "Be mine and no one else's?"

It was the most terrifying and wonderful thing I had ever heard in my life. I wanted Jake like I'd never wanted anything and hearing his frantic plea that I be his...

"And will you be mine?"

His grin split his face in two, "I already am."

I kissed the soft spot on his cheek where his invisible dimple was peeking out, "Then yes."

A knock on my office door brought reality crashing down on my memories. I looked up to find my boss standing in the doorway. Josh Norton was a few years older than me, handsome enough: six foot, thin, a little mousy for my taste. But he was a great boss. He'd taken me under his wing from day one, specifically tasked to make me part of the team. It had been an undertaking considering my first day was only two weeks after Jake's grand exit, but he had handled it brilliantly. We'd been friends ever since.

"You ready for this?"

I looked down at the stack of proposals. I was Director of Fan Experience for the Tampa Bay Rays, the Major League Baseball team based out of St. Petersburg, and we were adding a new tailgating and pregame experience outside Tropicana Stadium. For the next three hours Josh and I were going to be listening to the formal presentations for these proposals. I had my favorite, it was the last one, and I hoped the presentations matched the paperwork. I didn't like it when my expectations weren't met.

"I'm not looking forward to my ass falling asleep, but otherwise I'm prepared."

"Good," he smacked the papers he was holding against his hand. "Let's get this over with. I have a dinner date with the last presenter and he's taking me to Bern's. I'm gonna bleed the sucker dry."

I laughed. Bern's was a local favorite. A very cool restaurant with a nice high price tag. "I take it your favorite is also the last one?"

Josh made a face and held up his fingers, "The first one is way overpriced, the second one is pointless, but the third one is both interesting and on budget. It's just right."

"And paying for dinner."

Josh grinned. "Exactly. I'll see if he's willing to bring my Director along, too."

I rolled my eyes as I stood up, "I'm sure I'll manage to find food on my own."

The presentations went just as we predicted and Josh and I spent more time trading insulting text messages than actually listening to the bland presentations.

That was until Presentation Number Three showed up.

I wanted the earth to open up and swallow me whole. He was tall, dark, and *Jake*. My eyes flew down to the paperwork in front of me. *Spencer, Hamilton, and Associates* was the engineering firm and sure enough, the Chief Engineer was listed as none other than Jake Spencer.

How had I not noticed his name? I was apparently so taken with the plans I hadn't bothered to look at anything else. The devil was in the details, not the plans.

Josh shot to his feet, greeting Jake enthusiastically.

I stayed glued to my seat like I was strapped in by

a five-point harness. Jake casually looked over Josh's shoulder, his smoldering stare pinning me against the padded chair. He looked amazing. His three-piece suit was a light shade of gray and his green tie set off his eyes and tan skin.

He looked edible.

*Damn it.*

I swallowed and tried to stop myself from blushing. The way he looked at me was positively possessive and I could feel the heat surging under my skin.

"We are just so thrilled the head of Spencer, Hamilton, and Associates himself came out to do the presentation. We don't get that very often," Josh prattled on.

Jake's eyes never left mine. "No, I'm sure you don't," he murmured. "But this is my pet project, the Rays have had a special place in my heart since my college days."

*Damn. Him.*

"Oh, really?" Josh asked, oblivious to what was happening.

"Papa Joe was like a father to me."

I shot daggers at him. How dare he bring my father into this? Josh spun on his heel, "Then you must know our Eve."

I forced a smile onto my face and finally stood, "Oh, yes. Jake and I go way back." I tried to only shake his hand tersely, but that wasn't what happened. His fingers managed to wrap around mine in a soft but demanding way that sent a tingle so charged up my arm it took my breath away.

Josh looked from me to Jake and back again, "Okay . . ."

I snatched my hand back, "Presentation. Let's get this over with."

Jake moved to the head of the conference table with a ridiculously proud smile on his face. The fucker saw how badly he threw me for a loop. He had planned it all along.

I remembered how calmly he'd left my driveway three weeks ago. He'd basically warned me he'd be seeing me again soon. Stupidly I'd taken it as a general off-hand remark, not an actual scheduled meeting. Tampa was a small city and from the looks of his company, Jake and I would be seeing each other from time to time.

It only took him a moment to take over the projector, bringing his presentation to life. He was smooth and confident. And damn it all, but I could have watched him talk all day. I loved the sound of his voice and found myself closing my eyes just to absorb more of it.

I missed it. Those deep, rough, gentle vibrations were like a lullaby soothing my soul.

I'd already read the proposal and I knew Jake was brilliant. I didn't need any more information than that. Paying attention to the details was purely optional.

What I *was* learning, however, was how very, very different Jake was from the boy I used to know. The boy I'd loved in college was terribly damaged. He was

social and fun, but had an incredible lack of confidence. He was probably more screwed up than anyone
I'd ever met before or since. And yet I'd loved him with
everything I had despite his inability to function like a
normal human being. I'd never met anyone smarter.

But he hadn't understood how wonderful he was.
And every time we were outside our little bubble, he
struggled to function. He was full of doubts and incapable of recognizing his own genius. If I hadn't
watched over him he'd never have graduated despite
being able to ace every test he'd ever taken.

He was that smart.

And that screwed up.

But not anymore. He was smooth, confident in his
brilliance. I had a feeling I could ask him anything and
he'd answer me with a smile. Ten years ago he probably would have mumbled something, thrown in a few
swear words for effect, then stormed out of the room.

He really had changed.

I felt such a strange mix of happy and sad. Happy
was really the dominant feeling. Jake deserved to be
happy and to be brilliant. I was really glad he'd finally
managed to find peace in that.

But it made me incredibly sad to know getting
there took ten years on the other side of the world.

Away from me.

God, that thought hurt like hell. It was like this
hole in my heart was ripped open every time I thought
about it.

Jake grinned and winked at me from the front of

the room. I glanced at Josh and realized he was looking down, jotting notes on a notepad. He hadn't seen anything. Jake was flirting with me mid-presentation with my boss happily oblivious.

I snapped my attention back to Jake who was still talking as if nothing had happened, a huge, proud smile plastered to his handsome face.

He was a seriously cocky bastard. For some reason I was shocked by that. Really, I shouldn't have been. Jake was always cocky. Truth be told, it was one of the things I loved about him. There was just something about a guy willing to take his chances . . . it drew me to him like a freaking moth to a flame. But this... he was taking cocky to a whole new level. It was in every fiber of his being now. He oozed it. Cocky wasn't something he pulled out sometimes and used like a tool—it was who he was at all times.

And damn it all, I loved it. My heart was doing that stupid schoolgirl crush pitter-patter thing and yep, sure enough, I was tingling between the legs. I wanted the bastard.

I think 'drug' was a good description for Jake. I wanted him. I knew he'd be a fantastic high while he lasted. But it when I came down off that high, I would crash and burn.

Out of the corner of my eye I saw Josh look down again. His pen was waggling away as he scribbled more notes.

Jake smiled, all suave and seductive, and his eyes smoldered. He was practically beaming sexual thoughts directly into my brain.

Who was this man? I didn't know this Jake at all.

It happened before I could stop it. My mind took a trip down memory lane, desperate to find an answer to what happened between Jake and me. It went straight to that night. The night he left me.

I'd done a damn fine job of constructing a beautiful, elaborate wall in my mind. Behind it I hid all things Jake. Behind that wall was another wall where I kept my memories of graduation night. It had been an eye opening experience for me. It had shaken me to my core and opened my eyes to a world I really had no idea existed.

I didn't know a parent could really and truly not unconditionally love their child.

I did now.

I hadn't understood that some people, like Jake's father, were so broken and damaged by life, so desperate to obliterate their hopelessness, that they were capable of lashing out and destroying everything around them.

I did now.

Because that night Jake hadn't seen it coming, so he wasn't able to get me out of his parent's house before all hell had broken loose.

We were so happy, floating on a cloud of accomplishment and hope and promise. It had been such an innocent comment that started it all. Jake said, *"I'll make you guys proud, I'll do all the things you weren't able to."* He'd meant it in a good way. But Jake Sr.

hadn't taken it that way. To him it was an insult.

Jake's father snapped. A curtain immediately fell over his eyes and it was like the man who'd been there vanished and was replaced by someone else entirely different. I'd never liked Jake's father, he was always mean and angry, he thrived on intimidation, but that night I saw pure evil and I could honestly say I wished he'd died. He didn't deserve to live.

It was like it was happening all over again in my mind's eye.

Jake Sr. grabbing Jake and pulling him into a chokehold, sneering in his ear, "*You fucking piece of shit. Screw you. I'll put you back in your place.*"

Jake's eyes were wide and wild with fear. Not for himself, but for *me*. He knew what was coming and it was something he'd never wanted to touch my life.

I knew Jake usually let his father beat him up, it was easier to be the punching bag than to fight the inevitable. But not that night. I saw the fear and worry in his eyes as he fixated on me, and something snapped.

The fight that followed was terrifying. I'd seen fights growing up around ballplayers, but never anything like that.

It wasn't a pissing contest or a fight over a woman. This was a fight of desperation. It was a fight for survival.

The only thing that stopped Jake from killing his father had been Tom. He was close enough that when I called, he'd been able to get there in time. He pulled Jake off his father who was beaten unconscious at that point.

He was wild. I think a lifetime of blame and abuse had finally reached its boiling point and Jake simply couldn't take it anymore.

The minute he focused, Jake ordered me to leave.

The next day he was gone and everything changed. No phone calls, no explanations. Just gone . . . like we'd never existed.

I *knew* why he'd left. And really, I couldn't blame him.

I was glad his uncle had gotten him help. I even saw the wisdom in a change of lifestyle. But I didn't understand his logic in abandoning me, and that was what I couldn't seem to get past. At the very least he could have given me a choice. I think I hated him for choosing for me.

I was in a total fog and somehow when the presentation was over I agreed to join Jake and Josh at dinner. I don't really remember the drive, I was pretty lost in my head. St. Petersburg, or St. Pete, as we actually call it, is on the opposite side of Tampa Bay from the city of Tampa. They are sister cities and between the two of them they provide the area with a little bit of everything. Neither city is huge, but both sprawl for miles and miles. In St. Pete there's more of a small town atmosphere and the only sports team is the Rays. But on the Tampa side there's football, hockey, concert venues, and a casino. I loved my little cities.

But somehow I saw none of this on my drive over the bay. I drove on automatic; following Josh the entire way, not that I didn't know how to get to Bern's by heart.

As I sat and waited for the valet to take Josh's car, my door opened and a familiar hand reached in for me.

It was kind of surreal to see Jake so many times after all these years. The picture I had of him in my head was quickly transforming from the scrawny man-child who needed a haircut and something in his wardrobe other than t-shirts, into a strong, confident, put-together man.

"Thanks," I muttered grabbing his hand.

"My pleasure. Thank you for coming." He blocked my path so that I couldn't move without pushing past him.

I threw my hands on my hips in frustration, "Aren't you going to move?"

The corner of his lip pulled up in a smile that matched the delight in his eyes. "Do you need your purse?"

I rolled my eyes and huffed as I sat back down and grabbed my purse out of the passenger seat. There was no way I was bending over and giving Jake an eyeful of my ass. He stood there chuckling to himself, leaned casually against my door as the valet finally came around and handed him my ticket. I stood up and snatched it with an evil glare. I may be sympathetic to Jake's past and more than a little confused by my feelings toward him, but I was not confused by who was in charge here.

But as I stamped in a very un-ladylike huff in

through the restaurant doors I realized how wrong I was about that. Jake chose this restaurant on purpose—he was very much in charge of this evening.

We had a lot of memories here. It was one of my dad's favorite places for big celebrations. We'd eaten here with my family on multiple occasions, and alone a few times as well.

One anniversary in particular . . .

It was our third. We'd both just turned the magical twenty-one and could legally drink in public. We felt so grownup going out to a fancy dinner just the two of us and splitting a bottle of wine. They'd sat us at a tiny table for two on the main floor. Dinner had been foreplay. Every bite and sip was a sexual suggestion.

And then we went up to the dessert floor.

A very special feature of Bern's was the second floor—devoted entirely to dessert and dancing. There were secluded booths for each party, all different sizes to accommodate everyone, and in one room was a piano with a singer and just enough space for a few dancers.

We ordered my favorite: apple pie and cinnamon ice cream. I was a dedicated chocolate fanatic, but the cinnamon ice cream was my one exception. It was like crack and I couldn't resist ordering it. While we waited for it to arrive Jake pulled me out to the dance floor. The pianist was having fun playing a polka and we had fun dancing along.

Jake was a good dancer, he had a natural rhythm but no training, he just knew how to move. And after three years I knew how to move with Jake.

"Any requests?" the pianist asked looking pointedly at us.

Jake grinned and whispered something in his ear. The pianist smiled and winked at me, "We have a very special couple dancing up here tonight. They've been adorable and I just found out it is a special night for them. Ladies and gentleman please help them celebrate their third anniversary!"

There was light clapping from various booths across the floor and Jake pulled me tightly against his firm body. He tilted my chin up and gazed lovingly down into my eyes. He was smiling.

"Here is their song . . ." the pianist struck the first chords of *Can't Help Falling In Love* and Jake mouthed the words while we swayed together.

I always heard a strange mix of the Elvis Presley and UB40 versions of the song in my head. It was to the UB40 version Jake first told me he loved me. And just like that night he dipped his lips down to my ear and whispered, "I can't help falling in love with you." It sent a shiver of pleasure over my sensitive skin and made my body ache to be locked together with his.

He wove his fingers between mine and pulled our hands up to his heart, pressing them firmly against his chest. "I've never been so happy being a fool."

I laughed and snuggled into his chest, "It's fun being a fool," I agreed. But even then, somewhere in the back of my mind and heart, I felt the dread. We were so happy, but it had a limit. We both knew there was a dark cloud hanging over our happiness. Every one of those beautiful moments was always tempered by a pang of sadness.

After the song we returned to our private, dark booth and dove into my ice cream. Ice cream, it turns out, was even more sexual than food and wine. Before I knew it, I was gasping. Jake's hand was between my legs and he was working his magic.

"Take a bite," he ordered with a smile. His eyes were flashing and glinting with mischief.

I sucked in a deep breath and shakily scooped up the creamy white ice cream flecked with cinnamon. It melted on my tongue as Jake's fingers flexed and teased.

"Lick the spoon."

I smiled and did just as he asked.

Jake groaned.

I came.

We'd gone straight home from there and spent the whole night tangled together.

We'd been fools. That much I knew was true. But even with a broken heart I still remembered that night fondly.

Bern's was distinctive and imposing, dark reds and wood dominating everything from the moment you walk through the door. It was hard not to put every single one of those memories into their place as I glanced around.

"Miss Daniels! It is so good to see you, it's been a while," Marcus, the headwaiter chastised me.

I nodded absently, feeling once again overwhelmed by, well, *everything*.

"And Mr. Spencer, I see you've requested a table for three this evening. It is ready and waiting, if you'll follow me . . ."

I glanced from Marcus to Jake and back again. Marcus knew Jake by sight, as if he *knew* Jake.

"You've been eating here often?" I asked under my breath.

Jake smiled, looking as confident and comfortable as ever, "I like the food here and most of my clients seem to enjoy being taken out for a nice meal."

I stopped dead in my tracks. "How many clients are you bringing here? How can you afford this?"

Jake stopped beside me, placing his hand gently on my elbow and urging me to continue walking. "I hardly think this is the time or place to be discussing my financial situation."

I glanced around at the happy dinner guests and realized Jake had a point. Not one I liked, but I certainly couldn't fault him for not wanting to discuss his business beside a table full of Japanese tourists.

We were shown to one of the quieter side rooms. They were nearly private and excellent for conversation. At the moment I wished Josh wasn't with us. I had suddenly been hit by a wave of curiosity about Jake and I certainly couldn't ask the questions I really wanted to ask in front of my boss.

So I kept my big trap shut, sitting quietly as we ordered wine and appetizers. I observed. For the first time I started to put things together. Both times I'd seen Jake he was well dressed in gorgeous designer suits. He was the first named partner in his engineering firm. Sure he was still driving that stupid Bronco around town, but what had he driven today? I stopped to think about my blind drive over the bay and I couldn't remember seeing the orange beast. In fact, I seemed to remember a very throaty and nice looking F150 leading us on our journey. Was that Jake? How did he have not one, but two trucks, designer suits, and money to burn at one of the nicest restaurants in town?

Who was this man?

Thankfully Josh helped me on that.

"Jake, how are you enjoying living in Tampa again? I hear you and your partner have been taking the city by storm."

He chuckled and leaned casually back in his chair, "You know, it's nice to be back. I've missed the humidity."

"Is working over in the Middle East as hard as they say?"

"It is," Jake said. "You live and work by a different set of rules. But it was good for me, straightened me out."

Josh seemed to think it was all well and good, nodding and drumming his fingers on the table. It was one of his telltale signs I'd come to know well. When Josh was leading up to a bigger question he had a routine. Leading questions, feigned agreement, drumming fingers... and then the real question on his mind. "And the money? I hear they make it worth your while."

*Bingo*. Josh was fishing for information. It just so happened to also be the information I was looking for. I couldn't help but hang on his answer. Jake's eyes flicked to mine for a brief moment before he smiled stiffly and looked back at Josh. "Yes, the money can be very, very good depending on what you're doing."

"Your partner, Greg, he said you made a few key investments that helped get the new firm open."

Jake huffed, "Greg has a big mouth. Yes," he nodded, looking back at me again. It was as if he was as desperate to share pieces of himself with me as I was to hear them. "I got lucky. A friend of mine came to me with a good idea. I invested and not long after, it took off. The kid just sold it for a mint." He paused for a moment looking temporarily uncomfortable talking about himself. "I also helped another friend develop a key piece of technology. She was able to sell it to a military contractor that is developing similar forms of technology for the government. It was that investment in particular that made me very rich. I was able to bankroll most of what Greg still needed to get our firm off the ground here."

"You're a lucky man," Josh said.

"I suppose I am," Jake said suddenly looking grim.

Luck was such a strange and relative term. Was Jake lucky? That was probably the last thing I'd ever say about him. If he was as well-off as he sounded, it wasn't by some great turn of fortune. It was more like a payback for the years he'd already lost to a life he hadn't chosen.

He caught me looking at him. The moment he saw the look in my eyes, he stiffened. No, there was no luck at this table. Luck would have been Jake finding a way to stay, or a way home to me sooner.

"So, you and Eve . . . what's the story?" Josh asked the inevitable question. He really had no idea what he was asking.

Jake's eyes flicked over to me, silently asking if he should talk or if I wanted to take control.

I swallowed hard, pushing down the confusion I was feeling inside and looked over at my boss. "Jake and I dated in college, actually. All four years."

Josh's jaw dropped open. His eyes went so wide there was nothing but black from his pupils dilating. He knew exactly who Jake was. Everyone who worked in the front office at the Trop ten years ago knew who Jake was. Papa Joe had not taken his daughter's heartbreak very well. Not to mention I'd started working there two weeks later. The sad girl who moped around the hallways and cried through her lunch break every day tended to get a reputation. One I had gladly lost over the years. Being known as 'The Crier' was not something I'd enjoyed very much.

Josh was actually shocked into silence. But his stare was deadly. And it was saying everything he was thinking.

Jake cleared his throat and sat back, his eyes wandering back to me for a moment. "It was a helluva long time ago."

Josh finally closed his mouth and looked right at me. "Does Joe know he's back?" He stuck his finger out at Jake.

I shook my head. The only other person I'd talked to was my roommate Jennie, the one who had helped me pick up the pieces after Jake left. She was a child psychologist and, while I wasn't a child, her knowledge and wisdom had been essential in me pulling my act back together.

Josh reached into his pocket and pulled out his phone.

"What are you doing?" I asked him, knowing somewhere in my gut he was about to call my dad.

"Joe laid down the law. Anyone who sees *that*," he stuck his finger back out at Jake, "is supposed to call Joe immediately."

I put a calming hand on my boss. I was really touched he and everyone else I worked with cared about my family and me so much, but this was my problem to deal with. "Josh, please let me handle this. I'm not twenty-two anymore, I don't need my dad to kill my shit boyfriend for me."

Jake winced, I saw it out of the corner of my eye, but he didn't say anything.

Josh looked confused by my logic, glancing from me to Jake and back again. "Are you really okay with this? We can leave right now if you're not."

I smiled to reassure him, "No, I'm fine. Jake and I have talked and," I paused to take a breath, "we're fine."

We were not fine.

But for the purposes of this dinner, and for the sake of Jake's life, I would pretend. And the truth was things were okay. Not fine, but okay. I was confused and I was wary, but the meeting and sitting here at the table with him had shown me I was perfectly capable of functioning in social situations with this man.

Alone was another story. We weren't doing that again anytime soon.

Josh slowly put his phone back away, "Well . . . if you're sure."

I nodded reassuringly.

Josh turned back to Jake and gave him a cold stare that even scared the piss out of *me*, and I knew how sweet Josh typically was. Thinking of him in any other way seemed impossible, but that stare stopped me cold. "I will be watching you very, very closely. One toe out of line and I'll have the entire Rays line-up beat the crap out of your useless body."

And the thing was, that wasn't an empty threat. Baseball players were funny creatures, but very manly. They'd love nothing more than to defend my honor, so to speak.

Jake nodded slowly, his green eyes deadly serious as he spoke, "Trust me I understand completely, Josh. I will never, ever hurt her again. I can guarantee that."

An ache developed in my chest as I watched him talk. How could he guarantee that? I knew with absolute certainty having Jake around me would lead to *more*. And more would lead to heartbreak. It was just what Jake did to me. It wasn't his fault I loved him so deeply, so completely, there was no choice but to give him all of me. Just as it wasn't his fault that he loved me so passionately he couldn't control it.

But then his stare swung over to me. He looked deep into my eyes and straight into my soul the way only he could. I swear he could see all of me. I was naked in front of him, it didn't matter what I hid or wore, this man could see all of me. So when he spoke it wasn't just words, it was a promise between his soul and mine. "Ten years ago I ran away from my demons. I'm back to make those demons afraid of me."

The waiter returned with our appetizers, but Jake didn't look away. He had me trapped with his eyes. They were smoldering and intense, undressing me slowly and caressing my skin, the heat between my legs was pulsing.

Whoever this man was, he was a strange mix of the man I had loved and the man I always knew he could be, plus something else entirely. Something unexpected. He was darker and more intense, he knew what he wanted and I had the very distinct impression he never took no for an answer. This Jake got what he wanted. Period.

Panic ripped through me again. I didn't like this feeling, the concept he would win me back against my will. That I had no choice in what was going to happen between him and me. "Excuse me," I mumbled, clumsily standing up and tossing my napkin on the chair. "I need the restroom."

Josh didn't seem to notice the look of panic in my eyes, but Jake didn't miss it. His intense green eyes silently watched me as I left the room.

But I didn't go to the restroom, I ran to the kitchen. It was open and guests were welcome inside, but on a tour. I wasn't with a guide, so I stopped dead in my tracks, looking around. A chef smiled at me warmly as he looked up from his work. For some stupid reason that made me giggle and I wandered over to the fish tanks like I belonged there.

Poor ugly fish were hours or minutes away from being someone's dinner. I felt like one of those fish. I had been happily swimming along, blissfully unaware danger was right around the corner. Jake wanted me for his dinner and I wasn't sure how I was going to keep him from killing me.

A throat was cleared behind me. I expected to see one of the many waiters ready to request I leave the kitchen until a proper tour was scheduled, but instead, as I turned around my eyes fell upon Jake.

He was like a kid, no matter where I ran he kept turning up with a smile on his face.

"I didn't mean to scare you away." He kept a good five feet between us and his hands behind his back. He was making a conscious effort to seem safe and non-confrontational. "But I *did* want you to know how serious I am. Nothing about me is the same and I have every intention of righting every wrong I made before I left."

He was wrong about one thing, there were many

things about him that were the same. His smile was the same, his voice, and his heart. It may have been scared and buried beneath layers of crap parenting, but I'd seen it then as clearly as I could see it now. And Jake had a truly good heart.

Didn't make me any less terrified of loving him.

"Did you pick Bern's on purpose?" I asked. I noticed how straight he always stood. It gave him an extra air of confidence and control.

"Yes," he said flatly. "I told you, I'm taking my life back. All of it. Even if you don't want me back, I'm damn determined to make sure that's what you want. I want you to be absolutely positive. Doubts will tear a person in two—trust me on that one. So, yes, I chose this restaurant on purpose just like I chose to pitch to you myself. I'm not going away, but I'm not going to force myself on you either. I didn't expect you to fall into my lap and forgive me. This is gonna take time. Time I am more than willing to invest. Because it needs to be done right. When you tell me you don't love me, I want you to know it with every fiber of your being."

*Crap.*

## Chapter 3

*I* took a sip of my red wine and sighed as I looked out over my backyard. It was shady, surrounded by a mix of coconut palm trees and eureka palms. Hibiscus and other colorful flowers were intermittently dispersed, a water fountain soothingly dribbled in one corner, a small vegetable garden was in the other, and a covered hot tub sat just off the porch.

I loved my backyard; it was calming. My lounge chair was the fancy kind—weather-resistant wicker and big stuffy cushions. The kind that got soaked and nasty if they weren't in a relatively covered location like my wide, covered back porch. The sun was setting and Jennie and I were having an after dinner treat: wine and chocolate.

"I brought the bottle, you are going to drink until you spill your guts!" Jennie said, plopping the bottle down on the table between us and flopping into the chair beside me.

"Ha!" I replied. Eloquent, I know, but typical for me when it came to talking about my feelings. It was not my forte, to say the least. For some reason when it came to translating what was going on inside my head, the words seemed to get stuck somewhere between my brain and my mouth. Apparently facial expressions and gestures weren't enough.

"Seriously, Eve, if you don't start saying *something,* there's going to be trouble. You are going through a major life event and talking your way through your emotions is the best way to identify your true feelings."

I took a long drag of my wine and let it burn its way down my esophagus to warm my belly. "Said like a true psychologist, my dear."

Jennie snorted, "Thank you?"

In many ways Jennie and I were opposites. Where I tended to be logical and over think things, Jennie was a daredevil, willing to try anything. She was a leap first, look later, kind of girl. I tended to stand on the side and carefully find the best solution. She got me to take chances, I got her to slow down and think.

Jennie was bubbly, I was not.

Jennie was blond, I was brunette.

But she had a point. I hadn't said much about what I was thinking and really, I could use a second opinion.

So I took another big swig, refilled my glass, and turned toward Jennie. She grinned wickedly, her blue eyes twinkling with excitement.

"So, at dinner last night he made a couple of big speeches . . ."

Her grin grew even larger, she looked like the Cheshire Cat, gripping her glass with both hands and leaning closer, "What did he say?"

Why was talking so hard? It was like turning a rusty gear. Sure it moved with enough force, but it was hard, took a lot of muscle, and wasn't very smooth. "Round One involved something about how he would never hurt me again."

Jennie started nodding enthusiastically, "That's good! He's reassuring you." Her positive outlook on Jake was mildly annoying. From the moment I first told her Jake stopped by she had been gushing about us getting back together. Her professional opinion was that he had done the logical thing: removed himself from a bad situation and worked on processing his troubles. Now that he was better, he was reintegrating into society and starting a new life.

I hated her professional opinion.

"Whatever," I muttered gulping some more wine. It was starting to do its job—the warm fuzzies were reaching my brain. "Then he explained to me what he wanted."

I paused there because I knew Jennie was going to agree with Jake. I didn't want to hear her positive take on things.

Jennie swung her legs around and sat up, "Spit it out!"

I grumbled for a moment before giving in, "He says he's not going away until I am absolutely sure I don't love him anymore. He says otherwise the doubts will keep eating at me."

Yep, Jennie was grinning like a fool. I rolled my eyes and grabbed for the dark chocolate.

"Eve . . . he's being smart. You never really moved on—and don't sell me any crap about Sebastian. I'm your best friend, I know the difference between love and contentment."

My eyes flicked over to her blue ones, "Maybe contentment is what I should be looking for."

Her face fell, the blue of her eyes deepening a shade or two, and a frown pulling down on her delicate lips, "No, it's not. You of all people do not need a content relationship. You need someone as passionate as you are. Someone who can keep up with you and handle your crazy."

That stopped me in my tracks. I paused mid-chew, the saliva pooling under my tongue until I had no choice but to swallow. "Are you suggesting I find a man who can *handle* me?"

Jennie tried not to smile, really she did, but the more she fought it the more she giggled until she simply gave in and doubled over in laughter. At me.

"This isn't funny!"

She looked up at me, still laughing, "Oh yes it is!"

I huffed, "Seriously, this isn't helping me!"

Jennie stopped laughing immediately and sat up, wiping a tear from the corner of her eye and taking a deep breath. "No, I know it's not. I apologize." She grabbed her glass and took a sip, taking another deep breath before looking back at me with a calm and serious expression. "I am not suggesting you need a handler. That came out all wrong. But I do think you need someone who understands you. Sebastian never understood you—he tolerated you. He was amused by your quirks, he indulged them, but he didn't *get* them. You will never, ever be happy with someone like him."

She was right. That was why I ended things with him. The lack of excitement and passion in our relationship had felt like drowning. I needed air. And for me, air involved someone who needed adventure and was willing to die for the things he cared about. I needed the male version of Jennie. "Maybe you and I should just give up on men and get married to each other?"

Now Jennie frowned, "Don't take this the wrong way sweetie, but you are *so* not my type. Not even a little bit."

Well, she couldn't blame me for trying.

With my lecture complete, Jennie swung her feet back up onto the lounger and leaned back with her wine. "I think you should spend some time with Jake. Not anything that makes you uncomfortable, maybe in a group setting. Give yourself a safe place to get to know him again."

I hated when she said something smart like that. Because the truth was, I did want to spend time with him. As much as it terrified me, and as sure as I was that Jake was the embodiment of pain, I desperately wanted to be near him. I wanted to know who he had become.

"Fine."

I saw her smile out of the corner of my eye, "He left all of us behind, you know. It would be nice if the whole gang could see him, get a chance to catch up."

"You told them?"

She sighed. I could hear the exasperation in her voice. My inability to deal with the Jake situation was driving her crazy. "Yes I told them. They were . . . excited to hear he was back and doing well, but they didn't want to make you uncomfortable. They all agreed to wait and see what happened with you. We love you."

Intellectually I knew all of this, but my brain was having trouble seeing things clearly. "Fine, if a situation presents itself for Jake to come see the gang, I will make it happen, per doctor's orders."

"Good. Now drink," she commanded.

\* \* \*

I WANDERED INTO THE suite owned by my family at The Trop. It was empty. My parents never came up for games and none of my friends had asked to use it tonight, which wasn't unusual. Wednesday night games weren't the most popular with the working crowd.

But this was my job. Baseball wasn't just what I did forty hours a week, it was in my blood. I'd grown up on the fields. Dugouts were my playhouses, clubhouses were where I'd steal buckets full of pink Bubalicious Bubble Gum and sunflower seeds. The guys were my secondary fathers and "uncles", their wives watched over my sisters and I as we got lost under bleachers collecting whatever we could find in our empty Bubalicious Bubble Gum buckets. When there were other kids they were our cohorts in trouble.

Having the light dusting of clay on my clothes and skin was comforting. So was the bizarre mix of hot dogs, popcorn, and beer. I loved the sound of the crowd and the crack of the bat.

I'd been an okay softball player, nothing great. Not like my sister Cassandra. She played through college and even piddled around professionally before hopping over to the corporate side like me.

Working in the industry was a given for us. Our dad was a legend. "Papa Joe" Daniels had been a celebrated third baseman for the Twins before switching sides and becoming a scout. He had a natural talent for identifying a player who could handle himself on the field with a booing crowd, bases loaded, two strikes, and the game riding on their shoulders.

Joe joined the Rays when they became an expansion team. My dad was a favorite with fans as a father figure, carefully watching over his recruits and guiding their careers. It was how he'd gotten his nickname.

I looked out over the crowd—my crowd—and enjoyed being alone with my thoughts. Jake now occupied them all the time, even during working hours. I had to give it to him—his plan was working brilliantly. I hated he was manipulating me so easily. But I liked his logic. We both needed to know without any doubts. There was no more room in my life for regrets.

I'd rather he just stayed away, and I had a strong suspicion that if asked him to, he would. But he'd already done the damage, planting those seeds of doubt deep inside my brain. If I asked him to leave me alone I'd hear his voice in the back of my head, years from now, whispering *are you sure?*

*Damn him!* Damn him to hell and back.

And damn Jennie for agreeing with him. I felt outnumbered. Like no one was on my side.

Well, actually that was wrong. My family was on my side. Every single one of them had told me to slice his balls off. But their support was reactionary and not terribly helpful.

I kept going back to the beginning. Back to us before he left.

I had been young and in love. And incredibly stupid.

Love was an emotion, and I'd been totally and completely in love with him.

Die for him, have his babies, grow old with him, love.

I knew it was special. Sebastian and I never had that. I cared about him, but I wouldn't have dropped everything to be with him. I appreciated him, but I wouldn't have died for him. I wasn't even sure I wanted to have his children. It was the kind of loving relationship that makes you think it's love because there are so many wonderful things that went along with it. He was sweet, he took care of me, he respected me. We shared a lot of the same interests and hobbies. He liked boating and fishing, and was more than happy to indulge my food fetish.

But it wasn't earth shattering. I wouldn't have torn myself to shreds to save him. I wouldn't have given my life for his happiness.

I would, and did, all those things for Jake.

I didn't think I could live through doing it again.

Which was why I needed to find a way to end things with Jake once and for all. To move on in a healthy way that would allow me to find real love with someone I could trust.

We were in the third inning when I heard his voice from somewhere down the hall.

"Sorry, I didn't realize—" Jake said.

Sam, the security guard, replied, "How do you not know that? Have you been living in a hole?"

Jake chuckled, "Something like that."

He was standing across from Sam, casually dressed in a Rays t-shirt and dark jeans. He looked good. Casual was a very good look on him. The dark shade of blue made his tan skin stand out and his green eyes seemed greener.

"Can I help you?" I asked, startling both Sam and Jake.

Jake's jaw fell open with surprise and he took a step back, his eyes widening. He was obviously not expecting to see me. But that didn't stop his eyes from roaming up and down my body, drinking me in. My body instantly responded to his attention, heat flushing up into my chest and down between my legs. I wanted him to want me, to know what he'd given up when he left.

What he couldn't have back.

I was extremely glad I'd decided to wear my favorite jeans and custom made Rays t-shirt. It accentuated all of my assets. Assets that I stupidly wanted him to enjoy seeing.

"Sorry, Miss Daniels. This guy was trying to sneak into the suites. Don't worry, I'll take care of him."

I touched Sam's arm to stop him from grabbing Jake. "Don't worry, I've got this."

Jake and Sam both shot me a quizzical look. Sam because it was his job to deal with morons, and Jake because I was going against everything I told him I wanted. "Ma'am, are you sure?" Sam asked.

I let my eyes wander over Jake from top to bottom, letting my instincts rule my decisions instead of my head. My instincts wanted Jake to stick around. "He's an old friend of the family. I promise he's just an idiot, not a security threat."

Jake frowned at my insult, but didn't interject.

"All right . . ." Sam replied, looking both of us over carefully. I'll be on the radio if you need me."

I waited until Sam was gone before I looked back at Jake. "Did you really think you could just waltz into the suites, Jake?"

He shrugged his shoulders. "I've got a bit of a learning curve to make up for. A lot has changed."

I looked at him pointedly and crossed my arms, "You lived here for a full two years after 9/11. You should know this type of security is standard."

He sighed, "Eve, I know this is hard for you to understand, but that was a lifetime ago."

*More like two lifetimes ago.* "Well, you can't just wander around the luxury suites like you own the place."

His lips quirked up at that and a mischievous look twinkled in his eyes. "No, that's your job."

*Really?* He was going there?

In college Jake and our gang of friends teased me mercilessly. Not only about the way I acted at the stadium or around the team, but how the staff treated me. I knew it was all in fun (my friends certainly enjoyed the benefits that came with being a friend of Eve Daniels) but it had always succeeded in getting me good and pissed.

"Do you really want to start with that? Here I thought we were being friendly . . ."

Jake's smile didn't waver in the slightest, "Not at all, *friend.*"

Something about the way he said that word physically hurt. We were not friends. We would never be "just friends". He was my *best* friend.

The minute the thought flitted through my brain I froze. Jake *was* my best friend. Not anymore.

Suddenly my mind was flooded with snapshots of Jake and I, not as lovers, but as the close friends we always were. No one had ever understood me the way

Jake did. Things other people found annoying or strange, he always found adorable or simply one of my unique and fantastic qualities. There was no one else I ever turned to when I needed to be understood—not even Jennie. "Were you coming to check out our suite?"

He nodded, his eyes searching my face, wondering what was going on in my head. "I've been taking a tour of my past."

*Our past.*

I waved for him to follow me, "Come on. It's empty."

A lot of memories accompanied the two of us into the room. We'd been to so many games over our four years together. Sometimes alone, sometimes entertaining family friends, sometimes partying with our own friends. All in this suite.

We'd had sex in this suite.

My eyes flew to the bar—we'd had sex behind it once. My belly quivered at the memory, taking my breath away. It had been quick and exciting—and had led to a problem for us. Apparently we had an exhibitionist streak, and it all started there, behind the bar. My eyes shot around the room, remembering sex against the wall, on the chair . . . his hand on my jeans between my legs when no one was looking. I couldn't count the number of orgasms he'd given me between these walls.

I swallowed, trying to suppress my body's reaction to the memories, but it was too late. I was breathing heavy, a deep throb between my legs, and shiver of desire washing over my skin, wanting to be touched.

It made me incredibly aware of Jake's presence— his size and his warmth radiating out in the little room. Wherever he moved, I could feel him. There was a push and pull between us as our energies collided.

"Hasn't changed," he murmured, his eyes dark with their own sordid memories.

A bat cracked down on the field and the crowd cheered, drawing our attention to the field. It was a fly ball, center fielder caught it and sent it back in to the pitcher.

"Nope. Some things don't change," I murmured, watching him out of the corner of my eye.

His head snapped around to look at me. "True enough." His eyes searched mine, asking for more, but I didn't give it to him.

"We can sit and watch the game for a while if you like." I wanted to hold on to these feelings, the magical way my body felt just from being close to him. The black emptiness that always haunted my memories was disappearing.

Jennie was right, I needed to spend time with him. It was the only way I was going to process my feelings. Being *alone* with him probably wasn't my wisest decision, but I was trying desperately to follow the advice she'd given me. And seeing him at my place of work, even alone like this, seemed strangely safe.

"Sit," I demanded moving down the row and propping my feet up.

Jake hesitated, but then did the same. "I missed this, you know."

When I didn't reply he sat quietly watching the game.

Another high pop fly sent the crowd cheering. The inning was over.

Cue the uncomfortable maneuvering. We were both quiet for a few minutes as we watched the crowds below us rearrange themselves.

Just for a moment, I allowed myself a fantasy. The opportunity to picture myself happy with Jake. Maybe we could be together. Maybe we'd make it work this time. And maybe he'd run at the first sign of trouble. He claimed he wouldn't, but do any of us really know what we're capable of until we're knee-deep in the situation?

And that included me. But I knew the answer to that. Anything that involved Jake also involved me losing control. I'd tried to keep from losing myself to him, but I just wasn't capable. Jake was too powerful, his presence too strong for me. He was my weakness.

And he was right. I loved him too much. I always would. It wasn't healthy.

It was for that reason I could never let myself fall under the delusion we could be happy together. Eventually something would take it away. He wasn't the kind of guy I could recover from again.

"How's Papa Joe? I hear he finally retired." Jake didn't turn to look at me as he spoke. He kept his eyes trained on the field in front of us.

I pushed away my brief fantasy and focused on dealing with my present.

"Dad's good. I don't think he knows what to do with himself, but he's good. He needs a hobby."

Jake chuckled, looking down at his hands. "I can't imagine Joe with time on his hands. How is your mom taking it?"

"My mom is a mess right now. Dad is home and June started college this year. She refused to come home for the summer."

Jake's head snapped around, his green eyes meeting mine. "You're kidding?" he gasped.

I shook my head slowly. "Nope. June is really taking a stand on the whole independence thing. So, needless to say, my dad has gotten a free pass for the time being."

"Poor Junebug."

"Ha! I don't know who to feel more sorry for, June or my mom. They are going to kill each other."

Jake just shook his head, his eyes lingering on mine as if he didn't want to look away. He'd fit right in with my family from the start. Knowing about his crappy home life they'd taken him in as one of their own. He'd been a part of everything we did. He came home with me on holidays and long weekends, went out with us when we were doing things, and on vacations. He'd been the brother my sisters never had.

And he'd broken their hearts, too, when he disappeared. Not just because he broke my heart, but because they loved him and knew why he had left. They were as heartbroken as anyone that Jake's demons had driven him away.

"Cassandra?"

I sat up and leaned on my knees so I could look over at his beautiful face. The face that would never be mine again. "Married and living in Boston with a three-year-old boy named Teddy, and one on the way."

"Oh my god." His reaction was just as I expected. If he'd been here, Jake would have tormented Cassandra's husband. For as rough and laidback as Jake was, Timothy was groomed and tight-knit. Jake would have put him through his paces, made him earn Cassandra's hand. Been the good big brother.

"Yep."

"Boston? Seriously? June and Cassandra are both gone? Mara must be losing her mind."

To say the least. I'd been steering clear of my mom for months. "Timothy, Cassandra's husband, actually has my job, but up in Boston for the Sox. Cassandra is taking a permanent leave of absence for the next five or so years, and Junebug is at Yale. So, while mom is crazy, she's at least concentrating all the crazy up in the northeast."

"Are we taking bets on how long it is before she buys a condo?"

I laughed at that one. "No."

A comfortable silence descended between us. It was nice, actually.

We lasted two full innings that way.

"You like your job?" he asked. I had a feeling he'd

been working his way up to it for a while by the way his fidgeting had slowly ramped up to a full vibration.

"Love it."

"Good." He finally calmed down. "I'm glad you found your spot. You were so worried before graduation about not fitting in."

"True. It took me a little while, but it worked out. Josh is awesome and we work well together."

I could remember those nights lying on Jake's chest while he stroked my hair. I whispered my confessions against his warm skin. My fears of not fitting in, of being accused of my father getting me my job.

"You earned it, Eve. All on your own." He'd reminded me.

"Doesn't mean people won't talk."

"So give them something to talk about."

Jake was probably the strongest person I'd ever met. He always saw a solution, no matter how dark or impossible the situation. It was like he was missing the gene that allowed people like me to see the possibility of defeat.

Even with my broken heart I'd remembered his words during my first few months at work. I'd kept my head down and worked my ass off. I'd done a damn fine job and worked my way up to director all on my own.

I looked back at Jake. He was studying me as if he was debating whether to tell me something.

I raised an eyebrow, "Something on your mind?"

He shook his head and sighed. "I'm sorry I blindsided you the other day at the presentation. I'm really not trying to be mean. I just know you won't see me if I don't make you."

I came to a complete standstill. My heart stopped, even my breathing. I hated hearing him say things like that, as if I were someone he needed to manipulate. He looked away, back at the action on the field.

"Did you miss me?" I blurted. Something deep inside me needed to hear him say it again. I was too overwhelmed when he first came to my house. His words were still echoing in my ears, but they felt like a dream.

"Yes," he replied simply. He didn't look away from the field, but I saw the muscles in his neck and shoulders stiffen and his jaw lock in place. "You were my best friend, Eve. I loved you. You were the only good thing I've ever had in my life." He paused, his muscles working, "I lost all of that when I left . . . Of course I missed you."

"I think that's what hurts the most, Jake."

His green eyes swung to mine, they were deep and dark, so sad it broke my heart all over again. Would we ever stop hurting each other?

He didn't say anything. He just waited for me to explain.

"You were my best friend. I told you things I've never told anyone. We did things together I've never done with anyone else." The truth in that confession felt particularly exposing. It showed him just how profoundly he'd affected my life then and since. And I saw that realization flash across his face. "I let you know me in a way no one else knows me . . . and you left me. You didn't say goodbye, you didn't explain . . . you just *left me.*"

The energy between us was quickly shifting, twisting into something new. It felt good. We were talking and dealing with the hurt and resentment. It was helping to have those words out in the air between us.

"That's why I'm here now. To fix this. You didn't deserve to be hurt by my demons, but you were. And I'm going to fix it."

I didn't have any idea how that was possible, but I was beginning to see the wisdom in the advice I had been given the night before. "Jennie says you're right, that I need to know for sure."

Jake watched me intently, waiting for me to work out the things in my head.

Finally I said what I didn't want to, but I knew I needed. "We're having a dinner party at our house tomorrow night. Come over and we'll see if we can get through a meal together."

His eyes lit up. "Challenge accepted." He said it so fast it was like he had been waiting and begging for the chance.

## Chapter 4

"Should we have a code word?" Jennie asked. She was being entirely serious, too.

"Like *purple rain is falling outside*?" I asked, expecting her to laugh.

Instead she scrunched up her face as she thought long and hard about it. "No, no. It should be no more than two words. Like Rumpelstiltskin."

"Rumpelstiltskin?"

She nodded vehemently, "Just say that, and I'll know to have him thrown out on his backside. Ricardo will do it in a heartbeat."

That was a fact. One of our best friends was Sylvia Garcia. She had been a steadfast friend and early member of our "gang". Two years after we graduated she fell in love with, and married, Ricardo. He'd taken it upon himself to become the big brother of the group. He was fiercely loyal and had very set ideas on how women should be treated. He'd watched over all of us single ladies. If I needed it, Ricardo would gladly step in and rescue me.

Tonight's little fete was our once a month get-together for international food and drink. Jennie and I were hosting this month with a Brazilian theme. Jennie had gone all out, even redecorating the house. Besides Jennie, Sylvia, and Ricardo, there would be Jennie's friend from work, Heather, and her girlfriend Sharon. And of course, Jake.

I still wasn't sure if inviting him was a brilliant ploy to move on, or sheer stupidity.

"Did you taste the chimichurri sauce?" she asked.

Had I tasted it? Yes. Had I thought about drinking it? Quite possibly. "I put a bowl aside with my name on it. Touch it and die."

Jennie laughed. "Shall we reward ourselves for all of this hard work with a toast?"

"Here, here!" I agreed. The drink of the night was *Caipirinha*, a Brazilian rum cocktail we usually made for our weekend boating trips. It was delicious, cool, and could knock you on your ass if you didn't watch how much you were drinking. We'd made them weaker that usual for tonight since it was the middle of the week and we all had to be up for work in the morning.

"I've got a date tomorrow night . . ." Jennie drawled as she clunked her glass against mine.

"Really? Who is the lucky guy?"

I could tell by the flash in her eyes and the flirty way she was flitting about that Jennie was excited. "His name is Andrew. I ran into him at lunch today and he asked me out."

"What does Andrew do?"

She grinned, "He's a lawyer. Criminal defense. And he's *hot*."

Which for Jennie meant lean and extremely clean-cut. She and I could not be more opposite in that department. We both liked them tall and dark, but where I liked them rugged and down to earth, Jennie liked them well groomed and high-class. I wanted a guy who would spend the day on my boat. Jennie wanted a guy to take her to dinner and dancing.

A lawyer sounded just right.

"Where is he taking you?"

She beamed, "Mis en Place."

Crap, he would probably last a month, tops. If he was starting off at one of the nicest restaurants in town, he was trying way too hard. He was peaking too early. It wasn't love at first sight—it was extreme compatibility at first sight.

At least she'd have fun while it lasted.

The door opened and all our guests started pouring in.

Jake trickled in last.

He looked a little shy at first, getting the lay of the land. I watched him from the comfort of my corner. He was dressed in a white linen button down with the sleeves rolled to the elbows and dark jeans. His dark hair was wet and brushed back like he'd just taken a shower. He was just sexy. That was all there was to it.

Jennie flitted over to him, taking the bottle of red wine he offered and kissing him on the cheek. They whispered a few things to each other, Jake's face serious while Jennie smiled.

Jennie said something else and Jake finally smiled, his dimple appearing. I was instantly transported back to the night I first realized I was in love with him.

It had been a night like this, in this room, actually. It looked different back then, pre-renovation. We had a giant old square coffee table and a ratty old couch, a crappy rug on the floor. It was game night. Three different games were going on and all our friends were lounging around, drinking and talking smack.

Jake was sitting on the floor in front of the coffee table playing Risk. He was having a great time. I was curled up on the couch behind him, watching while I read a book. He was wearing a white t-shirt and jeans, not entirely unlike tonight, but he had on a baseball hat.

He was wearing it backwards.

His skin was tan, like it was now, and he was grinning. It had taken my breath away. He was so handsome and so happy that night. His eyes had been alive and his dimple . . . for that one night it seemed to be on his cheek permanently. All of his coloring was so perfectly in balance . . . *he* was perfect.

I couldn't take my eyes off him. I tried desperately to memorize every single thing about him. And I had never forgotten. Not the sound of his voice, not the rumble of his laugh, not the way he looked at me.

I had never forgotten the moment he turned to me with those bright green eyes and I knew I was in love.

My whole body suddenly ached, as if it were crying out in mourning for that moment. It actually hurt. A real visceral feeling I could quantify. Love wasn't just an emotion; it was a full body experience. One I was clearly not over.

I stayed on the edges watching Jake interact with our guests. They kept him busy for a full thirty minutes before we transitioned from appetizers to dinner. We ate in the living room around the coffee table. It kept the conversation flowing and casual.

Sharon and I were in a deep conversation about the merits of organic food when Jake came up alongside us. Every hair on my body stood straight up. Jake was like a lightning rod directing all the energy around us.

"The food is delicious, Eve. Did you cook?"

I smiled weakly up at him. My heart was racing uncontrollably. "Some. I made the chimichurri sauce."

He nodded, his eyes drifting casually between Sharon and me. "It's fantastic."

"Thank you," I said softly. Being near him was setting all of my senses on fire. Good and bad. Happy and sad. I was an emotional hurricane.

"Your mom's house looks a little different. You've been busy."

I took a deep breath and looked around the living room. I was so proud of my renovations. "It was a good way to keep me busy for a few years."

He nodded thoughtfully, dropping his eyes and clearing his throat, "Yes, well, it's amazing. I'm glad you've been able to keep it. I always felt like this house was yours."

As strange as that sounded, I agreed completely. As a child visiting my grandparents here I'd known this house would one day be mine. It felt like home every bit as much as the house I grew up in. My mom inherited it two years before I started college and with the little house on Davis Island's so close to the University of South Florida, it was a no-brainer. Jennie had moved in with me and a year later, Jake did too. Sylvia had lived with us one year, and a rotating list of our other friends over the years.

This house had always been the center of everything. And to a certain extent, it still was.

"Did you ever build your library?" he asked.

My heart skipped a beat. If there was anything I loved as much as Jake, it was my library.

I waved. "Follow me."

Jake's eyebrows shot up and he fell in line behind me.

"I'm gonna get another plate," Sharon called shaking her head. She knew better than to get between Jake and me.

I opened the door to a room that sat on the back of the house. The dark wood door matched the dark wood and brown leather of everything inside. On the right wall were tall dark bookshelves stuffed with books, knickknacks, and pictures. At the very top was a transom where light spilled in during the day. On the far wall was a bank of French doors that opened up onto my back porch. Above the French doors was another transom. I could pull the heavy dark red curtains and still have a delightful glow of daylight in my library. It was one of my favorite features.

The floor was dark wood that matched everything else in the old house from the forties and covering that was a thick red oriental rug. A long leather ottoman stood in the center of the room with a matching couch on one side and mismatched armchairs on the other. Blankets were draped over every available corner.

On the left wall was my enormous wood desk surrounded by more bookshelves. It was the exact library I dreamed of having.

"Just like I pictured it," he murmured.

"Sometimes I spend all day in here."

He nodded and walked quickly around the room, "It's like being inside your head."

The temperature in the room dropped. The electric pull between us was stronger than ever.

To say I was confused was an understatement. I hated the man standing across the room from me just as strongly as I loved him.

"We should get back to the party," I murmured, turning and leaving.

"You've done amazing things with your life, Eve."

I paused, part of me wanting to turn around, sit down on that comfy leather couch, and talk to my former best friend for hours. But I knew I couldn't do that. It would hurt too much. "Thank you," it was barely more than a whisper. My heart was being strangled by my rising emotions.

"You are very welcome."

I took a deep breath and rejoined the party.

We kept our distance for the rest of the night. I never had to say 'Rumpelstiltskin' or ask for Ricardo to throw Jake out on his backside. In fact, I was feeling pretty good. Yes, I was attracted to Jake and I mourned the loss of his friendship as much as I ever had, but all of it was surprisingly manageable.

Until my phone rang.

Things were put in motion that were about to change all that.

"What's wrong, sweetie?" Jennie asked. She was buzzing hard, a permanent grin affixed to her pretty face, and a non-stop stream of babbling pouring out of her mouth.

"That was Dad. He and Mom are hopping a flight to see June."

Jennie frowned, pulling her brows down. "Oh no. Is everything ok?"

I shrugged. "Probably. Apparently mom didn't like the sound of June's voice." Everyone chuckled good-naturedly at my mother's over-protectiveness. I probably shouldn't have said what I said next, but I'd had a few drinks and I was relaxed. I didn't think about the potential ramifications. "They were planning a cookout this weekend and all the food is going to go to waste, he asked if we wanted to come down and use up the food for them."

Jennie's face lit up immediately and she started a ridiculous bounce. "Oh, yes! Let's get the whole gang. We haven't had a party at your parent's house in what . . . two years?"

I nodded. "Yep, since Max destroyed the guest suite."

Jake's eyebrows shot up. "You've got to be kidding me."

Jennie shook her head. "Oh no. The party got seriously out of control. Stephen got lost on the beach and we found him asleep in a sand dune the next morning. Sylvia—"

She and Ricardo groaned, "No, please don't remind us!"

Jennie grinned. "These two knuckleheads had sex on the boat and passed out. Luckily the shoddy anchor job held. And poor Max . . ." Jennie looked over at me with the saddest eyes. She had the worst crush on the poor lunk head. He was an artist at heart, but usually veered dangerously close to rock star status without actually achieving it. His band had played for hours that night and somehow managed to trash one of my parent's guesthouses. Joe made the boys come back every weekend for a month to help the contractor piece it back together and redecorate it. Not to mention he made them pay for it. "Let's just say he's never lived that night down. Joe didn't let him come for Thanksgiving that year."

It was the perfect weekend to get away. The Rays were on the road until Tuesday, so my schedule was completely flexible. Maybe a nice weekend away with my friends would be fun.

Then Jennie said what changed everything. "Jake, you should come, too! You can see everyone that way!"

My heart stopped as all eyes, even Jake's, swung over to me.

Weirdness levels skyrocketed. We'd only just barely managed to survive a ballgame and a dinner party. Wasn't a weekend away—at my parent's house, filled with memories of our old life—pushing things too far and too fast?

Or maybe it was just what I needed. Push it hard and get it over with. If I was lucky, come Monday morning I would be able to confidently look Jake in the eye and tell him I didn't love him anymore. That he and I could finally move on.

"Let's do it," I said firmly and before I lost my nerve.

Jake's eyebrows shot up and cheers filled the room. Plans were quickly made, not that I listened to any of them. Jennie was taking care of it all.

Thirty minutes later the party started breaking up. Jennie and Sylvia were in the kitchen cleaning, Ricardo was putting our things back where they belonged and taking out the trash, Heather and Sharon had already left.

"You don't have to come," I said as I walked Jake to the door.

He had a sly grin, the kind that said he was more than happy to come for the weekend—and not just as friends. "I wouldn't miss it for the world, darlin'."

*Darlin'.* I swallowed at the way it sounded coming from him. Sweet and reverent. It promised to be both adoring and sexy. The way the letters rolled off his tongue and his voice gruffly vibrated behind them . . . it could easily change their meaning. I liked the way it sounded. I liked that it was directed at me.

Which was all wrong.

## Chapter 5

*It* was Thursday night and Jennie was out on her first date with Andrew. I told her to bring me home dessert. Meanwhile I was enjoying my evening alone. I had the music blasting, a pizza open on my bed, and I was giving myself a pedicure.

Because I was alone and expecting to stay that way, I was wearing dark gray leggings, a sports bra, and a giant racerback tank. My hair was piled up into a messy bun. I was twisted like a pretzel to reach my toes and singing at the top of my lungs, so I didn't hear him come in.

Not until I saw him lounging in my doorway, watching me with a look of pure amusement. "What the hell are you doing here?" I yelled at Jake over the music. "You scared the shit out of me!"

That only made him chuckle. He'd clearly just come from work. He was dressed in a very sharp three-piece suit. Dark gray, pinstriped, and obviously tailored to his frame. My mouth went a little dry as I looked him up and down.

The twinkle in his eye said he'd seen my longing look. *Crap.*

I pointed at the remote just out of my contorted reach and Jake smiled more, shifting away from the doorjamb to lower the music.

"Sorry I surprised you. Having fun?" His amusement at my position clearly giving him fits.

I glowered at him. "I was supposed to be having a nice night alone."

"I know. Jennie is on her date. She asked me to run by and grab some stuff for your parents house." He paused long enough to give me stern look. "You keep the key in the same place. Don't you think you should change that?"

I finished the nail I was working on and untwisted myself. "You could have knocked, or called, or texted. You do know how those things work, right? That isn't on your 'learning curve' is it?"

I noticed as his eyes longingly wandered over my pizza so I picked up a piece and shoved it in my mouth, intentionally baiting him.

"Yes, Eve, I know how to use a phone. I will try to give you a heads up next time, though I must say surprising you is working out for me so far." Cocky bastard. But he was right. So far his "surprise" visits had earned him multiple occasions to talk to me, the obvious confidence of my best friend, and now, a few uninterrupted moments alone in my bedroom, of all places.

I threw my pizza at him, which he, of course, deftly caught and stuck into his own mouth. "Thank you. I was hoping you'd offer. I haven't had dinner."

It just pissed me off more. Who did he think he was waltzing into my house and asking for my pizza? "Well grab your stuff for Jennie and go get some."

He didn't seem to like my choice of words. His eyes zeroed in on me in a way that took me back. It wasn't a friendly look—it was a lustful look. "Are you driving your car down?"

"Yes." What did that mean? How else would I get to my parent's house . . . wishful thinking?

"I'm taking the Bronco," he said looking down, then suddenly back up and into my eyes. "You are more than welcome to ride with me."

The idea locked my muscles in a death grip. I couldn't think of a worse idea. "I think I'll be fine in the car. With Jennie." And her very, very safe conversation. There was no chance Jennie was going to try to sleep with me or make me fall in love with her.

He shrugged as if my refusal didn't bother him and finished off the pizza. "Hot pink toes?"

His question annoyed me and I couldn't for the life of me figure out why he was in my bedroom. "It's summer, I thought it would be fun."

I watched as he looked around my room. When he'd lived here with me it had been one of four tiny identical upstairs rooms. When I renovated (and since I was single for the foreseeable future) I'd turned those four bedrooms into two: Jennie's was directly in front of the stairwell, mine directly behind.

I absolutely loved my bedroom. There was an enormous overstuffed chair in an alcove with a window that overlooked the backyard. A large bookcase held more of my favorite books and pictures. But my bed was my favorite. I'd spent a stupid amount of money on it. It was enormous considering I slept alone. A king-sized dark wood antique headboard, intricately carved with vines and filigree, and a dark-blue bedding set made of the softest fabric I could find. I don't even remember how much it cost because I'd had to block out the total. Otherwise I wouldn't have handed over my credit card. But it was worth it. I could get lost in my bed and I could sleep naked any time I wanted. It was like being held in the caress of a cloud.

"I love what you've done with the house. It really looks incredible."

I swelled with content pride. "Thank you."

He continued his uninvited tour of my room and I let him. For some reason seeing him in my intimate space had me paralyzed. It was like the past and the present were colliding in front of my eyes. The new Jake in my new room. It was so different: the suit, the swagger, the confidence... and it wasn't like I had cheap posters decorating my ratty walls anymore. He paused in front of a picture of all of us, the whole gang.

"I'm kind of impressed you didn't cut me out of this picture."

I smirked. "That's the replacement. You should

have seen what I did to the original."

He turned to look back at me, his hands back in his pockets, his eyes unmistakably seductive. "We're all grown up now. What are your plans for your life?"

His question confused me. I *was* living my life. But then again, it hadn't taken me until this year to figure myself out. "What I'm doing right now. I work, hang out with the gang, visit my family. What else is there?"

He was burning a hole right through me. "That's not what I meant. No boyfriends? You planning on settling down with Mr. Right and having kids?" He was so different. He was demanding, almost angry. His questions seemed more like an accusation than anything else.

Something flipped inside me. An anger erupted out of nowhere. "Jake, that is none of your damn business."

He grimaced. "I think it is. Why aren't you married, Eve? You are beautiful and smart. There are a million men lined up at your door, but you're here alone. So, I'll ask you again. What are your plans, Eve?"

I stood up very slowly, attempting to control the eruption taking place inside me, walked out into the hallway, and growled, "Get. Out."

"No," he replied just as firmly, not leaving my room. In fact, I was pretty sure I heard him sit on my bed.

"Get. Out." I repeated through my clenched teeth.

"Get. Back. In. Here." He growled back.

I rolled my eyes. Jake had definitely changed. He

never, ever would have stood up to me, let alone ordered me to do anything.

Suddenly he was in front of me and glaring down from above. "Please, just talk to me for few minutes. I promise I won't bite."

"I'm more worried about a kiss," I said before I could stop myself.

Jake's eyebrows shot up. "I'm not going to kiss you, darlin'."

A part of me was pretty disappointed at that piece of information. "Fine," I replied, stomping back into my room.

Jake strolled in behind me, sighing, "I just want to make sure I haven't completely fucked up the rest of your life, Eve. Why aren't you married?"

*Because I've never met anyone as good as you? There hasn't been a man since you who has made me weak in the knees or throbbing for his touch.* "I haven't met anyone worth marrying, Jake. You don't just put your name in a bowl and hope to be picked."

He eyed me, gaging my reaction, looking for the lie. "All right. As long as it isn't because of me."

*It is absolutely because of you.*

"You think you ruined men for me, Jake?"

He grinned his cocky half-smile I used to love so much. I loved it because it was one of the few times his dimple showed. My dimple. I couldn't help it, my eyes were drawn right to it, and he saw. I'm pretty sure he stopped breathing, his eyes burning into me.

"Eve . . ." he murmured.

My heart stopped. There was an explosive combination of lust, passion, and longing circulating around my bedroom. Anything would set us off.

"Do you need help with the things Jennie asked you to get?" I asked, trying to deflect what was coming.

He shook his head. "Just show me what to take." He didn't take his eyes off me. I didn't take my eyes off him. There was a running stream of *'He'll ruin you, don't do this, get out of here!'* going through the back of my mind. I was half listening to it. The other half wondering if maybe all my fears were unfounded. That maybe Jake and I had gone through all our bad already. That if we did get back together, we'd be fine.

But could I really take that chance?

"Then let me show you." I quickly left the room and practically threw myself down the stairs. I hadn't missed the disappointed look on Jake's face as I ran.

I could hear his heavy footfalls behind me. "Why are you running?" he asked. His voice was deep and full of emotion.

I spun around to find he was right behind me. "You know why."

"No I don't."

My barefooted view was of his chest. His wide, strong chest. The suit looked so good on him. Growing up suited him. He grabbed my chin and tilted it up so that I was looking at him. "Why are you running away from me?"

I wanted to tell him how I was feeling but I knew if he believed we had a chance he'd take it. So I lied.

"You're just too much, Jake. You fill up the room. You say you just want to make sure I know what I want. Even if it's not you, but I can see you want more. I can't give you more, Jake."

He dropped his hand away. "I'm sorry."

I turned as fast as I could and scurried out the front and around to the garage. Jennie had put two boxes aside. I had no idea what was in them. Just like I didn't know she'd asked Jake to pick them up. I was starting to suspect Jennie had a few tricks up her sleeve.

Jake picked them up silently and placed them in the back of the Bronco. I didn't know what to say to him after that and neither did he, apparently. It had been an assault to the senses on all fronts. He had just turned to me with his ruffled hair and confused eyes when Jennie pulled up, followed by another car I didn't know. I was guessing Andrew had come back for a drink.

Jennie hopped out of her car holding up my dessert. "Here you go!" She hurried to my side. "Dinner was amazing! He came to meet you!"

She was glowing, absolutely glowing. I had never, ever seen her like this. "Wow, you brought him home already? That's a good thing, right?"

Andrew stepped out of his cool, black sports car and my jaw dropped. Jennie was right. Andrew was *hot*. He was clean cut, perfect black suit and red tie, a head of dark hair to die for, piercing brown eyes, but what was truly magnificent about Andrew was his smile. It was earth shattering, make your knees weak, movie star quality. He even had *me* swooning and he wasn't anything close to my type.

"Shit, Jennie. He's gorgeous."

She giggled, "I told you. And he's wonderful. I'm telling you, I like this guy, Eve."

He and Jake shook hands. I noticed the way Jake was giving him a careful once over and the easy way Andrew introduced himself. He had an air about him that exuded confidence, but not in an arrogant way. He just genuinely seemed to know who he was and didn't care what anyone else thought.

"I brought dessert for everyone," Jennie said. "I was hoping you'd still be here, Jake." She had that mischievous glint to her eyes that told me she was in full matchmaker mode. She wasn't going to let the idea of Jake and I getting back together go.

I gave her a look that told her I knew what she was up to. But she just smiled sweetly holding up the bag of dessert, and pranced into the house.

"Didn't feel like dancing?" I asked as I closed the door.

Andrew turned. "I wanted to meet you all. Jennie couldn't stop talking about you."

That was when I realized Jennie was beaming and Andrew was looking pretty dreamy himself. He was obviously taken with my girl. Maybe Andrew was going to be around longer than a month after all. Maybe Mis en Place for their first date wasn't peaking on the first date. Maybe it was starting off on the right foot. I liked the way they looked together. But it also made me sad. I'd looked at Jake like that once upon a time.

"How long have the two of you been together?" Andrew asked looking at Jake and me. It was an innocent question, but so completely wrong.

I cleared my throat and pulled out my chocolate pie, letting Jake take the question.

"We're not together any more. We dated back in college."

Andrew looked surprised. "Oh, I suppose that's why you look so comfortable together. Did you all go to USF?"

Jennie was still smiling like a fool, "Oh yes. And most of the gang you'll meet tomorrow." She turned toward me. "He's coming with us, if that's okay with you."

That had me completely shocked. One date and Andrew was coming with us for the weekend? "Of course. There's plenty of room."

"Jennie said you guys were planning on heading out right after lunch, correct?"

I stuck a spoon full of pie in my mouth. "That's the plan," I mumbled, pulling the spoon out. "That way we can take the boats out before dinner." My parents lived on Captiva Island, a good two and half hour drive south. If we left at noon we'd have just enough time to take the boats out.

"The girls love the water," Jake chimed in with a wink at Jennie.

"I've been to Captiva before. And Sanibel a few

times. It's a great place. You must have loved growing up out there, Eve."

I had. It was an amazing life, as long as I didn't think about how often my dad was gone. But we'd made it work. His spring training with the Twins was down there in Fort Myers, and most of baseball season fell over summer so that we could travel with the team when we wanted. But for large chunks of time, I was fatherless. It was probably the only thing I could justifiably complain about. Otherwise, I'd grown up in a privileged paradise, with beaches and boats at my fingertips.

"My grandparents moved there and built the house before my dad was born, back when almost no one lived out there. No causeway, no access to the mainland without a boat."

"You don't hear many stories like that," he replied.

"Eve is old Florida on both sides of her family," Jennie explained for me. "This house was her mother's."

His eyebrows shot up, "Very, very rare indeed. My family moved here in the nineties from New York. Seems most of the people I meet are like me, not the two of you." He was beaming at Jennie again. They really did have it bad.

"Where did you go to school, Andrew? Stetson?"

He smiled politely. Even that basic smile was swoon-worthy. "For law school, yes. Florida Southern before that."

He had a good, solid background and all local. He

was sounding more and more like Jennie's perfect match.

"All right. Well, I have to get up early so I can escape work on time," I mumbled in a vain attempt to exit the room with as little drama as possible.

It didn't work.

Jennie perked up again, pulling herself from Andrew's enormous, gorgeous grin. "I'm riding with Andrew, Eve. Maybe you should hitch a ride with Jake. That way we won't have an extra car." She might as well have just handcuffed me to Jake and thrown away the key. It would have been easier, and probably subtler.

"Fine," I grumbled, dropping my spoon in the sink and shoving my box in the trash.

When I turned around Jake was behind me again. It was becoming a habit of his. "Walk me out?" he asked softly.

I shrugged, the fight going completely out of me. I was tired of fighting. Fighting Jake, fighting Jennie's secret schemes. For the rest of tonight I was going with the flow. Grumpily and with a bad attitude, but with the flow.

I don't think Jennie or Andrew noticed as we left, he was whispering in her ear and she was giggling. The feeling they were perfect for each other hit me again.

At the door Jake stopped and looked down at me, "You don't have to ride with me if I'm going to make you this uncomfortable. In fact, I don't have to go at all."

Something about the idea of him not going made me feel queasy. And I still liked the idea that it would be intense, that by the end of the weekend I would have more answers than questions. He needed to go. I needed to work Jake Spencer out of my system by overdosing. "It's fine. I miss the Bronco. It'll be fun to take her for a spin again."

Jake half-grinned. The damn dimple smiled at me. My heart took off again.

"She's just the same. I think I missed her almost as much as I missed you."

And now I'd stopped breathing. Not to mention how my insides were quivering being so close to his warm body.

His lids lowered and he leaned in toward me, just a little. "Eve, I lied earlier . . . upstairs."

It was like he was drawing me in toward him even though neither of us had moved. Or had we? Maybe I'd stepped in to him, because he seemed so much closer. So much more of his scent was wafting around me, making me dizzy. "Oh, what about?"

He loomed over me, his eyes fixated on my lips. "Kissing you. I do. I want to kiss you."

I was inside his arms now, my head tilting up toward his lips, my eyes gazing into his dark green ones. "I want you to kiss me," I murmured back.

And he did. He wrapped those big, rough hands of his around my face and pulled me to him. His lips grazed mine gently, kissing first my bottom, then my top lip. Then he claimed all of my mouth, kissing me deeply, his tongue gliding down along mine, searching for a way completely inside me.

I pressed my body flush against his, feeling every molecule of my body come to life for the first time in years. My breasts ached to be in his hands, my legs begged to be wrapped around his trim waist with him deep inside my wet body. I wanted all of him, here and now at my front door, with Jennie and her new boyfriend in the kitchen. I didn't care who saw us. All I knew was what I wanted. And it was Jake.

And then for some stupid reason he stopped.

Jake kissed the tip of my nose and my lips, then pulled away and looked down at me long and hard. "I want you back, Eve. I want all of you this time. I can give you everything and anything you desire. There is no more scared, hurt, screwed-up little jackass left inside me. I'm a new person through and through. Someone who can take care of you inside and out." His hand ran down between my legs. I was hot and swollen, so the contact of his hand against the thin cotton covering me was intense. I gasped and shuddered from the overwhelming sensations it sent through me. "I can be the man you always wanted me to be. But I want you to know it. I want you to want it." He pulled his hand away and I swayed. "Think about it tonight and we'll talk on the drive tomorrow."

And then he left.

And I was so damn confused.

## Chapter 6

$\mathcal{I}$ couldn't sleep, so I was curled up on the couch in the downstairs living room, watching on old movie. I had one of those fuzzy blankets wrapped around me, the kind that made you feel like you were on a cloud, and a giant bucket of buttery popcorn.

I didn't sleep that night. I don't call that restless, crazy rest, *sleep*. Sleep is restful and rejuvenating. What I did last night was relax my body while my mind went wild.

We kissed.

And it had rocked my world.

If I could understand what made Jake so different from every other man I'd ever known I might finally be able to grasp why he had such a firm hold on my heart. Or why I couldn't find magic like that with anyone else.

His lips were so soft. How was it possible for lips to be that soft? They had been like whispers against my skin. His tongue was like velvet as it stroked mine. His scent had intoxicated me to the point I couldn't see. I couldn't stop reliving those moments over and over again. Each time I thought of his lips my eyes automatically closed and my head tipped back as if I could physically relive the moment even without him there. Just the memory of it made me warm all over and the heat between my legs was almost enough to drive me wild.

I bounced back and forth between those memories and his final words . . . *I want you back.*

I was like a ping-pong ball all night long. I should be exhausted and yet, I was strangely awake. I was alive with an energy I couldn't explain. I felt like a live-wire, full of power and potentially dangerous to those around me.

Luckily I had work to do and I focused on it with a fervor—plowing through my obligations for both that day and most of Monday.

At least there was that.

By the time Jake texted me I was a bundle of nerves. He was outside, parked next to my car and waiting. This was it. This weekend was my opportunity. If I couldn't figure Jake out in my family home surrounded by my friends and our memories . . . well, then I was screwed.

The orange Bronco stuck out like a sore thumb next to my sleek graphite colored Nissan GT-R. I really did miss that old orange beast. She was rough and fun. Like Jake. He'd worked on her all through college and we'd taken her on all kinds of adventures. I was pretty excited to take another ride in her.

Jake was laid back in the driver's seat wearing green board shorts, a tight white t-shirt, a Rays hat, and aviators. He must have seen my approach because suddenly he was up and out of the truck and at my side.

I popped open my trunk.

"Just this bag?" he asked with a ridiculous crooked grin.

It sent a familiar shiver right through me. "Yes," I replied, not trusting myself to say anymore.

He grabbed the bag and set it carefully in the backseat of the Bronco. His shirt was thin and tight enough I could see every flex and ripple of his beautifully sculpted upper body. I'd always been attracted to him, but this newer, harder body was difficult not to openly appreciate. It was probably some sort of cavewoman instinct to be strongly attracted to tall and strong men—a display that they are capable of defending their family and protecting what's theirs—and mine was being triggered hard.

"You ready?" he asked turning back toward me, his cocky grin firmly in place.

I popped on my own sunglasses, threaded my ponytail through my hat, pulling it down and flexing the bill around my glasses. Then I smoothed down the tank top and shorts I was wearing over my bathing suit. "Yes. Let's get this show on the road."

He watched my fidgeting, I couldn't see his eyes

through his sunglasses but I knew his looks. He wasn't causally watching my movements, he was reading my body language. "It's going to be fine, Eve."

I hated that he could still read me. It made me feel vulnerable in a way that I didn't want to be. "Of course it will. We need this."

He took a step toward me, his long legs covering the gap between us in a single stride. "Yes, we do." He was so close I could feel the air shift, the hot Florida humidity was pushed aside by Jake's body, his heat replacing the air around me. He lightly grasped my fingertips, just my fingertips, inside his larger ones. "Let's go." He tugged me toward the passenger door, opening it and helping me inside, not that I needed the help. It was a sweet gesture, or at least it was supposed to be. Instead it just made me more nervous. Every second I was awash in his energy was another step toward losing what little control I had.

He backed us out and headed toward Interstate 275 which would take us south over Tampa Bay and the Sunshine Skyway, then south down I-75 to Fort Myers. He grabbed his phone, "Hey, we're on the road . . . Great, I'll keep an eye out."

After he carefully tucked it back into the console he explained. "Jennie and Andrew should only be a few minutes behind us."

In reality I didn't know why I was so nervous to be around Jake. We were each strapped into separate seats, the truck was open to the outside with the top off, and Jennie would be following us. It wasn't as if he was going to drag me off somewhere isolated and force me to love him.

And it wasn't as if I didn't like him. In fact, I was realizing the anger I'd originally felt toward him for leaving me was starting to fade. And yet I was still completely and utterly nervous around him.

Maybe it was because I knew I wanted to love him.

Jake smiled over at me after he merged onto the highway. "Ask me anything. The next two hours are yours, I'm an open book."

So it was Q&A time? "Did you like living over there?"

His large, capable hands gripped the wheel a little tighter and his biceps flexed. "Not particularly."

*Then why did you stay?* "What didn't you like?"

He chuckled softly, "You mean other than the eternal sun and endless desert?"

The bay was approaching fast, the cables of the bridge stretching up ahead. The salt of the air stung my nose. It was hard to imagine living somewhere so completely opposite of the only environment I'd ever called home. I loved the water and I didn't think I could survive without it. The salt on my skin and the waves rocking my body were my favorite form of therapy. I couldn't even adequately imagine what it must be like to live in a desert.

"Yes, other than that."

He sighed and shrugged his broad shoulders, "There are women over there, but it's a lot of guys. A *lot*. It can be a bit testosterone heavy, very competitive, and well . . . hard. Guys are hard, women are soft. The desert is hard . . . I think when I picture my life over there I think of it as hard."

*Then why didn't you come home to me?* "It sounds like a good place to work on yourself then."

"It was." He glanced at me and studied me for a moment. "I went to Germany for a week once every six months to see a therapist. Then it was phone calls and video chats in between." He paused and his face flinched and contorted as he worked through whatever was going on in his head. "I didn't dick around while I was over there, Eve. I worked. I worked hard. I worked on me and I worked on actual work. I made contacts, built relationships, and got really damn good at what I do."

"And what exactly is that?" He had a degree in mechanical engineering and was heading his firm here in Tampa—I knew that. But I didn't know what he *did*. I didn't know what made him damn good, better than everyone else. I wanted to know what he had finally figured out.

"Materials," he said with authority, the kind that makes you sit up a little straighter and listen a little harder because you know you are about to hear someone speak who really knows what they are talking about. "I have a gift for identifying the best materials for any project. You and Josh liked my proposal not just because you liked our design but because you liked the price." Which was true. "I design projects based on need. I don't design it to be made of the very best materials available—I pick the best for what you need. Not many people think that way, so my projects often come out more streamlined. I don't include extra crap and I don't over-design. It's helped me become very, very successful."

I arched an eyebrow of curiosity. I'd done my research after his blindside at work. Jake did have a good reputation and, despite his company being relatively new, it had an impressive client list. "How did you meet your partner?"

"Tom. Greg and I had both been working for him for years when I mentioned I was thinking of setting up shop over here. He and I are a good compliment and he likes the office a hell of a lot more than I do, so he handles the more bureaucratic side of things."

"And you?" I asked, already picturing him scribbling on graph paper or with his hands covered in grease, getting his hands dirty on one of his projects.

He grinned. "You know the answer to that."

His complete confidence in that fact sent another shiver through me.

"Where has the Bronco been hiding all these years?"

"Greg's," he replied matter-of-factly. "Tom ditched it there when we left town. He put her up on blocks and kept her nice in his storage unit. He got her out and had her all tuned up once we got the company up and running and he knew I was coming."

"Nice friend to have," I murmured.

We sat quietly for a few minutes. There was so

much to ask him but I was finding it hard to find my words. Jake drove in the slow right lane, taking his time and letting us enjoy the sun and wind. It felt surprisingly therapeutic whipping over my skin.

Jake had spent most of two years working on the Orange Beast. Most of it in my driveway. I had watched as he transformed her from an antique rust bucket into a smartly remodeled machine. She was practically weather resistant and ran like a top. I think it was one of his first forms of therapy. He'd bury himself in figuring out her quirks, getting lost for hours covered in grease and with pieces and parts strewn across the garage.

"What are you thinking about?" Jake's voice cut right into my thoughts like a knife.

"You working on the Beast."

He chuckled and reached out to caress the dash. "It's nice to have her back."

"Did you remodel trucks in the Middle East?"

He laughed good and loud, a nice belly laugh. "No. I did work on a few, though. But no remodels like this. I honestly didn't have time unless someone needed help. I was buried in work, usually up to my elbows in a machine of some kind."

It was too easy to picture Jake like that—his hands busy and his mind working. It was who he was through and through.

That ache in my chest started to throb again. It felt like mourning. There was lead in my stomach, the ache in my chest, and the overwhelming urge to cry my eyes out. It wasn't fair that Jake had such a rough life, a life he felt he needed to run away from.

But then again life wasn't fair.

Sitting here in the Orange Beast was a painful reminder of that. I remembered the day I came home from defending my honor's thesis.

My presentation hadn't gone quite as I'd expected. I was more than prepared to sit in front of five of the academics and professors I respected most to present my thesis, but the drilling had been merciless. By the end, I was exhausted, defeated, and on the verge of tears. It didn't matter that I'd passed or that I'd answered every question.

My brain was mush and my body was done. If I'd run a marathon I wouldn't feel that exhausted. The only thing I cared about was finding somewhere to collapse.

I pulled into my drive and wasn't surprised to see two legs sticking out from beneath the Orange Beast. Jake had suddenly gone nuts on the Bronco, taking her apart and replacing her piece by piece. I didn't know exactly what was driving his sudden need to renovate, but it was something. And I had a sneaking suspicion it had everything to do with his father.

It was the only subject Jake was still reluctant to talk to me about, even after three years together.

"Hey baby!" he called from somewhere underneath the hunk of metal.

I paused beside where I estimated his chest would be, plopped my bag down onto the concrete, and sank down. I would normally care about my nice suit, it was rare I got to wear clothes that made me feel so grown up, but at the moment the only thing I cared about was making eye contact with my boyfriend.

I laid out on the hard concrete and turned my head. He was smiling and covered in grease. In one hand he held a wrench and in the other he was holding some sort of bolt. He looked right at home.

The minute he saw my face, he froze. "Didn't it go well?"

I sighed, "It went fine. But it was brutal. I think I need to cry."

He pushed and rolled out from beneath the beast and a second later he was holding himself above me in a push-up. His strength always surprised me for someone so lean. He dropped first one, then two kisses delicately onto my lips. "If it went fine, then why do you look so defeated?"

His green eyes earnestly searched mine and that was when I realized Jake wasn't just covered in grease, he was covered in bruises. I sucked in a sharp breath. "You went home?"

He closed his eyes and rolled onto the concrete beside me. The evening sky wasn't too bright, but the puffy white clouds were still an intense contrast. He was quiet for a long minute and I knew he was gathering his thoughts. I'd learned the hard way to give Jake a minute. And space.

"Mom called and said she needed help with the stove. I thought I'd be in and out before he got home from work."

"But?"

"But he came home early. It's like the asshole knows when I'm home."

I swallowed down the freak-out boiling up inside me. The fact that Jake could stand his life at home was beyond me. I was just grateful he lived here with me and only went home when he had to.

"Jake . . ." I sighed as I rolled up onto my side.

His eyes darted to meet mine. "She's my mom. I can't say no when she calls."

I closed my eyes against the pain for just a moment, then studied the soft bruises that marred his beautiful skin. It wasn't too bad. A faint black eye, a small welt on his chin, and a few bruises appearing on his arms and body. I couldn't resist the urge to trace my fingers along their edges, wishing I could somehow take away the pain with my touch. But I also knew the real damage was inside. Those punches had come along with words. Horrible, hateful words that would change Jake for the next week. It always took around seven days for him to fight back to the surface.

He cupped my cheek. "Forget about it. We were talking about you."

"My problems aren't problems. They're silly."

He grabbed my chin and jerked so that I was forced to look into his eyes. "Don't ever say that, Eve. Our problems are different, this isn't a contest."

"I didn't mean it like that."

He shook his head and pulled me down onto his

chest, "You did. You meant my problems were more important than yours. And that's bullshit. Your problems are your problems, and I want to know all about them."

I sighed and burrowed into the comfort of his chest. It was my favorite place in the world. "It was brutal. It didn't stop the whole hour. I think they asked me about every single aspect of the project. They delved into my background research and my projections. By the time I was done I just wanted to run away and cry."

He stroked my hair softly, over and over as we lay in the driveway between our cars. "So cry. You just accomplished something that took you a hell of a lot of time and effort. You should be proud. And it is all right to be overwhelmed and exhausted, baby."

The tears trickled out of the corner of my eyes and onto his bare chest. His hand kept moving through my hair and up and down my back. His deft movements were the only thing that ever brought me that kind of peace. I had never thought of myself as a particularly tactile person before Jake, but he loved to touch and feel so much that I quickly discovered how much I loved it too. At least when it was Jake.

He comforted me, then I comforted him. He left the Bronco in pieces while we went inside and got lost inside each other.

I hated how unfair life was to Jake. I hated life had torn us apart.

Reality was stupid.

I watched Jake handle the Orange Beast as we glided down the interstate. I struggled to rectify the boy I knew with the man sitting beside me. I knew him, but I didn't. I wanted him, and I wanted nothing to do with him. Every minute near him I felt my heart breaking all over again.

It was heart breaking because I still loved him. I would always love Jake, I knew that. It didn't mean I could ever be *in love* with him, though. Those were two totally different things.

He glanced at me sideways and smiled, "Get out of your head, darlin'. Ask me something else."

I asked him question after question, slowly getting to know the man Jake had become. He answered everything without hesitation. Somewhere along the way I began to feel comfortable, like I'd slipped on an old t-shirt.

It was that easy, false comfort that lead to my demise.

\* \* \*

WE MADE THE BEAUTIFUL DRIVE over the causeway from Fort Myers to Sanibel Island, the pelicans diving as we passed, the boats lazily drifting beneath us in no hurry to get anywhere. This was my home. Time moved at a different pace here. When you drove through the tollbooth, transitioning from mainland to island, you left the real world behind.

The air was different, the light was different, the

sounds were different. I always felt the strangest sense of calm wash over me as we turned off the causeway onto the main drag and glided under the tree canopy. Hurricane Charley had done it's best to ruin that, but time moves forward even if you can't feel it; the trees growing back and erasing the scars of Mother Nature. We enjoyed the ride down the island in silence making the slight transition from Sanibel to Captiva. The beaches here were white sand and the waves were low. Because of the unusual orientation of the islands, high tide would leave behind treasure troves of seashells and there always seemed to be a slight breeze.

Our house was on the backside of the island—it was even calmer there. A large main house sat back from the shore, but four smaller houses lined the edge of the beach.

The four smaller guesthouses were assigned to my sisters and our friends. It was there my friends and I would be staying this weekend. We were not allowed inside my parent's home unless it was absolutely necessary, it was their line of privacy and one I rarely crossed.

Behind the main house was a massive outdoor kitchen and patio that gave way to the wide, white sand beach and the dock that stretched out into the shallow water. Two boats and two jet skis were moored to the dock and we'd be on those in less than an hour. I could barely contain my desire to be out on the water. It was a raw need at this point.

Jake parked in the gravel drive, an enormous grin

plastered to his handsome face. It was so large and so genuine I couldn't help but smile, too. "Welcome back."

"Thanks."

I felt like I knew him better now that he'd given me free reign to quiz him, but it didn't do anything to dispel the frantic nervous fear racing through my veins. It just confused me more. This new and improved Jake was amazing. He was sweet and cocky and confident. He seemed like the world was at his feet.

He seemed safe and inviting, a man I could trust and allow to see all the screwed up parts of me without judgment. But I felt that way about the old Jake and look what he had done to me.

The difference, I realized, was the man himself. The new Jake was, at his core, seemingly unflappable. That unwavering strength was the difference. If Jake really had become strong from the inside out, then he was really and truly someone I could learn to trust again.

But I wasn't convinced. And *that* was the problem. I didn't know what it would take to convince me or even if I could be convinced. That level of trust may be a one-time thing, once it's gone it can never be recovered.

Jennie and Andrew pulled up behind us and if it was possible, they looked even more in love than they did last night. They were falling hard and fast, there were no two ways about that.

I felt a pang of jealousy watching them. They were

falling in love so effortlessly. There wasn't a dreadful childhood to overcome or the pain of betrayal to work through.

They were simply two people falling in love. What would Jake and I look like if we had only just met? Would we be falling in love just as effortlessly? Would I be able to simply love him for the man he was now and not the man who left me?

His lips were at my ear. "Don't."

I looked up at him with surprise. He couldn't possibly know what I was thinking, and yet when I looked up at him and saw the depth of regret in his eyes, I knew that he was feeling the same longing I was. "Don't what?"

His eyes bored into me. "Don't wonder. We aren't them and we never will be. It won't make it hurt any less."

He turned and followed the path down to the guesthouses leaving me behind with my thoughts.

Regret, I realized, was a powerful thing.

Rum drinks and beer were out and being consumed in record time, as were the appetizer plates we found in the outdoor fridge. Once the sound system came on and the next car arrived, the party really took off.

There was the expected excitement as Jake caught up with everyone. He was the center of everything and I was glad. It gave me a chance to hide on the edges. It also gave me an opportunity to observe. I was a truly excellent eavesdropper. I'd used my powers to gather all kinds of useful information over the years.

I couldn't help myself. There was just so much I needed to learn about this man.

He was sitting around the empty fire pit laughing with Sylvia and Ricardo, drinks in their hands, relaxing. All three of them looked different. We were at that age . . . life was stressful. Jobs were demanding more and more and I knew from some quiet, intimate conversations with Sylvia that the struggle to have children was straining her relationship with Ricardo. Even the happiest couples had troubles.

It was really nice to see them all smiling.

"What the hell have you been doing for ten years, man?" Ricardo asked.

Jake shook his head and took a long drag of his drink. The muscles in his arm tensed and his jaw locked in place. He didn't like having to constantly answer that question.

"Learning."

"I've heard. You are making quite the splash in town."

Jake cocked his head, "Really?"

"Really. Apparently, you're a badass. Everyone's talking." He leaned and hunched his shoulders together and made his voice three octaves higher so that he sounded like a silly girl. "He's hot and rich and fantastic!"

"Now here I thought you were going to say something useful . . ."

Ricardo straightened back up. "Well, they are. But

the word around the golf course is you're a man who knows how to handle a club."

"We should play a round sometime."

"I've got Thursday open. Lunch?"

Jake nodded thoughtfully. "You're on."

Ricardo squealed in his girly voice again.

I was so busy listening to their conversation I didn't hear Andrew walk up beside me. He scared the piss out of me.

"Stalking?" His brown eyes were keen and observant as they studied me.

I was struck once again by the realization I really liked this guy. He seemed to be a very genuine person. I never got any weird vibes from him, no alarm bells signaling Andrew was anything but a happy, successful guy.

"Sort of," I admitted, my eyes wandering back to Jake.

A comfortable silence descended between us and I realized Andrew was the male version of me.

He was freaking perfect for Jennie.

"Jennie filled me in on the story of you and Jake. This can't be easy on you."

I shook my head, watching Jake laugh with Sylvia. "No, it's surreal. I keep expecting to wake up and find this was all a very elaborate nightmare."

Andrew's eyebrow quirked up. "Nightmare? Interesting choice of words there."

"Dreams involving Jake ended five years ago. That was my statute of limitations on torture." I explained.

"Everything since then is a nightmare. None of this seems real."

Andrew crossed his arms over his sculpted, distinctively male chest, and leaned back against the countertop. "Can I ask you a question?"

I knew Andrew and I were going to be friends, I could feel it in the easy way we were talking to each other. "Shoot."

"If you had a guarantee Jake would never leave you again, would this still be a nightmare?" He was quietly observing me, his eyes soft and unwavering. There wasn't a hint of malice or a hidden agenda and he seemed to be genuinely concerned for me.

Jake: nightmare or dream? It seemed to be the only question on my mind over the last month. Maybe he was both.

The reason I'd fallen in love with him was still the same. I was still attracted to him physically, but it was so much more than that.

We got each other. He always seemed to know what I was thinking and feeling. I didn't have to explain myself. I didn't have to change myself. To Jake, I was just Eve and I was perfect the way I was. He knew my insecurities and fears, but he never used them against me. He knew when to reassure me and when to stand back and let me do my thing.

And I was the same way with him.

He was an extrovert by nature. He loved groups of people and usually found a way to become the center of attention. Not because he needed the spotlight, but because he enjoyed people. I got that about him. It was so interesting to see the new Jake, just the same, but different. He didn't have that same anxious need to be with a group at all times, but he liked it. Even now as the group around the fire pit was growing, Jake's glow was growing, too. His smile was widening, his laugh was deepening—it was like he was coming to life.

So was he a dream or a nightmare? The more I got to know him, the more I was unsure of that answer.

One thing I did know, was that *I* hadn't changed.

I still only had two settings with Jake: off and on. If I flipped that switch, there would be no stopping me. I would have to love him completely. I just didn't know how else to love someone who I felt so connected to. And if we got that close again and he ran for some reason? I knew I couldn't come back from that kind of broken heart twice.

"No one can guarantee that, so it doesn't matter," I murmured.

"Jennie thinks you two are meant for each other."

"I used to think that, too."

"*I* think you two are meant for each other," Andrew stated flatly, his eyes boring into mine.

I took a step back, an actual step back, as my heart took off racing. How could he possibly say that? He'd barely met us.

"I have amazing instincts, Eve. It makes me a good lawyer and I have a long track record that proves just how good my instincts are. I've learned to trust them. The night we met, I assumed you and Jake were a couple because that was what felt right to me. You two vibrate on the same frequency, you communicate without talking . . . and since then, Jennie has told me all about you and Jake. It has me more convinced than ever." He pushed away from the counter, standing open in front of me, "I know it's not really my place to be saying things like this, not yet anyway. But trust me Eve, you don't want to look back and regret losing a man like him because you were scared. You are too strong for that and you won't like yourself when you look back."

Something in the way he said that last part made me certain Andrew had his own sad story. I wanted to ask him about it, but I was paralyzed. Every muscle in my body was frozen and so was the tongue in my mouth. The only thing working was my heart, and it was racing.

Andrew stepped forward putting his hands gently on my biceps, "Eve, trust me on this. I know people and I know how men's brains work. That man," he tilted his head toward where Jake and Ricardo were laughing with Sylvia, "loves you. I don't know who he used to be and I don't care. The only thing that matters is now, and I don't believe for a second that man would ever leave your side. He's not made that way." He squeezed my arms and smiled softly, dipping down so that he could look into my stunned eyes. "Think about it."

And then he left me to my thoughts.

One thing was on repeat in my head. *He's not*

*made that way.* Andrew had just described a man I didn't know. He saw a Jake I didn't know. *He's not made that way.* But he was, wasn't he? He ran. He left me. He wouldn't let me be there for him when he needed me most.

*He's not made that way.*

I stared at the man sitting between Sylvia and Ricardo. I wished I could see him like Andrew did. He described someone loyal and unwavering. He described someone hopelessly in love.

With me.

My brain was struggling to work when Jennie came running—and I do mean running—over with a look of terror on her face. "He didn't, did he?"

"What?" I asked, confused.

"Andrew. I told him not to, but I just saw him walk away and you look like you've been hit by a bus. Please, *please* tell me he didn't do what I think he just did."

I shook my head, taking a deep breath and focusing. "If you mean telling me his thoughts on Jake, then yes, he just did."

Jennie grabbed my hand. She tugged hard enough to pull my attention away from Jake. "I'm sorry, Eve. I told him not to, but he was just so damn insistent. He says he couldn't stand looking at you all torn to pieces when he knew in his gut you didn't need to be worried."

"What does that mean?" I asked.

Jennie shrugged, "He hasn't told me exactly. It has something to do with his parents, though. I got that out of him." Jennie paused, glancing over her shoulder at Andrew. "But he's right, Eve. I didn't think you were ready to get the tough love treatment from us, but it doesn't change the truth. Andrew is right. Jake is different."

The rest of the crowd arrived at that point and I was grateful. I'd had just about enough heavy, emotional conversation for the afternoon.

"I'm trying to see what you guys see."

Jennie squeezed my hand again and let it fall. "I know. I just want you to be happy, Eve. I've known you a long, long time. I knew you and Jake then and I've been your best friend all these years. I don't want you to be miserable—you know I don't. Give him a chance."

My plans to fall *out* of love with Jake were not going so well. Apparently the universe was conspiring against me.

Stephen, Jake's best friend in college, joined them around the fire pit.

I'd expected Stephen to be excited to see Jake. I was wrong. He was cool and distant. But then again, if anyone else had been really hurt by Jake's sudden disappearance, it was him.

Max showed up next. He was transfixed by Jennie and Andrew, but all I could think when I looked at him was 'you snooze, you lose'. Did he really think Jennie would wait for him forever?

I couldn't stop thinking about Andrew. His opinion mattered to me for some reason. Maybe it was the connection I felt to him—that we were two similar souls attached to the same wild girl. Or maybe it was his fresh perspective on my life. He wasn't tainted by the years the way the rest of us were. He saw Jake the way I wish I could. He saw me in a way I couldn't.

He called me strong.

That was something I used to feel, but hadn't since Jake arrived. Was I still strong or had I let all of this make me weak?

I was revolted by that thought. Eve Daniels was not weak. I may be hurt and confused, but I was not weak. If Andrew was right, if Jake and I were meant for each other, was I strong enough to love him again?

I wasn't sure.

# Chapter 7

*It* was three o'clock when we left in the boats. I knew we were pushing things—it was an incredibly hot day and the thunderheads had been building since at least one o'clock. But we went out anyway. Four on my boat, four on the other. Everyone else stayed back to rest on the beach. We shot over to Cayo Costa and we attracted dolphins so we made a few passes, inviting them to play in our wake before anchoring off the beach and wading in.

Cayo Costa was my favorite island. Period. It was a state park only accessible by boat and only a handful of people lived there; so it was one of the few places that still looked relatively untouched by man. The beaches were decent for shelling, especially after a good storm, and there was always cool driftwood along the southern point. I liked the weird horseshoe crabs that lived there, too.

I guess I'd wandered off too far, I'd let myself get too lost in my head, I didn't see how hard and fast the storm front approached. I didn't notice my friends calling for me, or the first boat leaving.

Leaving with everyone but Jake and me.

I only became aware of what was happening when I heard Jake's yelling as he ran down the beach. I finally looked up and saw how pitch-black and angry the sky was, how deep the rumbling from the thunder was. This wasn't the kind of storm you could ride out. It was going to be violent and long.

Well, long by Florida standards anyway.

"We've got to go, now!" Jake yelled as I started to run back toward him.

"No shit." I muttered.

The air was already sizzling as we pulled ourselves aboard. Jake hauled in the anchor as I lowered and started the engine, quickly calculating our chances of making it home.

The answer was easy: we wouldn't.

And the waves were already pushing higher and higher as the winds at the front of the storm grew stronger. We needed a backup plan. I yanked the cords of the blue bimini top free of their brackets and sent the canopy collapsing against the hull just as Jake dropped the dripping anchor on the bow.

"Ready," he yelled. The sun was gone and Jake had tossed his sunglasses onto the dashboard, so when he looked at me I could see how dark with worried his eyes were.

"Sit," I commanded, throttling forward. We were getting tossed around and it was not going to be a pleasant ride, but at least I knew where we were going.

The boat was hitting the water hard as we cut around the island, rising and falling with each wave. It was the kind of pounding that doesn't just jar you, but sends a stinging jolt up through your entire body with each and every hit of the hull against the waves. Trying to make it back home would have been ugly, as it was we'd barely beat the rain. It was going to rain hard. The wind was going to be fierce. And the lightning—it was already lighting up everything around us.

It was the kind of storm you really needed shelter to escape from.

There were a few different options we could have tried for, but the old fishing shacks on the other side of the island would only take us a few minutes to get to.

Once upon a time they had been used by fisherman, and I guess they still were. But only by locals like us as a stopover. It was a squat house raised up out of the water on pilings with a dock around two sides. We hit the dock hard as the waves rocked us and Jake deftly roped a pylon. As he secured the front, I scrambled around and did the same to the back. That was when the giant drops of rain started to fall.

The ropes would hold but the boat might not look so pretty after the storm. Or maybe it was the dock that would take the beating, you never could tell which way things would go during a storm. Either way, I didn't care. I just wanted to be inside, away from the wind and rain and intensity of the lightning. The air was alive, I could feel the tingle on my skin as the electric current wove its way through the air seeking a place to strike next.

"Stow everything," I yelled above the rumble of thunder.

Jake threw the white padded seat up and started shoving the loose towels and clothes that had been left behind inside. "You want your bag?" he asked.

I nodded and he shoved our things inside before tossing it up onto the dock.

Jake boosted me up first, then pulled himself up behind me. He was still shirtless so I could see every muscle in his beautiful body work.

His hands were warm against my exposed skin and his eyes were deep green and intense, like there was a storm brewing inside him just as powerful as the one swirling around us.

*What if you had a guarantee he would never leave?*

Andrew's question came slamming back into my head as my pulse quickened. Could I let everything go if I knew the fear was just in my imagination? This war in my head had to end. I was driving myself bat-shit crazy.

This guy I'd loved more than anything was back. He wanted me and I wanted him. The basic stuff was easy compared to the complications of my emotions. The bottom line was that Jake scared the pants off me. He was hot and handsome, cocky and confident . . .

and I knew this time it would be so much worse. I'd loved him with everything I had ten years ago, but that was a college girl just starting out in the world.

I was a grown woman now. Logic would have me think that my new experience and wisdom would make a relationship with Jake easier, but that was so *not* the case.

He was sex on a stick. He was triggering every sexual instinct I had. He was hot, successful, and he wanted me. Which made my body seriously want him. Not even my brain was helping in that department. It was older and wiser—which meant it knew just how fucking hard decent men were to find. Jake broke my heart and ran away from his past, didn't mean he'd do it again.

Otherwise he was a fantastic guy.

The only thing holding me back from all of this was my heart.

You know, the broken one.

It knew if Jake and I got back together we'd make our past relationship look like child's play. It would be a sweet footnote to this new torrid love affair. Jake and Eve 2.0 would be an uncontrolled explosion of sex and adoration.

Uncontrolled explosions were dangerous. Everyone knew that.

And yet, I couldn't seem to stop myself from wanting to play with the matches . . .

"Just in time!" Jake called, slamming the door shut and throwing his towel over a rusty folding chair.

"Fuck that was fun!"

His crooked smile did all of those things it always did to me. It twisted my belly in a delicious can't-feel-the-floor-beneath-me way. It heated my skin and sent my pulse racing.

Why did he make me excited when no one else did?

"What?" he asked, his voice suddenly hoarse. He was frozen, watching me watch him.

"Why?" I asked.

"Why what?"

"Why do you make me different?" I asked. "Why doesn't anyone else do that? Why *you?*" I simply didn't understand it. I'd tried so hard to find that spark with someone else. Hell, I'd even wondered if there was something wrong with me.

"Why not me." It was a demand not a question. Jake was making his case. "No one will *ever* love you like I can. You know it and I know it. Don't let the past keep ruining everything." His eyes wandered over my heaving chest and trembling body, growing darker and lustful. His fist clenched and his jaw went slack as his eyes zeroed in on me.

"I won't survive you a second time," I choked out.

"You know me better than anyone ever has," he growled. Jake was mad. At me. "Do you honestly believe I'd hurt you a second time? I did what I had to do, I *never* meant to break your heart." His anger softened into a plea, "I love you."

That was when I understood what I did to Jake. I

126

made him different, too. I wasn't sure exactly how I made him different, but I knew I did. I could see it in his eyes, in the hungry way he was looking at me. He craved that rush of being different as desperately as I did.

Somehow we made each other more.

I was strong and capable on my own. I'd proven that many times over. But Jake brought things out of me no one else could. He calmed me, gave me a special sense of confidence—he made me even stronger than I already was. It was a special gift. One I gave him in return.

Jake stood where he was, begging me to make the first move. It had to be my choice—we both knew that.

"Eve . . ." His voice was so deep and rough.

My name did me in. I wanted to hear him say it over and over again, in a thousand different ways. And right then, I wanted to hear him groan it.

I closed the gap between us in a second, throwing myself around him, my legs wrapping around his waist as his arms wrapped around my body. His hands on my skin were electric, shooting a thousand volts of pleasure through my body and taking my breath away.

I loved this man. I hated this man.

He would ruin me, maybe I'd ruin him.

But for that moment, locked away from the world alone in a fishing shack on the water, all I wanted was to feel him.

A rough grunt came out of Jake's throat as my hands wrapped around his face, kissing him deeper and deeper.

That was when he turned and slammed my back into the wall of the shack.

# Chapter 8

*M*y back was pressed to Jake's front and he was still twitching inside me. My arms hung lifelessly at my sides, the sweat rolling all the way down their length, dripping from my fingertips to the wood floor beneath us.

I was numb, every muscle in my body gloriously relaxed, every ounce of energy sapped away. I couldn't move or think. It was a wonderful change to feel nothing, to be lost to the oblivion of complete and utter satisfaction.

Just the sound of the rain slowing, the thunder drifting away, and Jakes heavy breathing.

When was the last time I felt this relaxed? I couldn't remember. And the more I chased that thought the more I honestly wondered: when was the last time I felt this good?

It all came crashing in on me at once. It had been

years, probably a decade. Not since Jake. Jake who was inside me. Jake who would leave me all over again, taking with him all of this good.

The panic flooded me so fast, flooding my veins with equal parts fear and fire, that I shot off of his lap, surprising him.

I'd made a mistake. A huge, massive mistake, by giving in to all of this.

I'd slept with my black hole. He'd sucked me back in, and I'd let him.

I scrambled to the bag I'd dropped by the door, finding my cover-up and sliding it over my head. I was in a pure, frantic panic. I wanted to run, but we were in this stupid shack. I wanted to explode into a billion molecules.

"Eve . . ." his voice was low and when I turned around he was up, naked, and his hands were out in front of him as he cautiously moved toward me.

"No!" I shouted, scrambling backward. He couldn't come near me, when he came near I became stupid. I started believing in silly things like happiness and futures.

I was such a fucking idiot.

He stopped dead in his tracks, "Calm down, darlin'. Everything is okay."

*Okay?* Nothing about this was okay. "This is pure stupidity! What was I thinking?"

He didn't blink at my insult, just continued to calmly stand on the other side of the room from me. "We had sex, Eve. We've had sex hundreds of times. It doesn't have to mean anything."

My eyes went wide—I felt it. "Doesn't have to mean anything? *Doesn't have to mean anything?* Jake, everything means something between us."

His hands fell to his sides and his jaw tensed as he stood up straight. "Trust me, I know that."

"Then why did you say it?" I shouted back.

He looked me dead in the eye with an intensity that almost made me want him all over again. Confident Jake was not someone to be messed with. "Because I don't want to scare you away before you give me a chance to show you who I am now." He stepped toward me, and this time I didn't back away or flinch. "Eve, let me show you."

I was flying apart, the sadness and fear exploding from the center of me out. "We are too much Jake. You and I aren't good for each other. I love you too much, remember?" *I will give you everything.*

"Do not throw my words back at me like that," he demanded.

"But you were right, weren't you? I do, I love you too much for it to ever be healthy. We destroy each other. We can never be enough for what we each need."

I believed in those words completely. What happened between Jake and I was so explosive there was no option other than destruction. Self-destruction.

"That wasn't what I meant when I said that, Eve." His voice was eerily low and even, as if he were using extreme restraint to control himself. "I needed your love so much, but not in the way you think." He pulled his fingers through his hair, ruffling up his long dark locks. Finally he blew out a breath and cracked his neck. "I was desperate. Desperate to survive and I would have done and taken anything around me to do it. I would have used you and abused you until there was nothing left of you." His fists were tightly clenched at his sides, every muscle in his body taught as he spoke. "I would have consumed you to save myself. And the worst part is I wouldn't even know I'd done it until there was nothing left of you to save."

The reality of what he was saying hit me hard. There was no win here. There was no scenario where this situation would have come out in my favor. The deck had been stacked against me from the beginning.

This was the only possible conclusion. There was only one outcome to loving someone so damaged.

Whether he stayed or left, the result was the same: my heartbreak.

I don't think I'd ever allowed myself to see that possibility. It was probably too painful to recognize our love had been doomed from the start.

And that led me to understand something very important. Jake leaving me was a conscious choice to love me, even if I didn't realize it until just now. To stay would have been selfish. He left because he loved me too much to destroy me.

*Oh fuck.* The realization hit me like the lightning we were hiding from. *He left me to save me.*

Suddenly I saw Jake in a whole new light. Despite everything he was going through he'd still been strong enough to leave me when he probably wanted me more than ever. That act of selflessness took my breath away.

"Jake . . ." The emotions were overwhelming me. I was confused, incredibly confused by the combination of things reeling through my mind.

I'd known from early on Jake had baggage. By the time I realized how deep his problems ran I was already hopelessly in love with him.

But that was what loving Jake meant. I had chosen to take on that responsibility. By choosing to love someone damaged, you accept the consequences along with it. And that meant I needed to accept all of this. That Jake hurting me was inevitable. That Jake had to leave and it was his choice to make. It had nothing to do with me. I had accepted those terms for loving him.

I needed to get over myself.

"Eve, I will never run again. I will say it one more time, and I want you to really hear what I'm saying. I am *not* the boy who ran away ten years ago. I dealt with my crap and I finally grew up. Nothing anyone— including my shit dad— *anyone* can do will break me ever again."

Then his eyes flashed with something wicked. Gone was the controlled anger from before. It had been replaced with something much more erotic. "And you are right about one thing: what we did wasn't just sex. It was you and me right with the world again. I know you still love me. And now that I *know* that, I will never leave you. If you run, I will follow. What we have is special . . . it's unique. You know how I know that? You

aren't married. I told you the other night you should
be. I see the way men look at you. You could have anyone you wanted. You should be happy and married, but
you aren't."

He took two more steps toward me. I felt like I was
being stalked. Jake was the predator and I was the
prey. He was tall and strong, his shoulders square, his
jaw and fists clenched, holding back the emotions he
was keeping at bay. He was gloriously naked, remind-
ing me with every glance how strong and powerful he
was, and how very, very attracted to him I was.

"You waited for me, Eve. I know you did. And I
will wait for you, just please don't take too long. I've
already wasted so much of our lives and I don't want to
lose any more than we have to."

Had I waited for Jake? Was that why no one was
ever good enough for me? Had I secretly been hoping
every night I would find Jake waiting on my doorstep?
I think I might have been—I think all these years I'd
been waiting for Jake to reappear.

I couldn't keep fighting all of this, but I couldn't
just jump back into love with Jake. "Ask me out."

Jake blinked. I think I'd really and truly surprised
him. He'd been pushing and he knew what he wanted,
but having me actually give-in a little wasn't what he
was expecting. It was kind of cute how surprised he
looked. His normally masculine, confident face suddenly looked shy and young. He straightened himself
up and looked around the room, grabbing his towel
back off of the folding chair and wrapped it around his

naked waist.

Then he took a deep breath, a mischievous twinkle gleamed in his eye, and walked slowly across the room to stand in front of me. "Eve, would you give me the pleasure of your company at a barbecue this evening?"

I tried to fight the smile on my lips. I really wanted to play this off a little cooler than I was, but hell, he was so damn adorable asking me on a date I couldn't stand it. "I'd love that."

He bounced his eyebrows and smiled just enough for his dimple to show. "One step at a time?"

I nodded, "I think so. I don't know you anymore and I want a chance to see all these changes you keep telling me about."

"That sounds smart. I think we should date. We never really did that, did we?"

I shook my head and laughed. "No, we most certainly did not."

"Think we can manage it this time?"

I thought about it for a moment. Considering we were both barely clothed, I had my doubts. *Serious* doubts. More than likely we'd get lost along the way. But damn it was gonna be fun to get lost with Jake again.

As long as he didn't break my heart.

* * *

"WE SHOULD GO BOATING more often. This is hot, darlin'," he murmured in my ear.

I couldn't help the sly grin that crept up on my lips. "You never called me that before. I like it."

He squeezed me close and I could feel every inch of his body. "Good. It just came out when I saw you and I can't seem to stop saying it."

For some reason, Jake having a new, special pet name for me was hot. I think it was helping me separate our past from our present.

"Then don't stop," I murmured.

By the time the rain ended and we managed to get our asses home, Jennie and Andrew were anxiously waiting for us on the dock. I could tell Jennie was hopeful that the time alone had done us some good.

"I see you guys managed to survive," she drawled.

"Mmmmm. We did. We holed up in one of the shacks."

"Oh . . ."

Jake started tossing bags and coolers up onto the dock and Andrew started hauling them back up to the house. Jake was watching me out of the corner of his eye, probably waiting to see what I told Jennie.

She suddenly had a mischievous glint in her eye and she smiled. One of those smiles that scared the pants off me because she knew something I didn't. "Did you have fun?" she asked.

"Yes . . ."

She nodded, "I can tell." Then she reached down and pulled paint chips out of my hair, crumbling them between her fingers and letting them fall into the water below. She cocked her eyebrow and waited for me to explain.

"Fine, we had a *lot* of fun. Happy?"

She nodded vigorously. "What does this mean?"

I knew she wanted me to say Jake and I were back together. She wanted us to live happily ever after and for the four of us to be the best of friends. But Jennie had the privilege of living in a world where magical things like that happened. Jake and I did not. Happily ever after had to wait, if it was ever coming at all.

"It means I have a date tonight with this hot new guy I just met. And we'll see what happens."

To my complete surprise she yelped and started jumping up and down doing some sort of silly girly dance. "I'm so happy!"

I rolled my eyes. Jennie was seeing wedding bells. I was seeing the possibility of getting laid again.

Andrew came back for the next load. "Uh oh, what's with the girly dance?"

Jennie rushed right over to him and whispered in his ear. I don't know why she whispered. It wasn't like it was a secret. Or maybe what she was telling her boyfriend was a secret Jake and I weren't privy to.

He smiled and winked at me.

I glared back at Andrew, "This is your fault, I'll have you know."

His eyebrows shot up and he pointed at himself, "Who? Me?" The grin that followed told me we were still on the same page. He knew I was serious and scared and happy.

"Yes, you. I'm blaming you for all of it, as a matter

of fact."

He pulled away from Jennie and gave me a brotherly hug as soon as I hauled myself up onto the dock. "Then I also get all the credit when this works out spectacularly well."

I pulled back and looked at him carefully. "Deal." I had a feeling Andrew was going to be around for a very long time. Maybe even forever. He and I were too much alike for him not to be perfect for Jennie. He fit in with us like he'd always been part of our group, almost like we had been missing him all of this time.

I immediately disappeared into my room to freshen up and change. Shack sex was hot and amazing, but it was hardly clean. We'd had unprotected sex, but I was on the pill and I knew Jake well enough to know he wouldn't have done that if he had anything I could contract. We certainly needed to have some sort of a conversation at some point if we were going to do that again, but for now I needed to get clean.

I felt disgusting, actually, with all that saltwater dried on my skin. So the cool shower was a little slice of heaven for my body, but my brain went on overdrive. I felt like I was going on a first date with all the butterflies wiggling around inside me. I think I was even feeling shy.

Why hadn't I packed something nice? I could hear my grandmother's quiet admonishment in my head. "Always pack for a special occasion, dear. You never what is going to happen next."

Right then I wished I'd taken her advice.

I pulled out a sundress, dried my hair, and twisted most of it back off of my face. I even went so far as to put on a little makeup even though it was ten thousand degrees outside and pure humidity. But I was going on a 'date' and I wanted to look nice.

When I opened the door Jake was leaned up against the side of the house with his foot propped up. He immediately hopped up and smiled. He'd showered and changed too, and was wearing a nice t-shirt and board shorts. He was just as simply dressed as I was, but it was an effort toward looking nice.

"You look lovely," he murmured.

God, it was stupid how much that pleased me. "You look very nice yourself."

He leaned in and kissed me lightly on the lips. Just one simple kiss, but it was enough to take the air right out of me.

The cookout was in full swing. Shrimp was boiling, burgers were grilling, and foil packets of fish were going on next. A game of bocce was rolling on one side of the beach, a game of corn hole with bean bags flying through the air was on the other, and a circle of talkers were around the fire pit.

I felt every eye on me the whole night. Well, except for Max, his eyes were still glued to Jennie. And Jennie's eyes were only on me when she could peel them away from Andrew.

But I felt like the show of the night to everyone else. They were carefully watching us, how Jake and I were together, how we were separately. I felt like a science experiment. Especially with Stephen. I was refilling my cocktail when he cornered me.

"Is it that easy?" he asked.

Stephen was six feet tall, solidly built, a little rough around the edges but a generally good guy. He wasn't as smooth and polished as Andrew or clever as Jake, though. He was that generally likeable good guy every group seemed to have.

"No. Nothing about this is easy."

He watched me intently. "It's been a month, Eve. Seems pretty easy to me."

I had the distinct impression Stephen's anger at Jake was going to keep him from hearing anything other than what he expected, but I spoke anyway. "Are you suggesting he needs to be punished before I am allowed to forgive him? Because I assure you Stephen, punishment has already been sufficiently doled out."

He snorted, "I highly doubt that. He disappeared, Eve. Vanished into thin air and didn't give any of us the courtesy of a note saying he was alive and well." He over emphasized the word 'well'.

Stephen's eyes shot up over my shoulder and I knew Jake was behind me. I could feel the change in the vibration of the air. What was it Andrew had said? Jake and I vibrate on the same frequency? I certainly couldn't argue that.

"Hello Stephen," he said. His voice had that deep, authoritative rumble to it I liked so much.

"Jake."

He moved between us, physically separating Stephen from me while he refilled his own cup. Jake glanced up at me, his eyes questioning. He could tell our conversation wasn't light and friendly. "So, how have you been?"

Stephen didn't even attempt polite conversation. It was at that point that I finally realized he was pretty drunk—the alcohol making him angry and stupid. "Fuck off, Jake."

Jake stood up tall, emphasizing the size difference between the two of them, and glowered at his former best friend, "Excuse me?"

"Inquiring minds want to know, did you trade in your friends and your girl for a boatload of cash?" If I had any doubts how Stephen felt about Jake's sudden reappearance, I didn't anymore. Stephen was practically oozing contempt.

"I think that is a gross oversimplification of the situation, Stephen." Jake's eyes locked onto mine and I could feel his mood shift. He was keeping his anger in check, but just barely.

"Bullshit. You think you can come and go as you please? Just walk back into your life and pick up like you never left?"

Jake leaned in close to Stephen. "No, I don't. Because you're drunk I'm not going to hold this ridiculous conversation against you. But for your information, I don't expect any of you to forgive me. I don't expect anything from anyone. But I *am* back and I *am* asking for your forgiveness. What you do with that is your business."

Stephen glared up at Jake for several long moments. "Fine." he spat.

But Jake put a hand out and stopped Stephen from storming off. "One more thing. Just so we're clear, if you *ever* suggest I traded Eve for money, I will beat you to a bloody pulp."

The deep seething anger in Jake's voice was terrifying and Stephen took a step back, the surprise obvious on his face. "Shit man, sorry."

Jake straightened back up and glared at Stephen, "Get out of here, go sleep it off."

We were alone for several moments before Jake turned around. The silence between us felt like an eternity. I couldn't tell what he was feeling so I let him be.

"Is that how you feel? That I traded you for my new life?" he finally said.

I froze as I carefully considered his question. "No, Jake. Even if I did, I don't anymore. I know you had to leave and it was as much for me as it was for you."

His shoulders relaxed. "Come here. Please."

I went right into his arms and let him hold me.

The music cranked up and Jake pulled me into the shadows. "Let's dance," he whispered. I relaxed into him, resting my head on his shoulder and shutting out the world. Our dance turned into three or four. When it started to drizzle with a second evening rainstorm. Most of the gang called it a night, retreating to their designated rooms. I heard something about a poker game in one guesthouse and a movie in another.

But Jake didn't let me go and I didn't ask him to. I liked the way the rain dancing on our skin felt. I liked the way it was washing over me. Yes, my hair was wet and dangling in a mass of knots down my back, knots Jake kept lovingly brushing away with his fingers. And yes, our clothes were wet and clinging to our bodies, but it was cleansing. I felt like it was metaphorically washing our past away.

I wanted it to wash everything away except the moment we were standing in.

## Chapter 9

The music faded away and all I could see was Jake. All I could feel were his hands as he cupped my face and studied me. All I could feel was him. He was everywhere, inside and around me. His scent was in my lungs.

I was in love with Jake.

Or still in love.

Or falling in love with someone I really didn't know yet.

*Damn.* I was so confused. And I needed to allow myself to work through all of that. I needed to feel what I was feeling and not what I thought I should be feeling.

"This was a pretty fantastic first date, Eve," he said grasping my chin and pulling my face up for a kiss.

He was intoxicating. "Definitely one for the record books."

He smiled. He was gazing into my eyes with millions of questions. I couldn't possibly answer them all. "We should get out of the rain before we get sick. It's cold, darlin'."

The mention of cold made me shiver. But what to do next made me nervous. You don't take men home on the first date. You just don't. Not even men you've known for as long as I'd known Jake.

But I wasn't ready for our date to end, either.

"Want to watch a movie in my room?" I asked.

"I'll meet you there in five minutes," he winked and disappeared.

By the time I'd dried off, *again*, and changed, *again*, Jake was back. He had on a pair of black basketball shorts and a white t-shirt splattered with a few raindrops. Plus that ridiculous smile of his.

For some reason I got nervous all over again. Being alone with Jake was still a rush.

I pointed to the big screen TV on the wall and the built-in shelf of DVD's beside it. "Your choice. I'll get the popcorn and chocolate."

The little guesthouse had a kitchenette with every tiny appliance I could think of. The cabinets were always stocked and I found the popcorn right where it should be. I grabbed two bottles of water and located the bars of chocolate while the kernels popped in the microwave.

Then I heard the TV roar to life. I wondered what Jake had picked, knowing somewhere in the back of my mind it was going to have meaning. Sure enough when I poked my head out of the kitchenette with our goodies I found *The Princess Bride* paused at the very beginning.

"You've got to be kidding me? Of all the movies to pick from, really?"

He shrugged. "It's our favorite."

I shook my head vehemently. "No, there is no 'our' anymore. We started over today. This is our first date. You don't know I like this movie any more than I know *you* like this movie."

He slumped back against the couch and propped his feet up on the ottoman, getting comfortable. When he spoke it was an affected, high-pitched voice. He was mocking me. "So Eve, I'm not sure what movies you like, but I picked *The Princess Bride*. It's one of my favorites and I was hoping we could enjoy it together." He rolled his eyes at me, "Is that better?"

*Ass.* I threw the water bottle at him as I plopped down on the opposite end of the couch, as far away from Mr. Sarcastic as I could get.

He, of course, caught the bottle and set it deftly on the coffee table before lunging for my feet and hauling me long ways across the couch, "If you're going to sit that far away from me, might I suggest a foot rub?"

I glared at him from my new position. "Suit yourself." If he wanted to give me a foot rub, who was I to complain?

Unfortunately I'd forgotten what a Jake Spencer foot rub entailed.

He had magical hands. Hands that knew every

point on my foot to make me gasp with pleasure. Points that had a direct line to my sex. Somehow, by the end of the second foot rub, I was both incredibly relaxed and incredibly turned on.

Jake was an evil genius.

"Did that feel good?" he asked.

"Mmmmm," I mumbled in my half-asleep state.

"Good." I heard him reply.

I dozed off after that, waking from time to time to Jake's fits of laughter or the sections he was reciting. My feet were still in his lap and he kept rubbing them from time to time.

It was so comfortable, so easy.

And then I was in his arms, so warm and strong, my face pressed up against his firm chest. "What's going on?" I mumbled.

He chuckled, the rumble vibrating against my body. "You fell asleep. I'm taking you to your bed."

I nodded and burrowed deeper into his chest. I liked it there. I wanted to stay there.

He laid me gently on my side of the bed, the side I'd always slept on. Somewhere in the back of my head I thought it was strange—or sweet—that he still remembered that. But as he pulled the covers up around me, I grabbed his hand. "Don't go."

He kneeled down beside me and brushed my hair back from my face. "Are you sure?"

I nodded sleepily. I knew what I wanted.

"Okay."

A moment later I felt the mattress dip behind me,

and a moment after that I felt Jake's warm body curled up behind mine with his hand on my hip. It was chaste and comforting. I fell asleep feeling happier than I could remember feeling in a very, very long time.

## Chapter 10

*W*hen I woke up the next morning it felt late. I could hear chatter outside my window and the sun was most definitely up.

And I was alone.

"Morning, darlin'," Jake's voice was deep and rough like he'd just woken up too.

I sat up, pulling the sheet up with me as I looked around for him. I found him sitting in the armchair at the end of the bed, sipping on a steaming mug of coffee. He half-smiled, his eyes wary as he waited for my reaction.

"Coffee?" I asked, suddenly desperate for a cup. My head was doing that dull thud thing it did when I slept later than normal. I was probably in caffeine withdrawal.

He hopped right up and disappeared into the kitchenette, returning a moment later with an identical mug.

I took a tentative sip—he even remembered how I took my coffee: just cream. "Thanks."

He sat carefully beside me on the bed, sipping from his mug. "How are you feeling this morning?"

I knew he was really asking if I was still okay with the way the night had ended. "Good. You?"

"Good. Best night of sleep I've had in a decade."

The reality of that statement hit me in the gut. All of this was a really big deal, for both of us. This thing we were trying, it wasn't just my heart on the line, it was Jake's, too. That was a lot of pressure on both of us. It wasn't as if we couldn't handle the ups and downs of life, but broken hearts—more than once from the person you loved most—those were damn near debilitating. "I slept really well, too."

"It wasn't too soon?"

I smiled at him. For as strong and sure as he could be most of the time, he was very tentative right now. And with good reason. I appreciated how much he cared about my wellbeing. "For sleeping in the same bed? No. You were right, we aren't total strangers and we shouldn't act like we are. I didn't want you to leave, and I'm glad that you stayed."

"Good, I liked it. I missed it."

Things were going to be awkward between us while we figured out our safe zones. Sleeping was safe, jumping back into sex might not be. Dates were safe, but I wasn't ready to live together. I didn't even think I was ready to be his girlfriend. I just wanted to get through a few days and see how things felt.

"One step at a time," I repeated and took a sip of my coffee.

He brushed my hair back from my face, his fingers lingering against my cheek and I saw him sigh. "I missed *you*. Last night, all of it," his voice fell away.

But he didn't need to say any more. I knew what he meant. The movie, the banter, the cuddling—all of that was who we were as a couple. "It's nice to have my best friend back," I agreed.

Jake squeezed his eyes shut and cupped my face with his large hand. When he opened his eyes I saw ten years of loneliness and I knew he saw the exact same thing in mine.

We were going to fall hard and fast, just like we did the first time.

"The gang is setting up on the beach."

I threw back the covers and downed the rest of my coffee. "Well then let's get a move on. Sun, sand, and sea wait for no man." My heart could only take so much of the emotions rolling between us. The beach and the sun, surrounded by our friends sounded like a very nice place to be right about now.

In a matter of fifteen minutes I was safely in a bikini and under the shade of a giant umbrella.

Jake and Andrew started up a game of beach beer pong with the guys which gave the girls free rein to grill me. Somehow I managed to answer most of their questions to their satisfaction. I don't know how, I felt like I was trying to share and hide at the same time. It was too soon for me to understand my own feelings, let alone tell someone else how I felt. So I stuck to the facts. Facts were good.

"You did it in the fishing shack, didn't you?" Sylvia asked.

"Yup."

"He's hotter than he used to be, is the sex?"

"Yup."

"How?" Sylvia had leaned forward in her seat, and everyone else was straining closer, too.

I shook my head. "You all are worse than the Rays locker room."

Jennie grinned. "And just how much time to do you spend in that locker room, Eve?"

I rolled my eyes, not that they could see it through my sunglasses and ball cap. "We haven't seen each other in a long, long time . . . we had a lot of pent up sexual energy, okay?"

I really didn't want to think about how skilled Jake was or how intuitively he seemed to know exactly what to do or when. That would involve me thinking about him having had sex with anyone other than me in the last ten years. And I was *so* not going there. Not yet.

Sylvia grinned, "He's so damn adorable around you, Eve. It makes me wish Ricardo and I were just starting out again."

"What do you mean?" I asked. "Ricardo worships the ground you walk on."

"Not like Jake," she stuck her thumb out at Jennie, "or Andrew, for that matter. You are both in that new love stage. I miss it."

A weird ache developed in my chest. Yes, it was nice to have that intensity that comes in the beginning, but at this point I wanted what Sylvia and Ricardo had: history. There were so many blank years in ours. I knew him, and yet I didn't. Underneath it all Jake was still the same man, the one I saw back then even when he couldn't, but he was also completely different. He'd lived a decade in a part of the world I'd never seen. He'd probably been places, tasted foods, had adventures I knew nothing about. In many ways Jake was a stranger, and that feeling was bizarre.

"There's a lot to be said for what you have with Ricardo." My voice sounded as sad as I felt and that changed the mood of everyone around me. They backed off on the grilling, eventually wandering off.

Except for Jennie.

"How are you doing, for real?" she asked.

I shrugged my shoulders and grabbed an icy cold can of beer from the cooler. "I think the appropriate word would be 'confused'."

She bit her lip and gazed down the beach to where the boys were cheering themselves on to victory. "They seem to be getting along."

I smiled. "Yes, they do. This is good."

Jennie smiled and settled back into her chair. "It is good."

I used Jennie's momentary silence against her, taking the opportunity to turn the tables. "And how is Andrew in bed?"

She raised an eyebrow over her sunglasses but didn't move a muscle. "I haven't slept with him yet. I've known him for, what? Three days?"

I chuckled. "You two are inseparable. I'm half expecting him to drop on a knee before we leave and whisk you away to Vegas."

She smiled and I think she liked that idea. "I will say this, we've barely slept since we met. We haven't stopped talking. I feel like I know him better than anyone else I've ever met."

I knew how she felt. Jake and I were the same way, even all those years ago. "I like him. He's a good guy."

"Do you really think so? Because I'm afraid I can't see straight."

That was probably the scariest thing about falling in love. It happens so hard and so fast it kind of feels like going crazy. And with your heart on the line, the stakes are incredibly high. "I do. I think he's genuinely a good guy and he really, really likes you."

Jennie smiled and sighed. She had it bad. "Please tell me if you get worried. I'm pretty sure I won't be seeing straight where Andrew is concerned any time soon."

A sense of unease hit me out of the blue, and I realized it was because as she said that, I was looking right at Max. Max who was gazing at Jennie.

I swallowed and debated what to say. "There is something . . ."

She shot up out of her seat so fast it scared me. "What?" She ripped her sunglasses off and grabbed my hands in a panic. "Tell me."

"Jennie, calm down." I squeezed her hands to re-assure her I wasn't about to drop some huge bomb that would destroy her illusions of Andrew. "It's about Max."

She cocked her head and scrunched up her eye-brows in confusion, "Max?"

"He's not happy about Andrew." I thrust my chin in Max's direction and Jennie turned to look with her mouth half hanging open.

"But he doesn't want me," she whispered.

"I don't think he knows what he wants. I don't think he's ever known. And right now all he sees is An-drew."

She turned back toward me, her eyes wide with confusion. "What does that mean?"

"It means nothing. He's had every opportunity to date you and he never took that chance. He's not the guy for you, he never has been and he never will be. But right now he's confused. And I just wanted you to be aware."

Jennie stared off at something past me for a long minute before looking back at me. "Okay. I'll make sure I pay attention. He may be an idiot, but I don't want to hurt him."

We settled back into our seats and stared out at the water. Tomorrow morning we'd be headed home. I wondered what that was going to look like. How was it going to feel having Jake in my life again? How was it going to feel having *anyone* in my life again? I'd gotten

pretty used to taking care of myself, not having to worry about how my plans affected anyone but me.

My happiness dependent on his happiness.

There was a certain amount of safety in loneliness.

## Chapter 11

$\mathcal{J}$ ake and I were true to form. We fell into a comfortable pattern as soon we got home. He was careful not to push my boundaries. He took me out to dinners and movies, and most nights he wound up in my bed. We lasted an entire three days before we had sex again. After that it was like opening a can of worms. We were in the glorious honeymoon stage of dating.

I'm not gonna lie, we spent a lot of time in my bed for the next few weeks. We both went to work, and that was about it. Every other available moment of the day and night was spent together. We weren't always having sex—we did a lot of catching up too—but there was a ton of sex.

It was that special, can't-get-enough-of-each-other, need-to-learn-and-explore-every-inch, every sound, every need, sex. We were insatiable. We started off nearly every morning with sex, occasionally met for more at lunch, as soon as work was over, and again before sleep.

Thank goodness it was such a physical workout or we would have wasted away.

I'd never been happier.

We glossed over the necessary things. There were certain assumptions we both felt free making. For instance, I'd always been psychotic about my birth control and monitoring my cycle, so Jake had assumed (correctly) there was nothing to worry about there. But we did go over it, along with a cursory declaration of our clean health. Neither one of us wanted to explore why that was necessary.

But it was the kind of thing that we couldn't run away from forever. Eventually the topic came up—and it was my fault. My curiosity finally got the better of me.

"What?" he asked.

I shook my head and frowned as I looked back at my iPad. "Nothing."

He set down his Kindle and raised a speculative eyebrow. "Bullshit. You don't look at me like that for *nothing*. You have a question on your mind."

I sighed and looked back up at him. I still wasn't sure if it was really the time to bring it up, but then again, it was going to come up eventually. I gathered up what little courage I had, set aside the iPad, and dove in. "I want to know about the women you were with between me and . . . *me*." It was odd to refer to that span as the time between our relationships.

He sat straight up and turned to face me, his eyes growing deadly serious. "I've been waiting for this." He threaded his hands together in his lap, taking in a deep breath. "I want to start off by saying I've never been in love with anyone but you."

The reassurance was nice, but he had already said that. "But . . ."

He contorted his face and I knew I wasn't going to like what was coming next. I don't know how I knew—it was just a gut feeling that hit me like a punch right in the breadbasket.

"I had a *friend* over there. We helped each other out in that department."

Yep, the world fell away as the wind poofed right out of my lungs.

I guess I wanted to hear he'd had a bunch of random women over the years. A *friend* kind of sounded like a relationship, and I hated the idea of Jake in a relationship with anyone. "For how long?"

I didn't want to know. I didn't want to know any of this. Why was I asking?

"Five years."

I had to move. I hopped off the bed and started pacing around my bedroom. Back and forth, back and forth, across the floor. My heart was thumping and my stomach was churning as my mind took off in a million directions—not one of them helpful. I wasn't so sure dinner was staying down. "That's a pretty long time."

Jake was following my movements across the

room, his hands folded carefully in his lap. "It was just sex, Eve. The way work shifted around sometimes we wouldn't see each other for months—but it was just sex. We had no romantic attachments. She had needs, I had needs . . ." his voice trailed off when I put my hands in the air for him to stop.

I had enough information and I needed a moment to process. And processing involved a lot more frantic pacing. I felt like I was coming apart. I had an overwhelming urge to run and escape, but I fought it back.

Finally I ended up at my window looking out over the lawn. I tried to picture what it would have been like. Did she call him? Did he call her? Did they randomly bump into each other and hit a bathroom? Was she pretty? Oh, god, I didn't want to know that.

Suddenly his arms were around me and his lips were behind my ear. "Only you, Eve. I've only ever loved you."

I leaned into his embrace. God I loved being in his arms.

"Why did it end?"

He squeezed me tighter, "When I realized I was ready to come home. About a year ago."

"You haven't had sex in a year or were there others?"

He sighed and rested his head on my shoulder. For the life of me I wished I would stop asking questions I didn't want to know the answers to.

"I've been with a few others since you." He didn't answer my question.

The world got a little spinny with that info and I pushed him off of me, beelining for the bathroom and emptying my stomach of all the wretchedness swirling inside me. Unfortunately it didn't help my racing heart. That was still pounding on the inside of my chest like it wanted out of my body.

Intellectually I knew Jake was young and sexy and over the course of ten years having sex with a few different women probably wasn't all that insane. And it wasn't like I didn't have my own list of partners. Of course we'd continued to live our lives. But I wish we hadn't.

He was mine and he should never have been gone from my side, never had the opportunity to be with anyone else.

I heard the faucet and found a cup of water in my hand a moment before I felt his hand on my back. "I'm sorry."

I smiled at him weakly as I picked myself up off the floor and brushed my teeth, attempting to get all the vileness out. I think it only partially worked.

"I don't really remember a whole lot about those first few years. What I know mostly comes from Tom. I told you I was wild and out of control, and that included women. I remember hating myself—"

I pushed him out of the way as I made a repeat visit to the toilet. The very idea of him being with another woman . . . I shuddered. But at least this time I was pretty sure I was done.

Back to the sink, my mouth clean once again, I

eased myself back onto the bed feeling like I'd just been through a marathon. "So, in summary, you fucked around for a few years, got yourself a whore, fucked around with her and a few others, and then decided you were healed so you cleaned up your manwhore ways and came home to me."

He stood a safe distance away in the doorway to the bathroom looking at me, but not looking at me. His mind was in his past, not here with me. "I wish I could stop hurting you," he said simply.

*I wish that too.* "Then explain it to me so I understand."

He grimaced and looked down at the floor, "I was lonely and angry. I acted out in every way I could, including with women. Eve, I honestly thought we were done. I never thought I'd be able to come home, or ever deserve you. I just tried to survive."

I closed my eyes and laughed at the way it hurt.

Jake sat down beside me, the bed dipping under his weight, "My five years with Ashley was nothing but two screwed up people using each other to get through life."

*Ashley.* That name was moving to the top of my Most Hated Names list.

"I only loved you."

I sighed and leaned into his shoulder. I wanted to blot out all that dreaded information, but I knew it was etched into my brain forever. And I knew it was a consequence of the path Jake chose. I had no power over that choice any more than I had any power over how he chose to recover. It was what it was. And my comfort was in the fact that he did, in fact, love me.

Didn't make the next few days hurt any less.

\* \* \*

I STRUGGLED, I admit it, with Jake's list of whores. *Ashley*. I hated her most of all. And it brought up every insecurity I was struggling with. I fought back my fear that Jake might leave again. I pushed back on my feelings of inadequacy. But my biggest problem was confronting my anger.

I was angry at Jake for leaving. Because he left, he'd also been with other women. I rationalized that if Jake had stayed he would have been just as screwed up and might have wound up acting out with women here. He may have cheated on me, left me, ruined our relationship. Done things that would have truly ruined our relationship forever. But it didn't help much.

I was pretty much just angry about the whole thing.

To Jake's credit, he gave me space. He fucked me if I asked for it, but otherwise was very tender, making love to me at every opportunity. It was very sweet and reaffirmed his words: that he'd only ever loved me.

Unfortunately it was nothing compared to what happened when Jake finally found out about Sebastian.

It was a Wednesday evening. Jake had brought home a ridiculous amount of sushi for the four of us. Andrew was stuck at work so the three of us got started without him. We were around the massive island in the kitchen: rolls, sushi, and sashimi splayed out, a bottle of *sake* was being shared. We were laughing and thoroughly enjoying sampling all the different treats before us when Jennie picked up a piece of tuna sashimi.

The rectangular chunk of raw fish was perched easily between her chopsticks as she held it up in front of her face and started laughing. "Oh Eve, are you thinking what I'm thinking?"

I froze as I realized exactly what she was thinking, and unfortunately I couldn't get my mouth to work in time to stop her.

"You screamed so loud! I think half of Samurai Blue jumped out of their seats! I still can't believe Sebastian snatched this," she wiggled the sashimi at me, somehow missing the look of complete horror on my face, "right out of your mouth. It was *so* not like him to kiss you like that!"

Jake was frozen at the end of the counter, his neck muscles working and his fists crushed around the edge of the counter. He didn't need to know who Sebastian was—Jennie had given him the only information he needed.

Her face immediately fell as her eyes went wide. "Oh my god. I don't why I just said that." She locked eyes with me, "I'm so, so sorry." Her voice fell away so that she was practically mouthing the apology.

I looked over at Jake who was off somewhere else in his mind. He was looking straight ahead, but he wasn't seeing anything in front of him. "Jake . . ." I started.

He didn't move, except for the muscles flexing in his arms, but his eyes shot to mine. "I need a minute." He finally released the counter from his grip and stepped back. "I'm going to go take a quick shower. You ladies finish your dinner." He looked pointedly at me. "Meet me upstairs in a bit?"

I nodded, swallowing down the lump in my throat. "I'll be up in a minute."

He nodded tightly, the sadness in his eyes so obvious I could feel it.

"Eve, please don't hate me," Jennie whispered, her face still twisted with regret.

I popped a piece of sushi in my mouth and carefully chewed, using the time to order my thoughts. "It was time, we've been putting this off. Don't beat yourself up."

She shook her head slowly. "I'm still sorry. It wasn't my place to push you where you weren't ready to go."

Maybe we weren't ready to go there, or maybe it was a dark pall that had been hanging over us for weeks. Either way, what was done was done, and a little part of me was relieved to get it all out in the open. It felt like one of the last big hurdles in front of us. Not the very last by any means—there was one much larger still to come—but this was next in line. It would be a good test of Jake's claim he wouldn't run.

When I got upstairs the shower was still running and I knew exactly how I wanted to handle Jake. The bathroom was foggy from the humidity and I quickly stripped naked, my work clothes falling in a trail from doorway to shower. He saw me coming, watching me silently strip with a dark, intense stare, drinking me in with each step.

By the time I reached him, the air was alive and crackling between us. I could feel him and the darkness around him. The shower door opened and his large hand wrapped around my waist, pulling me inside.

The shower was just barely big enough for two people to comfortably fit. The tiles had a rough finish and a design ran along the top. Glass enclosed it on two sides with a door closest to the wall.

Everything about our shower sex was a mix of pleasure and pain. The hot water stung as it hit my dry flesh, but I quickly got used to it, even welcomed the comfort it brought me from the chill of the air. Jake's fingers dug hungrily into my soft flesh. I would have cried out from the roughness with which he handled me, but I didn't want to stop him and I knew my cry would snap him out of whatever world he was lost in.

I wanted him to use me. I wanted him to have me in whatever way he needed me.

He spun my back against the wet shower tile, hiking my leg up as his tongue forced its way inside my mouth. He was intense and hard with every movement he made.

Unlike every other experience I'd had with Jake there would be no lead up to this. He was going to take me hard and fast with no foreplay or slow pleasuring.

He kept his head down on my shoulder—in fact I don't think he'd looked at me once as he forced his way inside me. I dug my nails into his shoulder as he desperately pumped into me over and over. Then he grunted deep in his throat, thrust hard and deep, then froze, dropping his forehead back onto my shoulder until he caught his breath. When he finally looked up there was no change in his eyes, they were still as distant and dark as they had been when he first pulled me into the shower.

That was when I knew we weren't done. We were only getting started.

He silently reached for my body wash, the scent of vanilla and honey filling the steamy room in an instant, and he slowly, thoroughly washed me. It wasn't until he was done that he finally touched me with the intent to please.

I hated the silence.

His hand followed the water, gliding down my belly and between my legs. He worked his magic until I came apart, shattering into a soft, but spectacular orgasm.

I was little bit relieved it happened quickly. I had a feeling Jake would have kept me nailed to the shower wall until I gave him what he wanted.

His lips found mine again, but he still wasn't right. "Let's get you clean," he murmured, the sadness still in his eyes.

I washed my hair while he dried off. When I was dry too, I found him sitting up in our bed with a pair of black pajama pants on. I grabbed a soft t-shirt and panties before joining him and I sat down carefully, unsure of how to handle him.

"Tell me about him," he said softly.

Knowing how well I'd taken Ashley and Jake's many others, I really, really didn't want to tell him about mine. I didn't want to relive the days or weeks of distance between us. I didn't want to see him run.

But we would always be tied to the past until things like this were out of the way. "His name was Sebastian Monroe," I said quietly. "He's two years older than us, he has blond hair and blue eyes. He is six-foot-one, probably one-seventy-five."

Jake shook his head, his eyes shining as they watched me. "I don't care about what the fucker looked like. Tell me about *him*."

I couldn't read the emotions on Jake's face, but I knew they were powerful—and directed at me. "He was a good man and he took very good care of me."

His eyes darkened and the muscle in his neck flexed. "Keep going."

It was torture.

"Sebastian was kind and loving, stable and had a good job. He's a lead architect for a big firm." Jake was watching me so intently it felt like he had me tied down. "We were happy together but I never loved him . . . I was content. He was someone to spend my days with and keep the loneliness from crushing me."

I could have sworn Jake was trembling. "How long?"

This was where logic ceased to exist. It didn't matter that I'd waited seven years before I took another relationship seriously or that I was simply trying to move on with my life. That wasn't what Jake was going to hear when I spoke. Instead he would hear I tried to love someone other than him, and that reality would hurt like hell.

"Sebastian and I were together for a year. He moved in here for the last six months we were together." Jake closed his eyes and lowered his head when I spread out my hands indicating Sebastian and I lived in this same room. "He would have proposed if I hadn't broken it off."

"Why *did* you?"

I sighed and closed my eyes, wishing he could really hear me, not all the fear and regret that was clouding everything around us. "I didn't love him, Jake. I *liked* him, nothing more."

"Did he make you come?"

The question was so abrupt and vulgar it threw me off. It was probably the last thing I expected him to ask me right now. "Ummm, yes?"

Jake took a deep breath but didn't pull his eyes off me. "Did he make you come like I do? Every time? Or did he leave you wanting?"

Jake's question was ludicrous. He'd clearly bypassed upset, gone right past angry, and nose-dived into jealous rage. "He wasn't an idiot, Jake. Of course he got me off. Just like *Ashley* got you off." I knew bringing *her* up was a low blow, but I got the response

I wanted, Jake flinched.

How did I make him understand that regardless of everything, Sebastian had never been Jake? "Did he make me tremble from across the room the way you do when you look at me? No. No man has ever made me feel like you do."

Jake was breathing hard, the bow of his shoulders accentuating the chiseled muscles beneath. When he looked up his eyes were intense in a way that said he wanted to possess me. "I want to erase Sebastian from your mind," he growled.

Jake looked like he was going to claim me and protect me from any other man who came near me.

And for some reason that raw animalistic possession was everything I'd ever wanted. It said he loved me and only me in a way that was worth killing and fighting for. It may have come later than I'd wanted, but at least it was here.

"So come make me forget his name."

He moved fast, pulling my legs out from underneath me and sending me flat onto my back. Then he grabbed me by the ankles and yanked me across the bed until I was underneath him. It was an adrenaline rush. "I hate him." His voice was so gruff, I wished there was some way I could reach inside his heart and make the pain go away.

"I never loved him, Jake."

He stilled. "Doesn't matter."

Then he buried his head in my neck as his hands ran over the thin cotton of my t-shirt. My nipples immediately tingled for more attention and Jake responded by sitting up on his knees and yanking my shirt up over my head.

He suckled and tugged, the sensations causing slick, hot, heat between my legs that ached for its own attention. "I want you," I gasped. I wanted him inside me where we could both feel a connection. That special connection that comes between two people when they are locked together in orgasm.

Jake responded by yanking down his pants and pulling my panties aside, slamming into me as hard and fast as I hoped he would. The sensation of being filled with him was so satisfying I sighed with relief.

"Oh no you don't," he purred, running his nose up the sensitive flesh of my throat to my ear, then tugged at my lobe with his teeth.

It sent another jolt of electricity straight to my sex and I moaned out loudly, "Oh yes . . ."

"More?" he asked.

I nodded vehemently and he complied, teasing my ear with his tongue while his thumb ran over my nipple and his cock pumped into me over and over. I was quite literally screwed, being teased from every accessible pleasure point simultaneously.

I knew I was being loud but I didn't care. I wanted Jake to hear how insane he was making me. My muscles were winding up, contracting with anticipation of my coming release. But it wasn't quick. The buildup was deliciously slow. My body rising and tightening as Jake worked me until I felt like a live wire pulled incredibly tight.

I snapped.

I called out Jake's name, I made sure of it, as I dug my nails into his flesh, marking him with evidence of my complete and utter satisfaction.

Jake pushed harder, pumping into me faster until I finally felt his own spasms of release. When he was satisfied, Jake rested his forehead against my shoulder. "You okay?"

I took his face into my hands, forcing him to look at me for the first time since he'd entered me. When his eyes locked onto mine I told him the only thing in my mind. "You make me scream, you make me see stars. When *you* make me come the whole universe stops while I fall apart. You do that. Only you."

He dipped his head down to brush a soft kiss against my lips. "There is a vast difference between getting a release and being pleasured beyond your wildest dreams, isn't there?" He kissed me again. "I know, because that's what you do to me."

I nodded slowly. "There is no one but you."

He swallowed. "Good. I want to be the only one you think of, the only one you turn to. I want to take care of you and I'll kill anyone who comes near you."

I realized there was a much deeper meaning to his words. They weren't just some possessive male power play, they were an intense need to protect something he loved and treasured from the evils he knew all to well. When Jake promised to kill anyone who came near me he wasn't thinking of the guys who might flirt with me one day, or even the Sebastian's in my life. He was talking about real danger. The kind of danger he knew as a child—the kind that would truly hurt me. I had no doubt in my mind Jake would protect from anything and everything. But I also knew deep down inside he was still worried.

"You will."

He nodded and kissed me hard, "You're damn right I will."

## Chapter 12

We weren't the same after Jake got all the sordid details about Sebastian, especially once he realized my former lover was still loosely connected to my life. While I hadn't seen Sebastian in the last year and hadn't had any conversations with him, I knew he was doing well. I knew that because he and Jennie still regularly chatted. Not to mention Sebastian and Ricardo were pretty good friends. The two met up for golf and Bucs games on a regular basis.

Then there was the fact that Sebastian was still friendly with my family—with June in particular. He chatted with her on Facebook and kept up with Cassandra. Hell, he even met up with my dad from time to time.

It had pushed Jake away from me and I knew why. It had as much to do with what Sebastian stood for as anything. Sebastian had been the stable, loving man at my side when Jake couldn't. Because Jake had been on the other side of the world, Sebastian had been part of my life, part of my family.

It didn't matter that Jake was here now. It didn't matter that I never loved Sebastian. It was the idea of it all. It was eating away at Jake.

He was distant. Some days it was as if he wasn't there with me at all. When we made love it was functional, mechanical. I was satisfied physically, but not mentally. He'd started sleeping on his side of the bed again, only holding me for the first five minutes of the night before kissing my head and rolling away.

But then it was if he'd suddenly wake up and realize how many days had passed with him in a stupor. He'd try to make up for being so absent by overwhelming me, showing up for lunch unannounced, bringing my favorite foods, buying me music, and fucking me senseless.

I felt like I was on an emotional roller coaster, never knowing which Jake would show up. I felt like I was starting to lose my mind. I was crying for no reason, avoiding Jake, staying at work later than I had to. The baseball season was winding down so it wasn't a complete lie, but I also didn't need to be there as much as I was. I didn't know how I was going to deal with Jake if the Rays didn't make the playoffs.

I was starting to get worried. All of this was exactly what I was worried about. If a former ex-boyfriend I didn't even love could push Jake so far away from me, what would he do with a real problem? Maybe love still wasn't enough.

The realization was terrifying and it was making me edgy.

It all came to a head over dinner one night. I met him at Estela's Mexican restaurant down the street from home. In my search for comfort I'd asked for a giant burrito. Jake was brooding over something, paying more attention to the messages he was getting on his phone than he was to me.

"Babe, if you have a problem at work, please go. I can get myself home just fine."

He set down his phone and glared across the table at me. "Don't be ridiculous. I'm off the clock."

How was I the ridiculous one? "Then can you put your phone away until we get home? I feel like you and your phone are on a date, not you and me."

Jake's brooding quickly became anger. It pissed me off he that was angry at me.

"I am not on my phone that much."

I snorted, "You believe your own bullshit if you want to, but I don't have to."

"Excuse me? Maybe we *should* go home if you are in such a bitchy mood."

That was it. I was done, that was the final straw. I slammed down my napkin and pushed back from the table, grabbing my purse, "How about this, Jake. You go to your apartment and I'll go to my house. Call me when you decide you actually want to be with me again . . . or better yet, don't. I'm tired of waiting for you."

His anger boiled over, fire burning in his eyes. "How dare you say something like that to me? You don't throw around shit like that. *Ever.*"

The problem was Jake didn't understand I wasn't throwing it around for fun. It wasn't a game. I really was sick of his bullshit. I understood how badly he hurt, it hadn't been a picnic to know about Ashley. But it was reality. There was an Ashley and there was a Sebastian. If he couldn't deal with that, if Jake was going to let it change the way he felt about me, I didn't want to be with him. I'd already waited too long for him as it was.

"Jake Spencer, pull your shit together or don't ever call me again. I'm done."

I stood up and stormed out of the restaurant before Jake and everyone else saw me cry. I was going to cry and it was going to be seriously ugly.

I heard Jake's footfalls behind me so I started to run. I wasn't that far from my car and I had a head start, if I hurried I could escape from him before he caught me.

But as I reached for my handle, Jake's hand closed around my arm just above the elbow. "Eve, wait." He spun me away from the handle and pushed my back against the car.

"Let go of me right now, Jake."

He glowered at me, equal parts angry and terrified. "Not if you are going to run away from me."

"Let go of me right now, Jake." I repeated through clenched teeth.

He studied me for a moment longer, but then released my arm. "Fine," he bit out.

I glared at him. "You can't keep me here. Figure out what you want, Jake. I think you've forgotten and I'm not in the business of standing by and waiting for you any longer."

I wrenched open my door and this time Jake let me leave. He just stood there on the side of the road watching me leave with a hollow look on his face. I was grateful for the speed and power of my expensive engine as my heart squeezed in my chest. I needed to flee. Jake was lost but it wasn't my job to help him find his path.

* * *

I DIDN'T GO HOME.

Instead, I went to work. It was after hours and there was no game tonight, but going home felt all wrong. Work felt safer. My office was one place that was completely mine and no one else's. Besides, there was plenty to do there to keep my mind from fixating on things I did not want to face.

Like the possibility Jake might really be gone this time.

The minute I stepped into my office I felt better. My dark wood desk stood in the middle of the long, large room. I wasn't a manager yet, I didn't have an office as enormous as Josh's, but it was a very comfortable size, more than large enough for my desk, the two leather chairs that faced it, a small bar and refrigerator to one side of my office door, a couch on the other, a book case along the far wall, and a gorgeous window looking out over the twinkling lights.

I didn't flick on the harsh overhead light. Instead I reached for the lamp on my desk, setting a soft glow to the room. I threw my bag in the drawer I always kept it in and plopped into my comfortable leather chair. I wanted to hate him, but somehow I couldn't find it in me. There was just hurt.

A lot of hurt.

I was disappointed. I knew he would be thrown by Sebastian and I knew we would have our setbacks in life. But I had really hoped he would handle all of this better. It worried me. If he could get this lost to his insecurities, to lock himself up inside his head away from me, then what would happen if something truly difficult came along? Like Jake Sr.?

I hadn't even dared let that name cross my lips and I cringed thinking it now.

Work. I needed to focus on work. I opened my laptop and gave it a moment to wake. My foot tapped nervously and my fingers drummed on the wood of my desk.

The moment my desktop appeared on the screen I navigated to the file holding my event notes, searching for last year's playoff notes. Our planning meeting was coming up next week and I was going to be so damn prepared no one would need to do anything else.

I spent an hour going over my old notes and making a plan. Then I thought of the new fan experience we were beginning construction on the moment the season was over. I thought of all the things we'd be able to do next season. And I thought of the lead engineer and his brilliant plans.

Damn Jake. Why couldn't he just stay out of his own damn way? I wondered where he went when I left. I wondered what he was doing right now.

My phone lit up with a text message. *Please let me in. I'm outside.*

My heart started racing. I'm not sure if it was with relief or fear, but it was racing out of control. I didn't think, I just grabbed my keycard and walked out to let Jake in.

He looked like hell. His eyes were haunted and his face was pulled down, a hard set to his jaw. But he was tall and sure, his shoulders were square and his back was straight. I could feel his immense energy wash through the air the moment I opened the door.

It hit me like a wave and took my breath away. This man, for all the things he'd done to me, all the demons he'd fought, still had something about him that made me utterly stupid in his presence. My knees were weak and I felt that delicious spin of dizziness I got when he is in full male mode.

"Can we talk?"

I stood aside to let him in, his arm brushing me as he walked past. He waited while I secured the door, waving at the security camera to let them know all was well, and then he placed his hand on the small of my back. Whenever I was in charge, when he accompanied me to my work functions or met with us here in an official capacity for work, he always assumed that position: almost a half-step behind me, but his hand possessively on my back. It connected us without being too intimate. It made my belly quiver with nervous energy and all the muscles between my legs clench like I was falling.

Neither of us said anything. Not until the door to my office was safely closed.

He pressed me to the door, his warm breath dancing across my lips. "I'm sorry baby. You are right, I've been gone."

I looked up at him through my lashes. I was relieved he was here, but I was still mad and hurt. "I never loved him."

Jake closed his beautiful green eyes and grimaced at the mention of Sebastian. He leaned into me and placed his hands on either side of me, trapping me against the door. "I hate that he took my place."

"*I* hate that he took your place. I thought you were never coming home."

He opened his eyes and they were burning. I felt all the emotion in them, I felt his regret wash over me. "I know. And I still can't help myself. I can't tell you how much I've beat myself up."

"I can't do this, Jake. I can't be with you if you're not going to talk to me. You can't just check out. You scare me."

He stepped back and ran his hand through his

gorgeous dark hair. "Eve," he sighed, "I should have gotten over myself and called. I should have done something. Ten years . . ." He shook his head, wandering across my office and settling in front of my window. For some reason I started to follow, but stopped at my desk. I felt like he needed space. "I still can't believe it took me ten years."

"But you're here now. Remember?"

He turned, his eyes pinning me where I was. "Yes . . . I am." He stalked toward me. Only stopping once he was pressing me into the desk. This was the intense Jake I'd come to know over the last couple of weeks. The primal one who took me as his, who possessed me at his will. I enjoyed this Jake as much as I enjoyed the sweet lover who worshiped me. I loved his two sides when they weren't being driven by his self-loathing. They were both passionate and merciless. He took my lips, his rough hands grasping my face and holding me while his tongue explored.

"I'm done. I will pull my shit together," he rasped. The husky quality to his voice made me quiver. He wanted me.

"I missed you."

I didn't need to say any more than that. I knew things would be right between us again. But Jake didn't. He still needed something more. He looked deep into my eyes and smiled, a wicked grin I recognized all too well. It was a side of Jake I hadn't seen in a very, very long time. It was a side of both of us that was very dangerous.

And as he left me to lock my office door I knew we were about to unlock something we might not be able to handle.

The click of the lock sent the familiar thrill surging through my body. We were going to have sex in my office. Every time I came in to work from today through the rest of time I would think of Jake making me come against this desk.

That thrill of excitement was like a drug, it was a high, the adrenaline flooding my veins as my heart continued to pump faster.

"Turn around," he commanded, his dark energy reaching across the room and closing the distance between us.

I wanted him so badly I couldn't seem to stop myself from following his commands.

He pushed up my skirt and slowly slid my panties down my legs, coaxing each foot up until they were free. Then he laid them out on the desk beside my hand.

His warm, firm body pressed up against mine. I could feel every muscle as they flexed against me and his erection as it dug into the small of my back. Jake was so damn sexy, everything about him turned me on, even his scent and demanding voice.

I ground back against him as his hands reached around to my front, pushing my head back onto his shoulder, running down my exposed throat as his lips found my skin. "Darlin' you smell so damn good," he groaned as his hands wandered to the buttons of my shirt.

I was helpless in his arms, and I liked it. The two of us together didn't need thoughts, just instincts, just pure reaction. His warm breath danced across the skin of my neck, tantalizing me as his fingers glided against my skin, button by button.

Then my shirt was open and his rough hands sampled all of my exposed skin. "Do you know what your skin does to me?" He pulled my body tight against his erection. "I can't think straight." And then his hand ran all the way down between my legs, where my skirt was still hiked up, and clutched me with his large hand.

I moaned, bucking into his firm grip.

I could feel him smile against my neck. "That's right darlin'. We're good together. Don't you forget that." Then his fingers reached inside first one, then the other, cup of my bra, pulling my breasts up and out for him to play with. The underwire of my bra holding them in the perfect position.

A glance down told me what I already knew: they looked damn good like that.

Jake chuckled, "I love it when you do that."

"Fucker," I purred back. I liked that he loved it. It was hot and it made me hotter. Especially between my legs, which was getting wetter by the minute.

His fingers closed on each of my nipples, sending a shot of pleasure throughout my body. I writhed against him, gasping for air. He played like that, pulling a symphony of noises and pleasures out of me until suddenly he was done, his hands sliding down my sides to my hips. "I'm going to taste you now. Bend over."

*Taste me?*

He pushed gently on my back as he dropped to the floor behind me. Was he really going down on me now, when I was so wet, so hot and bothered? His tongue running from my clit to my core was my answer. It was like fire. It was pleasure in every sense of the word. He was fucking crazy.

"You taste like heaven," he murmured. Like everything else with Jake, it didn't matter how hard I tried to fight it, my body loved what he did to me. I tried to ignore how good his tongue felt gliding everywhere and plunging inside me, but I couldn't. Just like I couldn't ignore my clit as it started to throb for attention. It was burning and pulsing. It was begging to be touched.

But instead, his hands glided up the back of my legs, spreading me wider for him. "Hold yourself just above the desk so that those perfect nipples hit the top while I blow your mind."

For some reason his words made me gasp. It wasn't like they should have shocked me, he was already as far deep inside me as he could get, and yet... it sounded so dirty, so crass. And my stupid body liked that, too. I felt the pulse deep inside me calling for him to do everything he had just promised.

So I did just as he asked, repositioning my bent torso so that my dangling breasts just barely brushed the cool surface of my desk.

First one, then two fingers slid inside me. My breasts swung gently back and forth, the nipples catching the surface and sending little spikes of pleasure everywhere, making the muscles in my core contract with anticipation of more, getting wetter and wetter with each glorious movement.

And Jake was clearly enjoying himself. Occasional grunts of approval vibrating against my clit, his tongue doing glorious things to the most sensitive parts of my body, until I was shuddering from the waves of pleasure and the promise of yet another powerful orgasm.

That was when he pulled me hard against his mouth at the same time he pressed his fingers inside me. It was what I needed. I came hard, collapsing on the desk as my body throbbed. Jake teased every last ounce of pulsing pleasure out of my core until I shuddered one last time against the cool desk.

I was dazed, but I heard him stand up behind me and unzip his pants. They fell to the ground and I saw them as they were tossed to the side. I knew what was coming next. At least I thought I did.

So I was surprised when his hand gently glided over my throbbing sex, his fingers diving inside for just a moment.

There was a pause and then he was beside me where I could gaze at his perfectly chiseled body and fully erect cock. "You see this?" he asked. "This is all you. I am this hard because I want you and no one else. And this?" he ran his hand up and down his entire length. It was glistening. With *me*. "All of this is from you, every single bit of it. You are so . . . fucking . . . wet." His eyes rolled back in his head as a wave of pleasure shuddered through him.

I was hot all over again.

Then he moved back around behind me, pulling off first my shirt, then stripping me of my bra. Finally my skirt fell to the floor. "So I'm going to fuck you now."

He plunged inside me and the heated throbbing started off like a racehorse again. I called out his name as my body bucked up off the desk. He stilled for a moment as we locked our bodies together and he gently ran his bare hands down my back and over my bottom, "Oh your skin . . ."

Then he hooked his hands around the front of my hips and started to move. Slow at first, but he quickly picked up speed. I was definitely still wet for him and my body was quickly responding to his pounding. I started to push back looking for more, using the desk as leverage.

He took advantage of my change in position, sliding his hands around until they found my breasts, seeking out my already swollen and used nipples, pinching them between his fingers and rolling until I cried out. I didn't know how much pleasure I could take, but Jake seemed bound and determined to find out.

And then suddenly he stopped, pulling out of me and pulling me up. "I want to see you." His eyes were dark and full of a possessive need I'd never seen in him before. He picked me up and deposited me on the desk, thrusting back inside me hard. I arched my back and barked his name again, something I realized he enjoyed very much. It made me smile.

"Do you need to lie down?" he asked as he moved slowly in and out while watching me intently. I was so swollen I could feel every vein and ridge as it glided over my skin.

"No Jake, I don't." I used his name on purpose. To my extreme satisfaction his eyes burned with need. Need for me. Need for the woman who was saying his name.

"Good," he growled, bending me back so that he could have full access to my breasts. His warm mouth closed over my nipple just as he glided fully back inside of me so deep I didn't think he'd ever come back out.

But he did. Over and over as his tongue worked my breast. First his warm tongue would run over my nipple, then his teeth would tug and pull, only to be replaced by his mouth sucking. In and out my nipple went just as his dick moved in and out of me.

And then the first pulses started deep, deep inside my body. Not an orgasm yet, just the early promise of one about to erupt. Jake felt them, because he smiled against my breast. With my red and swollen nipple between his teeth he looked up. "That's right, darlin' give it to me. Just give in to it. I've got you."

It was if he knew how powerful the coming orgasm was going to be. That it was going to wring every muscle in my body, that it would tear me from the inside out. I'm not sure how he knew, but he did, and he was ready.

With one last lick, nip, and suckle on my breast, he stood fully up so that he was looking down into my eyes as my body split in two, pounding harder than ever, pulling my body up and down against his, as it took over, coming apart at the seams, and folding around his hard body.

My muscles squeezed powerfully around his firm cock as it plunged back inside, locking and holding him in place. I pulled his body against mine, my muscles shuddering, my nails digging into his skin, as I called out his name.

That's when I felt his release. The pulsing of his cock only spurred my orgasm on, taking it further and longer. I tossed my head back as the next round of contractions hit, "Oh fuck!" I called as Jake managed to pull back and thrust all the way inside me one last time.

It was then that he set me back down on the desk and pushed as far into me as he could. It made me throb even more, calling out more noises and curse words.

Jake finally barked out a final curse, leaning his sweaty forehead into mine. We were locked like that for a minute while our bodies calmed down. He held me up so that I couldn't escape.

"Tell me Sebastian made you come like that. Tell me *any* other man has ever made you come like that."

No. No one had ever made me feel anything like Jake did in any way. "You're the only one," I replied quietly. I would tell him that as many times as he needed to hear it.

He melted around me, gathering me against his body. "I won't run again," he whispered against my kisses. "I won't ever hurt you again."

## Chapter 13

"*I* come bearing gifts!" I declared as I stepped into my family suite at the Trop. Jake and his partner Greg were using the suite to schmooze some clients. Clients, it turned out, who came with good news of their own. Spencer, Hamilton and Associates had been awarded a big contract for the engineering to expand the Channelside Entertainment District.

"No!" the larger man, I think his name was Frank, exclaimed. "You are just too much my dear!" He looked at me with lust. I couldn't imagine a man like him ever treating a woman with respect. Women were meat to him. Warm places he could stick his flesh and find temporary comfort from his pathetic life. I flinched as his hands moved toward the box I was holding.

Jake seemed to notice my discomfort and wrapped his arms around me from behind. "You didn't need to do this," he murmured in my ear, pulling me away from Frank.

"I know," I said, turning in his embrace to wrap my arms around his neck. "I think I get some sort of thrill out of giving people free crap."

He chuckled and the rumble from deep in his chest resonated from him to me. It made me feel warm inside.

I hung out in the suite for a while, admiring my boyfriend in his element. He commanded the room, more so than anyone else. The men seemed to want to be him. I could see the admiration in their eyes as they looked over Jake's three-piece suit, his broad, firm frame, and me on his arm. But it was more than that. Men like Jake didn't just get respect for no reason. No one told the men in the room to admire him. Jake commanded that from the people around him. They could sense his ease and confidence. They knew he deserved the reputation he had, they could hear his brilliance, and they knew I was by his side out of choice, not because he had money or because he had some hold over me.

"I have to make some rounds, grease some palms, make some other fancy men happy," I winked at Jake. "I'll be a little while."

"I wish you could stay . . ." he murmured, and I didn't miss the rough way he said that. Things between us had been good since the night in my office. He and I were back to being easy and happy with each other. We'd decided to accept our past for what it was.

But something else had happened that night. We'd unlocked an old ghost. It had started to appear more and more often—the thrill of sex in unexpected places was exciting to us both.

It was becoming a challenge, an addiction we were seeking out more and more often. And the way it had started for us was glaring me in the face at the moment. Jake was pressing his erection into my back while my hand rested on the very bar he'd fucked me behind the first time we'd gotten that sexual high so many years ago.

I really didn't have that much work I needed to do right now. But I did need to get away from Jake and this suite during my working hours. The temptation to push our boundaries was getting too high.

"I'll see you soon," I murmured, pushing him behind the bar where he could adjust himself before I left.

He smiled down at me as he laughed and tucked himself behind his belt, the glint of longing in his eyes unmistakable.

"No, sir. You stand down right now. You have clients and so do I."

He shrugged his shoulders. "Darlin' sometimes I want to whisk you away, go live on an island for the rest of our lives, and fuck ourselves stupid."

I put my hands on my hips and glared at him, knowing full well Frank had just overheard us. "I never said that wasn't an option. But I think we'd get bored."

"You and I have enough money that we can do

whatever we want," he said pointedly.

While there was some truth to that statement, I was not ready to start planning 'ever-after' with Jake. Not yet.

"I'll see you soon." I repeated for the last time, pecking his soft cheek right where my dimple liked to hide.

"Love you darlin'," he called loudly enough for all the men and women in the suite to stop and smile at us.

I didn't see it coming. We were in the seventh inning stretch, I'd made all the rounds I needed to make, and I was taking a walk around the outfield concourse when I decided to step out onto the deck. I'd picked a corner hidden in the shadow of the lights. The Rays were winning handily and most of the stadium was beginning to empty. In fact, most of the outfield was a ghost town, real fans having moved to better, emptier seats.

It was a nice moment alone. I wrapped my hands around the cool metal of the railing, stretching my back and smelling the air. The Trop was a dome so it wasn't the same as an outdoor stadium, but it was close enough—especially with the traditional organ music playing at the moment. I closed my eyes and listened to the sounds of my life. The music, the shouts and chatter, the announcer's voice, even the occasional call of the vendors offering up last call on soda, ice cream, cracker jacks, and peanuts.

So I didn't notice him coming until he was behind

me. But I knew who it was the moment his arms slid around my hips. I knew the smell of Jake. I knew the vibration he put in the air. "I'm done with my clients. What about you?"

I leaned back into his embrace, resting my head on his broad shoulder. "Yes. I'm done."

"What are you doing out here?"

I sighed as the announcer came over the loud-speaker announcing the bottom of the seventh inning. "Relaxing."

Jake sighed into me, "You know you are a rare woman, right?"

I chuckled but didn't open my eyes. I was enjoying resting against Jake as much as I'd been enjoying listening to the stadium a moment before. "Because I bring your clients gifts?"

Jake growled in my ear, "No. Because you relax in the outfield."

There had to be something to that, I couldn't argue his logic. He held me for two batters before his hands started to roam. I was so relaxed I forgot where I was, I didn't even think twice as his hands roamed over my breasts. It wasn't until his hand glided down between my thighs that I gasped and my eyes shot open, taking a moment to focus on the green field ahead of me.

"What are you doing?"

He nuzzled my neck, "Having fun."

Suddenly, a memory as vivid as the field in front of me, flooded my mind. We were twenty-one, in this same outfield, in a similar situation. It was late in an easy-win game, the stadium was nearly empty and it was cold as hell. We were huddled up under an enormous Rays fuzzy blanket.

We'd had sex in the outfield.

Slow, under that blanket, over the course of the entire eighth inning. Well, we'd pleasured each other anyway. It was all Jake's fault. Him and his magical hands. Surprisingly I'd been the fast one that day. Maybe it was the excitement of what we were doing, or maybe he was just really on his game. Either way he'd gotten me off with those hands of his in seemingly record time, all with his eyes carefully trained on the field ahead.

It had taken me much longer to get him off. I'd taken that badly. I was young and stupidly felt it was a deficiency on my part. Jake claimed he'd just been enjoying himself too damn much to come any sooner.

But that was then. Jake's hands caressed my backside lovingly, smoothing over the roundness. "This is a dark corner, Eve. We could do it."

"No," I said firmly. I was not having sex with him here. It was one thing to be young and stupid, it was quite another to do it where I worked, out in the open, in the middle of a game.

His hands instantly left me. "As you wish."

I felt naked and I realized how hot I was. My core was throbbing, my nipples tingling. I was panting. And with Jake's light touch gone, I felt bereft.

"Come back," I choked, my hand reaching out blindly behind me.

"As you wish," he repeated. I felt his smile as he kissed my neck and the warmth of his body enveloped me from behind. "I'm not going to do anything crass," he murmured. "We aren't kids hiding under a blanket. You are at work and looking damn fine, I might add." He leaned in so that his lips were at my ear at the same time his hand traveled up the front of my loose skirt. "No one will know what I'm doing to you, but *you*."

Stupid or not, I wanted it. I let go of my last inhibitions and relaxed against his palm.

"That's right, darlin', just let go," he whispered, his warm breath dancing across the sensitive skin behind my ear.

And I did. I relaxed against the railing in front of me and opened my legs to his hand, allowing him to touch and caress whatever he wanted.

"Just look at how beautiful the field is from here, Eve."

It sent my heart racing. The thrill of being pleasured out in the open was energizing me. My blood was pumping with excitement. My skin was tingling from the rush and a deep throb was pulsing low in my belly.

Jake wanted to hear my strangled rasps as I fought to keep my pleasure a secret. He liked hearing the struggle, it was part of the thrill for both of us, but Jake especially, to know it was because of him I was panting and wild and desperate not to get caught.

I liked pleasing him too much. I was using this situation and I knew it. Things between us were good, but there was still a wall, and I was using sex to hide behind it. I had a feeling Jake knew, but he was afraid to push me too hard. Any time things got too intense, any time I felt Jake probing into an area I wasn't ready to go, I'd offer myself up to him, distracting him from his questioning with my pleasure as prize.

I could see the disappointment that flashed through his eyes just before he replaced it with desire. He was letting me hide behind my wall, I just didn't know for how long.

Jake stilled his large hand, his two middle fingers buried deep inside me, and I pulsed several times. He pressed me to him so I could feel his erection, "You are so, so very beautiful when you're aroused," he growled in my ear.

I pulsed again.

His free hand caressed my backside, sending an electric current over my sensitive flesh, before smoothing up the arch of my back and hooking over my shoulder. His mouth was at my ear again and I was all anticipation, being held captive at the edge of orgasm. "Come. Right now, Eve." he demanded, pulling down on my shoulder at the same time he thrust up with his fingers inside me. The sudden pressure was my undoing. I came hard, my sex squeezing and savoring his large fingers inside me. He turned my head, thrusting his tongue almost painfully into my mouth to quiet my cries. He held me tight while I fell apart, his strong arms destroying and protecting my body simultaneously.

The moment I was calm again he slid his fingers

away and my skirt flitted back down into place. His free hand on my hip spun me to face him and I leaned lazily back against the rail, still weak. He stepped between my thighs, his arm all the way around my waist holding me close, and locked his green eyes with mine.

I was caught in his stare, completely unable to look away as he raised his glistening fingers and licked them clean. "Dessert," he murmured.

I don't know why it was so damn erotic that Jake liked the way that I tasted, but it was. Knowing that the most intimate part of me drove him wild to the point of distraction and lust was *hot*. It just was.

"I'm glad I could help with that," I replied huskily.

He grinned wickedly as he licked the last of me from his fingers and pulled me tight against him, "Can we go home? I'm ready to fuck you in our bed like a good boyfriend."

I bit my lower lip as a fresh wave of excitement rushed through my veins. "As you wish."

* * *

JAKE TOOK ME OUT for a special dinner. Dinner turned into a walk along the water. His fingers were threaded through mine and a small smile played on his lips.

"You're happy tonight," I murmured.

"I am," he agreed.

I looked up at him questioningly and he chuckled. "I've got a couple of good things to tell you, actually."

I paused, turning toward Jake. The sun was set,

but the sky was still glowing a brilliant orange behind him. I loved the long summer sunsets. It made the days seem so eternal and the nights so short. "You've been holding out on me all night?"

Jake looked down at me with a satisfied look, "Darlin', there is a time and place for everything."

"Spill it." Sometimes I really hated how patient Jake could be.

He chuckled, the warm sound of his voice washing over me. "I landed a very, very large contract to develop a new piece of equipment. It will require both Greg and I to oversee a whole new division at the company." He shoved his hands casually into his pants pockets and shrugged his shoulders, "I beat out a lot of major firms for this."

"That's fantastic!" I cried jumping up and hugging him. He laughed heartily and put his arms carefully around me, his head dipping into the crook of my neck. I felt him breathe in my scent. The tender gesture made my heart race and I hugged him closer. "I'm so proud of you."

He squeezed me and whispered in my ear, "I've got something else, too." His lips grazed my earlobe before his teeth tugged, sending a shot of pleasure through me and making me gasp, "Oh really? Do tell Mr. Spencer."

He pulled back and grabbed my chin between his thumb and forefinger; studying me with a gaze so intense it scorched my panties. "Are we okay? Since my little freak out?"

I nodded slowly, incapable of looking away from

his intense stare. "Yes, we are. But I do wish you'd talk to me more. I feel like I'm still trying to get to know you."

"What do you want to know?"

I laughed, "Jake, so far I've got lots of sun, lots of sand, that you worked a lot, occasionally went to Germany, and fucked a girl named Ashley for five years. It's not a pretty picture in my head right now."

Did he really not understand how his lack of information was confusing me?

He let go of my chin, but didn't move away. His physical presence was a little overwhelming. "I was lonely." It was a confession and one he wasn't comfortable providing. "I had Tom, who was busy as fuck running a company. He worked my ass off and when I wasn't working I was looking for an outlet for my anger. I was always looking for something to make me feel like I wasn't alone. I went to Dubai, I went to Germany, but otherwise I stayed in Iraq and Afghanistan almost entirely. I didn't want to be anywhere else because the only place I really wanted to be was here with you."

When he said shit like that, it made those ten years we spent apart seem eternal.

"You were lonely?"

He took a step back away from me and sighed, running his large hands through his messy hair. "Yes, Eve, I was lonely. I had no family except a man who was often more like a stranger than a relative. And I had you."

"Greg?"

He nodded. "Yeah, he and I really got friendly about five years ago. We hit it off pretty well and he was probably one of the first consistent people I could really count on." Jake looked up at the darkening sky, the pain and confusion clear on his handsome face. "He's kinda the big brother I always wished I had. I mean, we're more friends than anything, but for a couple of years he was the guy I looked up to."

He stepped away to talk and I felt like there was a mile between us. Maybe it was easier for him to tell me these things if I wasn't so close, but I couldn't stand it. I needed to be touching him. I slid my fingers inside his hand. "I love Greg then. I'm glad he could be there for you when I couldn't."

Jake's eyes snapped back to me, clear and intense. "I don't think I'll ever be able to explain to you how much you *were* there for me. We weren't together, but you and everything we were . . . that was what kept me sane in the end."

I'd been knocked on my ass a few times. Jake had been the one to do it most of those times. Even if you combined each and every one of them into one giant push, it wouldn't come near how floored I felt by what Jake just said.

There were declarations of love, and then there was that.

I was stunned into silence as his eyes bored into mine. "Eve, you were always with me. Always in my heart."

I wanted to burrow in close to his heart, listen to it beat and feel the rise and fall of his chest as he breathed.

"I love you Jake."

He'd said it to me a hundred times since we'd gotten back together, but I hadn't really felt comfortable saying it back. I did now.

And I meant it. For some reason, hearing him say I'd always been with him, even after years and thousands of miles . . . I needed to say it.

His arms came around me hard and fast. He held me so close it hurt, but I didn't care. Hell, I'd probably be happy if he accidentally melded our bodies together permanently. He could crush me against him all he wanted.

"I love you, too," he said simply, a painful smile on his face. But it was his eyes, so deep and green and boring into my soul that took my breath away. He really could see straight into my soul.

I opened my mouth to say something, but nothing came out. I tried again, but when the words didn't come, I giggled.

Jake cocked his head to the side and smiled. "I know," he said simply, his eyes lowering to my lips.

"Just kiss me."

His smile fell away as he tenderly brushed his lips against mine. I melted against him as my knees went weak and desire rushed through my body. I wove my fingers up into his messy hair, needing to feel him any and every which way I could. His gentle kisses did more to turn me on than anything blatantly sexual. He could be buried deep inside me with any part of his body and not do what his lips just did with that kiss.

"You have another surprise?" I asked breathlessly. The mood between us was thick and ripe. If I didn't deflect some of the intensity we'd really start pushing our luck with the whole 'sex in public' thing. It may be dark but this was a wide-open park and I was not about to test that boundary.

Not even for massive declarations of love.

He loosened his grip slightly, his painful smile transforming into something truly happy . . . and seductive. "I do." He reached into his pocket and pulled out a small black journal. "It's actually two surprises." Jake was perfectly still for a moment and he looked off at something past me when he spoke. "One of the things the therapist had me do was write. I wrote a lot. This journal is probably the most important of them all."

He let go of me and took half a step back, flipping open the black book to a page that was bookmarked. "I don't need these anymore, but I think they'll help you understand me better."

He was giving me his personal thoughts. There really wasn't anything much more intimate or telling than the words you scribble down at your weakest moments. Giving them to me meant he wasn't worried about anything. He was willing to share every piece of himself—he wasn't going to hold anything else back.

"Thank you."

"It comes with one stipulation." He cocked his head and eyed me. I nodded. "Read it when I'm not around. I'm more than happy to answer any questions, but I don't want to see you read it."

"Okay," I agreed. I was floored. This was incredibly heavy and intimate stuff. I had never expected him to let me this far into his past.

He smiled a genuine smile. "Well then, you earn the second part of this surprise." The bookmark wasn't really a bookmark—it was a necklace. At the end of the chain was a beautiful golden sun. "I was going to give this to you at graduation and I never got a chance." He swallowed and took a deep breath as he stared at the sun pendant. "I was wearing the damn thing—I didn't want to lose it with all the chaos at graduation. So when Tom took me, it stayed with me." He stared at it as he held it up for me to see. "At first I couldn't look at it, you know? It hurt. But then . . . I couldn't live without it. It kept you close to me."

I touched the necklace and took it from his hands, holding the sun in the palm of my hand. "Why a sun?"

He didn't answer so I looked up and found him smiling at me. "Because you are my sun. You light up everything in my life. I wanted you to know what you meant to me then, and I need you to know that just as much now. I don't need it anymore since I actually have you." He snaked his hand around my waist and pulled me against him. "I want you to finally have it."

I was speechless as he took the medallion out of my hand at put it around my neck. He smiled approvingly at the way it fell between my breasts. Normally I'd roll my eyes and punch him in the arm. But not this time. This was far too important.

## Chapter 14

We turned our exhibitionism into a game. It could be initiated by either of us, and it always started with a phone call. Even though we didn't come right out and say *here's how we're having sex tonight*, it was clear from the sound of either of our voices what those phone calls were. It could be dinner or just an after-work event—it didn't matter. But from the moment the call ended, the foreplay began.

We reveled in the anticipation, in the maneuvering and the planning. It was a high. The call had come in at two o'clock. His voice was deep and husky and the way he spoke so low and quiet turned me on the instant he said, "Hey, darlin'."

"Hey," I murmured back.

"We've got to stop by the club and make an appearance. Greg is schmoozing some new client. Can I pick you up at five?"

"Of course. But you'll have to bring me to work in the morning."

I could hear his sly grin through the phone. "Nothing would make me happier. We'll have breakfast together as well."

"Nothing would make me happier."

"I'll see you at five."

By the time I set my phone down my panties were damp and my nipples were tingling.

Three hours of anticipation.

I couldn't be happier with my clothing choice of the day. I was in a sheer white blouse with gorgeous folds where it opened at the front. Beneath was a thin matching camisole, underneath of which was my bra. My skirt was a black, high-waisted pencil skirt with a gold belt, and three-inch snakeskin heels.

I was going to have so much fun with this.

I stood up, seductively fluffing my hair and turning my camera phone to the front-facing lens. I took three pictures and sent one to Jake. "*Do you think this will do?*"

To my extreme satisfaction I got an immediate response. "*You look delicious . . .*"

At four-thirty I went to the executive bathrooms to freshen up my makeup. I took the eyes up a notch and painted my lips with nothing but lightly tinted gloss (because hot red lipstick leaves too many clues behind). Then I went into the stall and carefully removed all my underwear.

The lack of barrier between my nipples and shirt

set them tingling again and my naked sex started to throb with anticipation. I was going to be in trouble if I couldn't get myself under control. So I spent a moment calming down with deep slow breaths before I returned to my office.

The bra went into my giant computer bag, but the lacey panties? Those went inside a Rays handkerchief. And that handkerchief went inside my clutch purse.

My eyes caught on the black journal tucked inside my bag. I still hadn't opened it. I knew I was being a chicken, but the words inside that journal were important. I knew they'd change the way I saw Jake, and I was scared it would change us. We were good and I was desperately holding on to the comfortable pattern we'd fallen into. Part of me was dying to see a side of Jake that was always just a little out of reach, but the other part of me wondered if it even mattered. If Jake could leave his past behind, maybe I should too. But then, he'd given it to me for a reason. I think he knew I would always have questions, questions he wasn't always capable of giving me answers to. This journal was a compromise and I was saving it for when I needed it. Until then, I was going to enjoy having Jake in my life.

At precisely five o'clock Jake knocked on my door and swept into my office with a smart, authoritative air that promised a night of fun was ahead. His three-piece suit looked fantastic on him, as usual.

"Are you ready?" he asked, his eyes intent on me.

I blushed, knowing instantly what dirty thoughts were in his head. "I think so." *Was that my voice?* If it was, I was a hussy.

I liked it.

Jake's eyes longingly lingered on the side of my desk where he had fucked me so well, weeks before. I raised an eyebrow, "Now, now . . . we can't be doing that. This is during business hours."

He smiled at me wickedly, "When does that stop us?"

I shook my head and stood, walking around to press him into the side of my desk, our warm bodies connecting for the first time since this morning. "Never, but I try to be good at work."

He grabbed my ass hard—it sent a thrill through me—and he smiled his cocky smile. "To cocktails . . ."

The ride there was quiet, we could both feel the excitement building in the air, our libidos tightly wound, our senses on fire. At least mine were. And by the stern look on Jake's face, I knew he was working hard at controlling something. My money was on his desire for me.

Once inside we made the necessary rounds and when Jake got pulled into an intense conversation with the owner of some development I could have cared less about, I took my opportunity to explore. It took me five minutes to find the perfect dark corner. It was a hallway off the main room that lead to a ballroom, or at least that was what it looked like to me. The room was empty with stacks of chairs up against the walls. The lights were out and the hallway was very dimly lit. Along the left wall was a long table with two giant fake trees on either side. This hallway was our spot.

I made my way back to the bar, snagged fresh whiskey for Jake and gin and tonic for me. I found him in the same spot I left him, but the conversation had clearly turned toward simpler things.

"There's my girl," he smiled at me warmly, but I could see the heat emanating from his eyes.

"Hey baby, here you go," I murmured, pulling the handkerchief out of my bag.

Jakes eyes zeroed in, dark and intense. "Thank you, darlin'," he murmured, taking the gift and turning in to me so no one else realized what he was really doing. And what he was really doing was pressing the open side of that handkerchief to his nose and breathing in my scent.

He sighed and whispered, "Fuck you smell like heaven, Eve. I'm hard right now."

I grinned with victory as he shoved the handkerchief into his pocket and spun me around in front of him to hide his erection.

"If you'll excuse me Lawton, my lady saw some art she's in love with."

Lawton barely noticed us leave as he rushed to another unlucky victim. He certainly didn't notice that Jake had his firm erection pressed to the small of my back.

Jake breathed in my hair as he drew his nose up the skin of my neck. "I love you . . ."

I smiled even though he couldn't see it. "I know."

I led him down the hallway and we practically

shoved our cocktails and my clutch onto the little hallway table as Jake manhandled me into the dark corner. I loved it when he was so turned on he couldn't help himself, when he didn't know his own strength.

"Perfect," he purred.

"I know," I gasped as he pressed me into the wall, one thigh between mine.

"Are the panties the only thing you took off?" he panted, pulling back enough to look down into my eyes.

I shook my head and bit my lower lip. "No."

He sucked in a gasp, his eyes rolling back in his head and his hands convulsively seized my arms. "You are so fucking hot."

All that was well and good, but what I wanted was for him to touch me. I'd been waiting hours for his touch, so I reached up to his left hand, peeling it away from my arm, and placed it on the thin layer of fabric.

He sucked in a breath, "Shit, it's like there's nothing there."

It was incredible how naked I felt under this blouse, my nipples on fire for his attention. He gently, teasingly, ran his hand over the soft fabric and I immediately started panting, my nipples begging for more. I thrust my chest up higher.

"Oh, baby . . ." he moaned as his tongue snaked into my mouth, its velvet caresses taking away all my sense of reality. His large thumbs ran over my nipples and they peaked against the fabric, adding to the multitude of sensations I was feeling.

He teased me until my nails dug into his shoulders. Then he pulled back, nothing but black want in his eyes and let his hand travel down to my thigh.

I flattened my back against the wall and took a deep, deep breath, slowly letting it out as his fingers traveled up. I swallowed the moment his fingertips touched the slick coating my sex.

Jake thrust his jaw out as he tried to control his own breathing and slowly brushed against me. I closed my eyes and shuddered as he did it again and again. Light touches getting stronger and stronger until he stopped. "Look at me," he commanded.

And I did. I opened my eyes, panting hard, my nipples riding up and down against the fabric of my blouse, taking in the open surroundings of the dark hallway, looking down toward the faint sounds of the party. We were alone . . . for now.

I swung my wide eyes back to Jake and at the exact moment he had my full attention he finally thrust two fingers inside me. I bit my lip just in time to quiet the cry that escaped my throat.

Jake leaned in closer, his hot breath dancing across my lips. "That's right . . . shhhhhh."

This was what we loved so much: the high that came with being together in public. Any little thing could ruin it. A wayward sound could reveal us just as easily as a lost guest.

I nodded, still panting, my lips pressed tightly together as he worked me, bringing me hot and swollen right to the edge of climax, but no further.

He was panting heavily now, too, and I knew he was ready. I focused just enough to find his belt, sliding the leather free, unbuttoning and unzipping, diving inside his boxers and finding his hot, throbbing cock.

He shuddered, leaning in to me as I palmed him, working my fist up and down his length several times until I felt his shoulders stiffen. His hands slid up my thighs, hiking my skirt up, then under my arms to press me up while I guided him deep inside me.

I bit my lip again, suppressing the cry of pleasure that so desperately wanted to come out at the same time Jake buried his face in my shoulder, muffling his own groan of pleasure.

He had me so hot, so swollen and ready for release it only took two strokes, two glides of his perfect dick inside my slick body, for me to come apart. My arms tensed around him, my head back against the wall, my thighs squeezing his waist, as wave after delicious wave roared through me.

And Jake was right behind me, taking only a moment longer, his cock kicking as he pumped into me. The moment he was done I slid my feet back down to the floor and Jake reached into his pocket to retrieve the handkerchief and panties.

He pressed the fabric against me and pulled out, tucking himself back into his boxers. I squeezed the handkerchief between my thighs as his hands disappeared to do up his pants.

The minute he was buttoned up he pressed his body against mine, his forehead to my shoulder, while we came down off our high. He nuzzled my neck, his hands massaging my bottom and hips. I loved his after sex caresses, they were always so loving and attentive.

"Good choice," he murmured, admiring the location I'd selected.

"Thanks for the invite."

He chuckled, a deep rumble inside his broad chest, "We weren't supposed to come, but when Greg mentioned it, I couldn't resist."

I smiled, enjoying the feel of him. "I could tell by the eleventh hour invite. I was so hot today waiting for this."

He growled, flexing his hips against me. "You were not the only one."

He kissed me, long and tender, his fingers tangling in my hair before he went back up my skirt and fished out the handkerchief.

His fingers trailed down the exposed skin of my thigh before repositioning my skirt and sticking the handkerchief back in his pocket. "Good as new," he murmured.

It was then an older gentleman wandered down the hallway, he stood perfectly still and he didn't seem to notice us as he mumbled something about the bathrooms and turned to leave.

Jake's smiled at me slyly, finally stepping back and offering me his elbow, "Shall we?"

"We shall," I replied. We rejoined the party as if we hadn't just fucked in the hallway.

# Chapter 15

"Come here," he purred seductively. It was late on Saturday afternoon and we were in my laundry room out back behind my house. It was an outdoor room with screening for walls. It mostly kept out the roaches. Mostly.

I sauntered toward him feeling like pure sex. He saw me and only me, his eyes locked on my body and his muscles taut with tension. Jake needed me.

It didn't matter that we'd had sex two times already today. We were insatiable. We'd woken up having sex. And he'd had me while I sunbathed on the bow of my boat. We should be satisfied. We should have had enough sex to at least get us through the end of the day, but no. Here we were, attempting to put our nasty towels from our day in the wash and all either of us could think about was being naked.

Naked with Jake deep inside me where he belonged. I couldn't seem to shake the feeling he belonged nowhere else, that we were two beings who should never have been separated—we were meant to be one.

His index finger ran along my arm and up my shoulder finding the knot of my bikini top and tugged. My top fell down, exposing my tan breasts. Did I mention my top had been off most of the day?

Jake grinned wickedly, his green eyes lighting up with delight. He may have seen them all day, but he never seemed to get enough. I waited for him to continue my undressing, something he loved to do with a great deal of flair.

He leaned back against the washer and stroked his stubbled chin. "If I were an artist I would paint you," he purred. "Instead I'll just memorize you."

Then his talented fingers untied my bottoms and he finally turned me around, pressing my body flush against the cool metal of the washer, and released the rest of my top. It fell right inside the open machine. I rolled my eyes. "You planned that."

Jake chuckled, "Actually I didn't. I just happen to be that good." His body left mine for a moment. Then his trunks and my bottoms made their way into the washer, too. He pressed his erection into my backside as he reached up to the shelf for the detergent, carefully measuring out the correct amount, closing the lid, starting the cycle, and all the while grinding me into the machine.

Little spikes of pleasure hit me with each movement and I was wet and wanting by the time the machine started. Which only made me gasp and moan. The machine vibrated just enough to heighten my excitement.

"Fuck me, please," I groaned.

But he didn't comply. In fact, Jake decided it was time to torture me, placing a hand on the small of my back to hold me in place while his fingers trailed a tantalizing path between my legs. Then he slid his hand up my back to press between my shoulder blades, lowering my chest until my exposed nipples danced along the cool metal of the vibrating washer.

I started panting harder. Jake had a knack for discovering new and exciting ways to pleasure me. And I knew how much he liked the challenge. Jake seemed to get as much pleasure from pleasing me as he did from actually fucking me.

Which was just fine with me.

Because as much as I liked making Jake happy, I liked being teased more.

"How does that feel?" I could hear the breathless way he asked.

"So good," I replied. I was very close, but the pleasure was exquisite. I didn't want it to end. I wanted to draw it out as long as I could.

"Let me up."

Jake stiffened. "What's wrong, baby?" His voice

was laced with concern and his hand immediately came away from my back.

"Nothing," I purred, turning toward him. Nothing a little fun of my own couldn't cure. I fell to my knees and grinned up at him.

To my extreme pleasure his eyes rolled back in his head. "Well, then . . ." he sighed.

I wrapped one hand around his fully erect cock and ran my tongue all the way up its length, tasting the Gulf of Mexico.

"Oh baby, do you know what you're doing to me?"

"I hope I'm making you feel good."

He ran his hands through my hair and smiled down at me with the most mischievous half grin on his handsome face. "Like heaven."

I raised a very pleased eyebrow and locked eyes with him as I slowly wound my mouth around his warm cock. The connection between us was electric as I used my mouth to please him. He watched me, every single move I made. Every glide of my tongue, every suckle of my mouth, every sigh.

He watched as I used my other hand to draw out my own pleasure. He wanted this to last as long as I did—the long, sweet torture of standing at the edge of orgasm was as exquisite a feeling as anything else.

But then we heard the sounds of a car out front and the happy lilt of Jennie's voice. She and Andrew were home and we were naked out back.

Jake hauled me up off my knees, turned me toward the washer and plunged inside me. The sudden invasion of his erection into my swollen and ready sex sent me gasping for breath. My knees buckled out from underneath me but his arm was around my waist, holding me up. I threw out my hands, bracing them against the vibrating washer and lowered my nipples back down to the cool metal. The combination of Jake thrusting into me from behind combined with the shot of cool sensation from my nipples ripped me in two. My entire body contracted as a pulse from deep inside my body tore out from the center.

I squeezed my lips together, muffling the scream that threatened to burst from my throat. Jake placed his hands on my hips and thrust deep inside me one last time. He grunted, stiffened, and finally relaxed, his hands starting their usual after-sex caresses.

Even through the fog of complete satisfaction I was blindingly aware we had a problem. Jake and I had to stop ignoring our issues. We had to stop trying to get caught.

\* \* \*

JENNIE AND ANDREW HAD our dinner laid out on the kitchen counter by the time Jake and I came down from showering.

"Barbecue. Perfect after a day in the sun. I could eat a whole pig myself," I grumbled, grabbing a piece of cornbread to stop the obnoxious growling my stomach was making.

Jake made some noises of agreement.

"Well eat something fast because we have an announcement to make and I don't want you passing out."

I stopped mid-chew and stared at her giant blue eyes. Jennie was ridiculously happy. Over the moon, vibrating with excitement, happy. Andrew wasn't so bad himself. He was watching her, just like he usually was, with a satisfied smile on his face.

They'd gone to visit his family today.

"Well, spill the beans," Jake exclaimed.

I looked at Jennie expectantly wondering if she was actually going to make me eat a rib before she told us the news.

Her eyes danced. "I'm moving in with Andrew. You need a new roommate."

She squealed after that and we did what girls do: we hugged and jumped around and said a lot of things in really high voices. The guys did the much more manly thing and shook hands.

"When?" I asked.

She shrugged her shoulders, "Now. I don't think that you've noticed, but I've barely been around for a while now."

Had I noticed? I thought back over the last few weeks and realized I'd been pretty caught up in Jake. "I suck, don't I?"

She shook her head and hugged me again. "Not at all. I'm obsessed and you," she paused, holding me back so she could look me in the eye, "have been happy. Finally."

Oh, if she only knew how much we were still holding back. "I think we need a night away from the testosterone, my friend."

She looked at me with raised eyebrows. "You have made an excellent suggestion. Soon?"

"Soon." I promised.

Then Jennie did what only Jennie could get away with: she carefully pranced around the counter back into Andrew's arms and dropped her bomb. "Now Jake can officially move in here."

I stopped with the rib halfway to my mouth and glared at her. Andrew looked helplessly at me. He was as incapable of stopping her as I was.

"He sleeps here every night as it is," she said looking at us both and clearly expecting one of us to join in her celebration.

But I didn't and neither did Jake.

"Okay, well. I'm going to take a load tonight and Andrew and I will come back tomorrow to clear out the majority of it. I'll just keep making little trips as long as that's okay with you, Eve."

I nodded. "Of course. It doesn't matter where you live, you know this will always be home."

After we ate, Andrew cornered me. I'd allowed myself to indulge in a couple of glasses of the expensive champagne Jennie opened and I was feeling more than a little buzzed. Life seemed to be getting away from me these days.

"I'm sorry, she's such a ball of fire . . . I can't seem to rein her in sometimes."

"Don't worry, none of us can. It's just Jennie. And that's why we love her," I said with a shrug.

He clinked his flute to mine. "Here, here." A comfortable silence fell between us before he continued. "I'm gonna take good care of her, I promise."

And I believed him. For some reason I couldn't explain, I'd been comfortable with Andrew since the beginning. "Wedding bells coming?"

"Very soon. If she'll have me."

"I'm pretty sure you two are meant for each other, Andrew. I've never seen those sparks before, it's been fun to watch you two."

He studied me for a long moment and I thought it was because he was trying to decide whether or not to tell me what was really on his mind.

"I spook easily, Andrew, but I don't scare often."

He cocked his head and held up his glass. "Interesting point. I might have to remember that one."

"Spill it. What's on your mind?"

"Have you looked in the mirror lately?"

I studied him long and hard for a moment. "What do you mean?"

The way he smiled at me made me wonder how much of my own life I wasn't seeing. "You and Jake are meant for each other. I can only hope to make Jennie light up around me the way you light up around Jake. It has been very educational for me to watch the two of you. I very much want what you two have. I think Jennie and I have it, but I am constantly learning how to take better advantage of it by watching you two."

My jaw fell open with surprise. "What?" My eloquence was epic.

"I don't know if it's the time you two have on us? I'm not sure. But you two have no inhibitions. You are you and Jake is Jake. And anyone who has ever spent any time around the two of you knows that there is no getting between you two."

I watched Jake as he laughed with Jennie. As if he could feel my eyes on him, he turned and smiled at me. Maybe we did feel the vibration of each other through the air.

"And," Andrew said, shifting to move back toward Jennie, "you two should move in together. Officially."

"You know, you're awfully opinionated for a newbie."

His eyebrows danced, "Just callin' it like I see it, Daniels."

\* \* \*

MANY HOURS LATER the guys were smoking cigars on the back porch. It was raining, but a light drizzling rain, the kind that lasts for a few hours while the sky lights up over and over with lightning dancing quietly from cloud to cloud far, far above.

Jennie and I were huddled up with wine in the corner of the porch chatting and listening to the drip of the rain. "Seriously, Eve. What is up with you and Jake? I expected you two to elope by now, but instead the two of you practically flinched when I suggested you officially move in together."

I hid behind my glass of wine. Why was something as simple as sleeping arrangements so complicated? Why did it hold so much meaning? I decided to deflect. "Why are you moving in with Andrew? I thought it was a rule of yours, no living together without a ring?"

I realized I'd stumbled into something big at that point. Jennie's eyes unfocused and her mouth turned down in a frown. Frowns always looked so terribly out of place on her normally happy face and I was worried about what was putting it there now.

She licked her lips and her eyes shot up to mine, making contact. "The ring is coming, I know it is. So, I'm not worried about what order things happen in . . . but a ring isn't going to happen today." She took a deep breath letting it out slowly, "Today was just too emotional and the whole moving in together thing was a whim. It wasn't planned, it just happened. It naturally grew out of everything that happened today."

"What happened?" I asked. I was completely lost and starting to get worried.

"Today was Andrew's mother's birthday."

That didn't seem like a bad thing. "That's wonderful. Isn't it?"

Jennie's frown deepened. "She died seven years ago. Today they had a big celebration in her memory." She reached out and grabbed my hand. "Even now it is so clear how much his parents loved each other. It breaks my heart for Andrew. He said they were the disgusting parents who only seemed to want each other more over time. His dad is still heartbroken she's gone. He's here and he's a part of his kid's lives, but it is so obvious a part of his soul is just . . . gone. And I think Andrew is afraid he's going to lose his dad to a broken heart at some point."

I couldn't help but look down the porch to where the guys were sitting. It explained so much about Andrew and I felt like I understood him so much more. "I'm glad you two found each other, Jennie. I really am. And I think you two are going to be just as disgustingly happy as his parents were. It will be a beautiful way to keep her memory alive."

She squeezed my hand, her blue eyes were so sad I wanted to hug her but I knew it wasn't what she wanted or needed. She just wanted to be able to make Andrew's pain go away.

"Thank you. I think so, too." But then she locked eyes with me again and brought me back to the question she'd asked in the beginning. "So what is up with you and Jake?"

I sighed. My heart hurt thinking about all of this. In fact, it was pretty infuriating to think how much time we'd lost already and knowing we couldn't move our relationship any faster than we were. I thought about what Jennie had just said, that she wasn't worried about the order things were happening in. "We're still working through some stuff."

Her eyebrows shot up as she waited for me to elaborate. "I don't need to know details, Eve. In fact, I'm pretty sure I don't *want* details . . . you two are kind of gross. Talk to me about what's going on under-neath."

Damn shrink, wanting to make me talk emotions. Emotions and feelings I still couldn't quite grasp my-self, let alone talk about with the only one it mattered to: Jake. But some of it I understood and I could at least talk to her about that. "I think I glamorized our old relationship. I forgot how screwed up Jake was, how sad we really were most of the time. It was easier to remember how much I loved him, how much he loved me, how perfect we felt together . . . and just for-get everything else." I checked to make sure she was following and Jennie smiled with encouragement. "But it was hard. And things weren't all shiny and perfect. I've been mad at him for a long, long time and not just about leaving. I've been mad at it all."

"You should be. None of it was fair, to you or him."

"The thing is, he left and worked on his issues, but now that he's back we have to work on *our* issues. We've had a lot to overcome, not just my anger, but trust issues and dealing with our mistakes." I took a moment to drink some wine and let everything I was thinking and feeling settle around me.

Why was the idea of Jake officially moving in caus-ing me to feel so defensive? "Falling in love is intense, you know? It feels so good and you want to hold on to that, keep it for as long as you can. You'll do anything to keep it." I laughed, not because it was funny, but be-cause of how important the things I was trying to say were. "You don't even realize what you're doing. I didn't realize what I was doing. Jake said it himself, he left me because if he'd stayed I would have done any-thing, *anything*, to save him."

I looked at Jennie hoping for comfort in her deep blue eyes because my thoughts were scaring the crap out of me. That was why I'd been avoiding things with Jake, keeping up that wall and hiding behind it. It scared me how close I came to destroying myself for him. How easily I could do it again. "There is nothing healthy about a relationship where one of you is bro-ken or using each other for happiness or validation. You each have to be complete. Only two whole people can truly have a happy relationship."

It was one of those crazy things. The math would never, ever add up, and yet it was true. To truly be one, Jake and I each needed to be separate and whole.

"That's good, Eve. That's healthy. You know, it's one of those things people ignore. They focus on the process not the people. The people and their relation-ship are what really matter. A list can't teach you how to have a healthy relationship. Only the two people do-ing the work can do that. The people are what matter, their relationship and how they treat each other. You have to focus on you and Jake and do whatever you two need to have a healthy life together."

She leaned in and took both my hands in hers. She looked down at them for a long minute before taking a deep breath and looking up into my eyes. I felt like I was on the edge of my seat waiting for some invisible bomb to drop out of the sky. "There is no rush. He's not leaving again. Take your time and don't lose you because of some preconceived notions about how relationships should work. You aren't a love-struck college girl anymore so I don't think you are in danger of that. You are Eve Fucking Daniels and you are a badass."

I hugged her. I wrapped her right up and hugged her for a long, long time. I had no idea how desperately I needed to hear someone say that. "Thank you," I whispered.

She squeezed me back. "We can't let ourselves get swept up in the love fog anymore. You and me, we need a night every week without the guys."

I sat back and composed myself, smoothing down my clothes and sipping the wine—anything to keep me from looking up. I knew Jake was watching me, I could feel his gaze as sure as if he were touching me. "I think that's a great idea."

To Jake's credit, he left Jennie and I alone for a full minute before he was at my side. "Everything okay over here?" His voice was rough and yet it somehow soothed me as his hand brushed up my arm. He squatted down next to me so that I was actually looking down at him. It was a strange change of position for us.

"Yes," I replied. "Everything is fine, just catching up with my best friend."

Jennie smiled and stood with her drink. "I'm going to go check on my roommate." She squealed, "That is so cool to say!"

"Get your ass over here woman!" Andrew yelled.

Somehow Jennie's grin grew before she scurried

off to Andrew's lap.

Jake placed his hand on my knee and ran his thumb back and forth. His eyes were dark and sad. He was worried about me. "You don't look okay."

I loved the sound of his voice. It was so deep and gravelly, it sounded like a man should. And something about that was unmistakably sexy. "I will be."

He studied me a for a moment longer while he looked for the answers I wasn't giving him. "Let's go to bed."

In Jake's arms was just about the best place in the world to me. But a small part was still hurting, still wondering how to get over this last wall. I stood and let Jennie know we were done. She smiled and promised to lock up before they left.

"Come to bed with me darlin'," Jake purred, pulling my hand as he headed toward the kitchen. I memorized his face in the dark that night with the rain gently patting on everything around us. I wanted to always remember how handsome and sure he was as he asked me to join him.

## Chapter 16

Sunday morning was overcast. The entire sky was gray, the bay was choppy, and the air had a weird cool charge to it. It was still early and I was draped over the armchair by my window, reading my favorite book. It was one I'd read a hundred times since high school and for some reason I couldn't quite explain, kept coming back to. It was like an old blanket, familiar and comfortable.

"Is that the same book you used to read?" Jake asked quietly. I realized he'd been watching me. Propped up with pillows on the bed, his pajama pants on with no shirt, his six-pack on full display, his bare feet surprisingly sexy against my blue sheets, but his hands were clasped in his lap and I could tell by the probing look in his eyes I wouldn't be able to distract him with sex.

I should probably talk to him.

"Yes," I replied, looking at the yellowing pages. They had that old book smell that I loved but hated.

He studied me and I studied him, a silent warning passing between us. Jake wanted to bring down the wall I'd erected, one I didn't even know why I put up.

"What's it about?" he asked.

I pulled my ancient bookmark out from where I'd tucked it in the back and slid it into the page I was reading, closing the paperback. It was beginning to fall apart and I'd read it more times than I could count or remember. I'd taken it on trips, kept it in my desk and my car... it'd had a rough life. The cover was separating from the spine and many of the pages were permanently deformed.

I bit my lower lip as I studied the cover. "It's about a woman finding herself. In an unexpected place and an unexpected time in an unexpected way."

Well, that explained a whole lot.

I don't think there was a more obvious sign for how I was feeling.

I felt out of control. Since Jake came back into my life I'd been flying by the seat of my pants and I wasn't quite sure who I was anymore. I'd gotten swept away by the intensity and urgency of everything and somehow gotten lost along the way.

Suddenly he was beside me, squatting beside the chair so that he was just below my eye level. "Talk to me," he pleaded. "I feel like you're slipping away from me. Please come back."

The earnest hope in his green eyes tugged at my heart in a way only Jake could. Where I held back from everyone else, I felt compelled to talk to Jake. He did something to me that took away my fears and opened my mouth.

One of the reasons we hit it off so quickly was his ability to see my thoughts even when they were stuck inside my head. Jake had a unique ability to get through the block between my brain and my mouth and know the turmoil underneath just by looking at me. He could read my emotions like no one else.

"I'm struggling." I finally confessed. I don't know why it had been so hard for me to realize this, let alone talk to Jake about it, but it was.

He moved his hand to cover mine, gently stroking the skin on the top of my hand. It instantly relaxed me and I sighed, "I'm stuck."

The sight of his fingers stroking my skin reminded me of a night fourteen years ago—the night Jake met my family. We hadn't even been dating a week. He was still this strange, mysterious new enigma in my life. But he came with me to a family dinner. We were talking to my mother. I'd made a stupid throw in from the outfield playing intramural softball and wrenched my elbow. It hurt. Jake was talking and without missing a beat, pulled my hand into his and started massaging the damaged muscles. He and my mother never broke their conversation and Jake didn't stop until he was satisfied my arm had been sufficiently massaged and my mobility restored. He squeezed my arm and smiled warmly.

After he left, my mother appeared at my side and announced Jake and I were meant for each other. I had been shocked into speechlessness. I hardly knew Jake and she knew him even less. But she smiled knowingly at me and told me there was only one man her strong, opinionated, independent daughter would ever love and that was the man who I would instinctively let take care of me.

I told her she was crazy, that I didn't let Jake take of me. Then she'd pointed to my arm and asked me what I called the arm massage. The thing was, I hadn't even realized he'd done it until she pointed it out. That was how naturally I'd let Jake take care of me—I hadn't even been aware of doing it.

And here he was, so many years later, sitting at my side with his hand on the same arm relaxing me enough to talk. I think it might be why he could get me to express myself when others couldn't. He had the unique ability to make me feel safe enough to open up my heart.

"I'm stuck, we're stuck . . . I'm scared, I'm mad . . . I'm a mess," I sighed.

Jake smiled warmly and kissed my hand. "Let's start with scared. What are you scared of, darlin'?"

"You, your dad, losing what we have."

Jake stiffened, his hand clenching around mine. "Why are you scared of my father?"

I realized how what I'd said sounded to Jake, "Oh,

babe. I'm not scared of *him*. I'm scared of how he could affect us. I'm worried he still might show up one day and you'll run off again."

Jake probably did the one thing that would reassure me right then—he rolled his eyes. "Don't worry about it. Trust me, please."

All right, I could give him that . . . for now.

But the time was coming where he and I were going to have to have a serious discussion about his father. I couldn't simply keep taking his word for it. I needed a hell of a lot more information to really feel comfortable on that front.

"Why are you mad?"

This was why I kept dodging Jake. This was why I liked hiding behind sex. Sex made me feel close to Jake and like we could ignore our problems for a little longer. I didn't like feeling mad. "A few reasons, actually."

"Start with one." He was getting impatient and I didn't blame him. I was acting like a child.

"Ashley." I spit out her name, I didn't think I'd ever be able to say that name any other way, ever again.

Jake raised his eyebrows. "Really?"

I sighed with exasperation, "Are you going to be angry about Sebastian for the rest of time?"

Jake nodded, "Good point. I completely understand what you are saying. Now, reason two?"

"We lost so much time. It fucking pisses me off every time I think about it."

"It should. You have every right to be mad. Number three?"

I sighed. "I'm mad at you. I still just get so *fucking* angry that you left me. You didn't give me a choice, you just . . . left."

There was nothing but silence after that. No witty comebacks, no soothing words. Just silence. Jake was looking through me the way he always did when he was thinking. I started to wonder if he was going to say anything at all when he startled me. "You should be angry. It's okay if you're angry about that forever." He looked up at me and shrugged. "I can't change what I did. I wish I could, but I can't. And I think you need to get angry. Really, really fucking angry. You need to let some of it out, Eve. Keeping it in isn't going to do you or me any good."

I shook my head. Letting anger like that out wasn't easy for me. It never had been. I preferred to keep it in and let it slowly dissipate over time. But this anger wasn't dissipating. It was growing. I was afraid if I didn't let some of it out, I might explode.

"I'll try."

Jake scooped me up out of my chair, spinning around so that he was in the seat and I was in his lap, cradled in his strong arms. He ran his nose along mine and pressed his forehead against me, looking up into my eyes, "Let's get away. Right now. Let's just pack up and go somewhere for the rest of the day and call out sick tomorrow." His eyes zeroed in on mine and his voice dropped to a soft, husky whisper. "I think we need this, Eve. We need to reset."

A reset. I liked the sound of that. In fact I liked it

so much I wanted to run out of my house in the direction of freedom. When had my life started to feel like a cage? "Take me away, Mr. Spencer."

\* \* \*

WE DIDN'T WASTE A SECOND. It took us all of five minutes to throw on our bathing suits and head downstairs to the hotel pool. We'd booked a last minute room at the J.W. Marriott hotel in Orlando. It was a short hour-long drive from my house. It was the kind of hotel you didn't need to leave if you didn't want to. There were restaurants, a gift shop, and most importantly a pool with a winding lazy river that wandered from pool to pool, around and back again. All we needed was to buy a tube and float.

The only stop we made between our room and the pool deck was at the bar to get drinks.

I was stuck in this weird limbo between getting out of my head but needing to be *in* my head to figure myself out. I was shifting back and forth between being totally and completely present in conversation with Jake and then suddenly staring off into space as my thoughts wandered off.

But I was relaxing, the cocktail and the sound of the water both helping. Jake looking all hot and sexy wasn't hurting, either.

"What?" he asked in his rough and sexy voice.

"I think you should walk around for me, let me ogle some eye candy."

He raised an eyebrow up over his shiny sunglasses. "You want to ogle me?"

I nodded vehemently. *Oh, yes. I wanted to ogle.* "It will help relax me if I'm distracted by your six pack and pecs."

Jake took a long sip of whiskey and tonic and cocked his head to the side, examining me. I wasn't sure if he thought I was crazy or having fun with him. Not that it really mattered—I was enjoying myself thoroughly.

But then he carefully set down his glass and leapt up, straddling my chair. "How about I just come over here and make out with you?"

Now that wasn't a terrible idea either.

"How about we make out in the lazy river instead? That way we can rotate around the people we're grossing out."

"Deal," he said holding out his hand for me.

I was grateful the sun had burned through the heavy morning drizzle. It was a hot and humid day, which made it nice to be in the cool water of the floating stream.

Jake snagged a tube and held it still while I hopped on. "I love this suit, by the way," he growled. Even though I couldn't see his eyes behind his mirrored lenses, I knew he was taking all of me in. I'd picked a very unpractical but very pretty bikini. It was strapless and very, very tiny. The upside to being out of town in the tourist district of Orlando meant we didn't know anyone here. We were just another couple in a mix of tourists from all over the world.

There was every level of dress at the hotel from women completely covered head to toe, to women wearing less than me in tiny Brazilian thongs. There was absolutely no reason for me not to wear whatever the hell I wanted to.

And I'd chosen the latest fashion. My bottoms were very tiny, the kind that tucked between my cheeks and displayed most of my ass. By the bob of Jake's eyebrows and the ridiculous grin he'd been wearing since I stepped out of the bathroom, I was pretty sure he approved.

There was certainly nothing to complain about his attire, either. Dark green board shorts were all he was wearing—his tanned body on full display for my enjoyment. As he leaned over the side of the tube the muscles of his shoulders and arms were flexed. I couldn't take my eyes off them.

He traced an invisible design along my skin, resting his chin on the side of the tube. "It's interesting how much you look the same, but different."

"I could say the same thing about you. Didn't they have anything to do but workout in Iraq?"

"Are you complaining? Do I need to drop some weight?" Jake chuckled. "Because you seem to enjoy the advantages . . ."

*Oh, yes.* The idea we could have sex just about anywhere at anytime in any position? It did things to me. We'd tested those limits again and again. Walls, counters, chairs . . . the list went on. Jake's new strength was a definite advantage. "Fuck off you cocky bastard. You know I like them."

Oh, that smile of his, it was so nice. I loved how much he smiled now. Yes, he was cocky as hell, but it suited him. And it was so much better than sad and doubtful.

"You've put on a lot of muscle, too," he said quietly. His fingers were still moving along my skin, sending sensations everywhere as he moved. "You were always so skinny, it's nice to see strength along with it."

"It helps me keep up with you," I murmured.

The next thing I knew Jake was dragging me to the wall. "What are you doing?"

He picked me right up out of the tube and that was when I realized Jake was aroused. The bulge in his trunks was obvious. "No!" I shouted. "Put me down, we are *not* doing this!"

Jake set me down immediately and there was no missing the complete shock on his face. "Baby, what's going on?"

"Sit." I demanded, pointing at the wall. Jake sat immediately, but he pulled me with him, positioning me on his lap to hide his erection.

"Talk," he demanded.

"Have you noticed we have sex in public just as often as we have it in private?"

Jake was silent for a long moment and I began to panic a little bit. What if I was blowing this out of proportion? What if I was starting another fight on top of all the others?

"No, I hadn't realized." His voice was very low and questioning. "But you're right. I thought we were just having a lot of fun, but you're right."

I smoothed my hand over the stubble on his cheek, "We are having fun. But it isn't healthy. It's one thing when we can't keep our hands off each other, but I think there is something more going on here."

I don't know if it was being in Jake's lap or having a space to think, but my brain finally seemed to be working. We were two passionate people who couldn't get enough of each other. "I think we're both looking for magic."

Jake pushed his sunglasses up on his head and did the same to mine so we could see each other's eyes. "Magic?"

"Magic," I repeated. It was overwhelming how much I loved him. So much so that I wanted desperately to be connected to him. "You and I are magic together, Jake. It doesn't matter where we are or what we're doing... it's magic. And I think right now we're desperate to have that connection. I've been distant and I've let a lot of things get between us. It makes it hard to connect the way we need to. You and I are the same in that. When we aren't connected both physically and mentally, everything feels off."

Jake pulled me to him, kissing me deeply. His tongue snaked between my lips and his hands knotted in my hair. "And when we drop everything to have sex right where we are it's more intense than anything else we do."

Alexis Anne

I nodded, "Exactly. It's you and me and that over-load of passion. We drop everything, we ignore every-one, and we—"

Jake's erection pulsed underneath me. I had to admit I was pretty wet and throbbing, too. Talking about how badly we needed each other was almost as hot as actually being together.

"We *connect*," he finished for me, pulling my body against his cock. "Does that mean you don't want me right now?"

He was kidding. He knew full well I wanted him right now. I was flushed and panting. That was what his need for me did. It made me want him every single time. "Oh, we're totally doing it as soon as we're done talking."

"Oh, babe . . ." he groaned, "I love how kinky you are. Seriously, I'm the luckiest fuck on the planet."

His eyes caressed me with the love he felt for me. We weren't just sex and passion—there was an intense love and appreciation, too.

"I don't want to stop having fun with you. I love," I looked right into his eyes and mouthed the word *love* again, "that we are the couple that drops everything because we can't keep our hands off each other. But we've got to rein it in. Fits of passion are one thing, looking for an answer to our problems is another."

"I agree," he said with a firm nod. "We will talk about our problems and fuck for fun instead. Sound good?"

I rolled my eyes. "You get what I mean?"

Jake sighed and looked into my eyes, speaking very seriously, "Yes, darlin'. That's exactly why we're here. To talk. We will figure out what is really going on and get back to using sex for pleasure, not therapy."

"All right then, we seem to be on the same page."

"Good, can I fuck you now?"

By the throb of my body I was pretty sure if we didn't have sex right then I was going to spontaneously combust. "You have a plan?"

He shot back up with me in his arms. "Oh, baby. You know I do."

A minute later I was in the middle of our tube, resting with my arms wrapped around the top, my body dangling in the water below, and Jake was behind me. My bottoms were pushed to the side and Jake's cock was sliding deliciously slowly in and out of me as we floated down the river.

In and out. Slow and steady.

The lazy river was fairly empty, the gloomy morning had tempted a lot of the tourists to the theme parks, so we only had to watch ourselves when we drifted past the lifeguards and pools. Everyone else seemed to be content to be left alone, just like us.

His forehead rested on my shoulder and his arms encircled mine. His long, hard body pressed to my back and I could feel his six-pack with every curl of his body into mine.

In and out. Slow, so slow.

It was delicious, relaxing torture. We slowly climbed higher and higher, chasing our orgasms. It was the most relaxing thirty minutes of my life. There was something so incredibly therapeutic about being slowly teased and tortured.

And he was enjoying himself, too. Jake was sighing and groaning, caressing me lovingly and whispering sweet, romantic things in my ear.

My climax came out of nowhere and Jake followed me. It was the only time we were jerky or noisy, but we couldn't help it. He buried his face in my back, grunting into my skin as he thrust deep inside and locked himself in place while my body pulsed around him. I only wished I could have held him while I came. I wanted him in my arms. I wanted that extra piece of connection to the man I loved.

But he had me. His arms circled mine, holding me tight to his body as he came. "Fuck, Eve," he grunted. "You feel perfect every single time. I don't think I'll ever get enough of this. Not ever."

## Chapter 17

"*D*o you have any Graycliff cigars?" Jake asked the manager of the hotel gift shop.

The man's face lit up. "Yes sir. We have the purple label. Their Chateau blend."

Jake took the cigar the man handed him and smelled it, closing his eyes and looking quite pleased. "Perfect, I'll take two."

"Yes, sir. Will you need any of them cut?"

"Both, please."

We strolled out toward the pools where Jake could sit and enjoy his purchase. He carefully lit it up, the smoke a billowing white cloud as it came out of his delicious lips. The smell was so familiar.

"Do you remember the Graycliff?"

How could I forget my favorite vacation of all

time? "Fondly."

Jake's lips curved up, but his eyes were sad. "We should go back."

The very idea of spending a holiday with Jake in the Bahamas, of going back to eat on the porch at the Graycliff, of snorkeling, and relaxing on the beach . . . "Yes. As soon as the season is over."

Suddenly I didn't want the Rays to make the playoffs, or to at least perform very, very badly and make it a quick series. I had a hot vacation waiting for me.

Jake was looking at me with as much longing as I felt. There was a certain magic the last time we were in the Bahamas, something incredibly special about the night we ate at the Graycliff. And neither of us had forgotten it. There are some nights that are just magic. Where everything is perfect and you can feel the love in the air. And that was our night at the Graycliff.

"Get me the dates and I will make the arrangements." Then he looked right into my eyes in that special way he had—when I felt like he wasn't just looking at me, but into my soul. "I will take you to the Graycliff for dinner every night if you want."

The air around us was charged with the electricity we were putting off. If Jake didn't stop looking at me like that I was going to jump him there on the pool deck. He looked like he wanted inside my body and to stay there forever. Desire ripped through me, pooling between my legs with a throb that was begging for attention. His attention.

"Stop," I breathed.

His eyes widened with fear, "Stop what?" Then Jake saw me. And I mean he really saw me. He knew what was happening. He moved very methodically, putting out his cigar, collecting himself and holding out his hand. "Let's go upstairs, darlin'."

The anger was seething beneath my surface. It was hot and alive. My blood was pumping and my head spun. The very mention of vacations and happy escapes sent me over the edge. Something inside me snapped. And I think it had something to do with wanting to be free.

We couldn't go on vacation with so many things still holding us back.

He held my hand, guiding us to the elevators. He sighed as he punched the button for our floor. He stood quietly beside me with his head held high as he prepared for whatever was to come.

It was going to be ugly. I'd held back too much for too long.

As soon as our door swung shut, I attacked.

"You left me," I hissed. "You fucking left me here all alone."

We were standing in the middle of the hotel room: Jake on one side and me on the other, the bed between us. He turned to face me, shoving his hands into his pockets and a hollow look in his eyes. He'd put up his defenses, not because he didn't want to take everything I was about to dish out, but to survive it. He was listening but he was being careful about it.

"Keep it coming, babe." Jake didn't interrupt—he didn't even flinch. It was like he was grateful for the beating.

I unleashed it at that point. It all started pouring out of me. Ten years of anger and hurt. Everything I'd ever thought about saying, whether it made sense or not. "You broke my goddamned heart and didn't come back to make sure I was okay. You were so damned hell bent on saving yourself you left me behind."

That one got to him. His eyes flared and his teeth clenched. And for some reason, I liked that. I wanted to pick a fight with him. I wanted him to get angry.

"Come on Jake," I said through my teeth, "Say something."

The muscle in his neck bulged as he tensed. "This is for you, not me."

"You were so fucking selfish."

"Damn you, Eve. Don't go there."

But I couldn't stop. I had him on the edge, if I just pushed a little more he'd snap and give me the anger I wanted to hear. "Do you know how abandoned I felt? How alone?" The way he disappeared, it was like I'd been dumped on the side of the road. A footnote on Jake's flee to freedom. "It didn't feel like I mattered."

"You had a family, Eve!" He yelled it. "You had a fucking family that loved the hell out of you. You weren't alone for a second. You never were and you never will be." His eyes were wild. The only time I'd ever seen him like that was the night of our graduation when he sent me away.

*I had a family.* There was nothing to say to that. We stood across from each other, angry and hurt. But he was right. I did have a family. They took care of me and loved me. They helped me get back on my feet and get to work. They encouraged me to date and have a life. He was right—I was never alone.

But they weren't him.

"You are my family, Jake." I choked as the tears started flowing. "I am your family. You had me."

I was suddenly in his arms. They were wrapped around me in a death grip, his head was bent into the crook of my neck and he was breathing hard.

Yes I had a wonderful family, but Jake was my world. He was my family every bit as much as the ones I was related to. He was my blood and my heart from the moment I fell in love with him. "Jake," I murmured, running my hands through his hair, but he shook me off. He held me tight against his body while he worked through his emotions. So I spoke instead. "I'm sorry. Baby, I love you. You have me forever. We're our own family, you and me."

Things got intense from there. Jake was completely silent, I don't think he could speak. His emotions were in charge and so were mine. We were hands and tongues, ripping our clothes from our bodies, desperate to get to the skin underneath. I needed him and he needed me. I could feel his desperation and I knew the one thing that could fix it was my body.

He pushed me back on the bed and ripped his pants down, hauling himself on top of me and thrusting home in a single movement. It felt like he'd torn me in two, the sudden invasion so fast and large. I yelled out and sank my nails deep into the skin of his back. I needed somewhere to let out the pain and pleasure, and I also wanted him to know I didn't want it any other way. I didn't want him to stop or think. I wanted him, all of him, hard and fast and deep. So I held him tight against me, using every ounce of strength I had.

"Shit!" He yelled out as he buried himself inside me. But it wasn't a pleasurable cry—it was a cry of pain and anguish. He kissed me deep and hard, his tongue reaching as far inside me as his cock. He was coming at me with everything he had from above and below.

His hands wove into my hair and tugged. Not a gentle, playful tug like he did sometimes, but a harsh yank. It sent a jolt straight to my sex, one we both felt, and brought tears to my eyes. But I didn't mind it. In fact, I kind of liked it. I wanted to feel everything—the more sensations the better. Pleasure, pain . . . it didn't matter. It was all one and the same for me at that moment.

My soul was as on fire as my body. So much hurt and anger at Jake and our past. About the things I never had any control over and the things we'd never be able to fix. It was all coming out in the way we were slamming into each other.

I was thrusting my hips up to meet his with every pump, my hands and nails were constantly looking for somewhere new to land. His back and his ass each getting an equal amount of attention.

He snaked his left hand under my ass and grabbed on to my hip, seizing control and taking me as hard and fast as he needed.

I was going to be bruised. He was scratched . . . we were going to be a mess. But hopefully a whole lot freer.

He started grunting and his thrusts started to stutter until finally he slammed into me one last time and I felt his release. The pulse and throb brought me right up to the edge of my own orgasm, and as he collapsed on top of me I writhed against him searching for my own release.

A moment later Jake realized what I was doing and started kissing my neck, thrusting with short quick movements against me. "Come on baby. Come on, I can feel you, you're right there." His hand was still wrapped around my hip and with one quick caress he gripped me and held me tight against him.

It sent me right over the edge, my body contracting and pulsing, wrapping myself around his large sweaty body as I cried out. He wrapped his arms around me and held me, one hand around my hip, one around my shoulders, and I buried my cries in his neck, the taste of salty sweat dancing across my lips and tongue.

When I finally relaxed, Jake shuddered and started to gasp, "Oh god, Eve. I'm so fucking sorry." He buried me under a blanket of wet kisses. He kissed my neck and jaw, my cheeks and lips, before finally resting his forehead against mine. "Did I hurt you?"

I shook my head. Hurting me was the last thing he'd done. "No, it was perfect."

\* \* \*

WHEN I WOKE UP THE NEXT MORNING, Jake's hand was resting on the middle of my back and his foot was tangled between mine. The way his hand delicately rested against my skin... it was like he couldn't bear the thought of not being connected to me, even in his sleep.

I didn't dare move—I didn't want to lose that feeling—I even tried to keep my breathing even.

I must have fallen back to sleep because the next thing I knew light was streaming into our room, a cart was beside the bed with two covered trays and a carafe of coffee. A little white mug was filled and steaming. But there was no one beside me and the bed felt enormous and empty. I glanced around the room and found Jake standing naked at the window. He was looking outside and sipping from his mug. His back was a mess—lines and marks from my nails everywhere.

I was sore. As soon as I moved I felt the ache of my muscles.

"Come back to me," I murmured.

He turned at the sound of my voice, a sly smile curving his lips. "Morning, darlin'." Then he sauntered back to the bed, all sexy and male, his eyes locked onto mine. "I called down and extended our reservation. There's no rush, we have all day."

All day . . . with Jake looking that sexy there were a lot of things we could do with that kind of time in this bed.

He eased down onto the mattress beside me. "There was no way I was letting you, all naked and beautiful, out of this bed before you were ready."

I set down my coffee and reached out for his cheek. He'd gone so long between shaves his stubble was turning into a beard and the rough hair felt good against my skin. I pulled myself up, letting the sheet fall away, and kissed him. His hands ran up my bare back.

"You up for a little morning exercise?" I asked knowing full well what the answer would be.

He smiled against my lips, hauling me up and onto his naked lap, bare skin against bare skin. "Always."

I moved against him, my hands bracing against his broad shoulders. I felt his immediate response between my legs as his cock began to harden. "Oh, babe," he groaned. His hands kept brushing through my hair as his lips traveled down my neck. He found all of my most sensitive places—every lick taking my breath away and making my belly quiver.

But then he stopped, wrapping his hands around my face and holding me back to look into my eyes. His were deep and dark and they made my heart stop. He looked sad or worried. Some emotion I couldn't quite place. "What?" I asked. Whatever Jake was feeling, I didn't like it.

"I just want you." His voice cracked and his hands

253

tightened around my face.

"You have me," I replied, but there was a completely different, deeper meaning below his words.

"Last night you said you were my family."

I wasn't sure where he was going with this and it scared me a little. "I am."

"Eve, I want you to know that every single day I feel the responsibility of loving you. I know what a gift it is."

He didn't let me talk after that. We had another intense round of fucking. There were certain things we were working through that just didn't seem to have words.

## Chapter 18

*I* knew we couldn't really move forward until we officially let go of the past.

One very important thing finally happened. Jake went out of town on a work trip, all big and important as he was these days, and I was nice and alone with my thoughts. I finally cracked open that black journal, suffered through the panic and dread, and started reading.

I had only known the parts of Jake's past he was capable of sharing in extreme moments of desperation. Otherwise he kept his past hidden and I got the impression it wasn't just from me.

I knew he was emotionally and physically abused, and I had a feeling the physical abuse was a footnote to the emotional damage Jake Sr. caused in Jake's life.

He spoke of being beaten up, the broken bones, and scars as if they were nothing. I remember going over his body with a fine-toothed comb one night, inspecting and kissing each scar. To my surprise, Jake simply smiled and explained each one.

"This?" I asked kissing his elbow.

He shrugged, "Pushed off the back porch, landed on a rock and broke my elbow."

I was horrified.

Jake laughed.

"I got a blue cast and I was the only kid in my school with a broken arm. I had fun with it."

I moved down his arm to his hand. There was a hooked scar along the back of his hand. "This?"

"A lesson in why I wasn't allowed to touch anything without permission."

I raised my eyebrows, "With?"

"A knife."

I shuddered at the image of his father intentionally cutting his son's hand to teach him a lesson. I moved to his firm abs. They weren't a rippling six-pack like there were now—back then he was skinny but muscular. There was a weird collection of scars near his hip. "These?"

This time he took a moment before answering. "It's my dad's spot. He always gets me there. It's his go-to . . ."

*Oh.*

The rest of his body was more of the same. Stitches, broken bones, falls all at the hands of his loving father.

What Jake never talked about was how controlling his father was. I knew he used words as effectively as any punch or knife. I had heard his skill in the few minutes I'd spent with him over the years. Carefully placed sentences designed to kill. Constant reminders that Jake was merely his plaything.

But as I started reading, I finally got a look inside Jake's head, inside the conflict and torture he lived through. I realized how very little I actually understood about the power of brainwashing.

One entry in particular seemed to explain it all. It was actually a night that had been a turning point for us. One I had gone back to over again and again in the years since he left. So this particular entry hit me hard.

*Today is my one year anniversary of therapy. It's been an interesting year. A good year, I think.*

*A long way still to go.*

*Today we talked about what changed me. Dr. Marks wanted to know why I rejected my father and his way of life and started on a new path. What was it that made me realize I wanted a different life? I'm supposed to write about all that stuff until I see him in six months. I'm pretty sure this is gonna suck, but I'm going at with everything I've got. What do I have to lose? Anyway, here I go:*

*My dad controlled everything. I couldn't do any-thing without his permission. Hell, sometimes I* couldn't piss without asking first. The first time I was ever really away from him was college and I'd barely managed to pull that off.

Dad let me know who I was—and I was nothing outside of him. He made sure I was constantly aware of how unwanted I was. That I was worthless and, by nature, bad. I wasn't fit to be around normal people, I'd corrupt them. I wasn't good enough. He made sure I knew no one would ever love me but him, and he didn't really love me. He took care of me because he had to.

Then I met Eve.

And it made no sense whatsoever, but she fucking loved me. At least I thought she did. It felt like love. It was certainly different than anything else I'd ever felt in my life. But then I went home for a weekend and my dad set me straight.

He showed me the truth—that Eve was a rich bitch and I was her new toy. I was just too stupid to be able to understand stuff like that. It was his job to take care of me and protect me from the world. He made sure to remind me I would just ruin the people around me and that the only safe place was home with him.

So I went back to school that Sunday night with every intention of dumping Eve.

But that wasn't what happened. When I got to her dorm room I slipped inside and saw her curled up on that stupid uncomfortable dorm couch with a blanket, reading a book. The minute she saw me she smiled. I mean she really smiled, like seeing me was the greatest fucking thing ever.

How could someone who didn't care about me smile like that? If I was just her toy she wouldn't be so happy to see me... right?

But I reminded myself how stupid I was and that I didn't understand women. So I kept on with my plan. I told her we were done and that I didn't want to see her anymore.

You know what she said to that?

No.

It was all she said and then she sat there and glared at me with her arms crossed.

"What do you mean... no?" I asked.

"No." she replied again, her voice going up a full octave. "You cannot break up with me. I don't allow it. No."

Could she do that? Could she refuse to break up with me? And more importantly, why?

"I think it's for the best, sweetheart. We aren't good for each other."

She sucked in a sharp breath and I really thought she was going to light me on fire with her eyes. "SWEETHEART? Did you just call me sweetheart?"

She kinda scared the piss out of me so I just nodded dumbly.

"No," She repeated. "I don't know who's brainwashed you into believing we aren't good for each other, but it's a load of bullshit."

Brainwashed. It was the first time I'd ever really let that idea sit inside me and move around. I'd wondered, doubted, had friends over the years mention it... but it was the first time I'd really stopped and thought about it. Eve planted a seed that night that hasn't ever stopped growing.

"No, we're bad for each other."

"How? Name one way I'm bad for you... No? Can't name anything can you? I help you study, I walk with you to class when you don't want to go, I make you happy... how can you fucking say I'm bad for you?"

"I don't know." I said. "But I know I'm bad for you."

She started crying at that point and I knew something was terribly wrong—and that thing was me.

"How are you bad for me? By making me awesome? I'm happier than I've ever been in my life, Jake. You make me feel amazing. Like I'm special... how can you say you're bad for me?"

She was kind of hyperventilating at that point and I knew I should hug her or something. That was what I wanted to do, but my brain wouldn't let me. It was at war. My reality was splitting in two.

I knew my dad was right. I was worthless and unlovable. But here Eve was, crying and I knew—I knew deep down inside—she loved me. And I loved her.

How could both things be right?

Or maybe they were both in my head. Maybe it was all made up. Maybe the shit my dad was selling me was a bunch of bull and maybe Eve's tears were *the silly tears of a girl who only thouyht she was in love. But if they were both fake, if I had to choose to live in one false reality... well I was choosing Eve every time.*

*At least with her love seemed like a good thing. With her I felt like I might be more than a useless pile of bones. Even if she broke up with me and left me... I still think I'd rather live in that world than the one my father gave me.*

*But I still wasn't sure what to think. I had no fucking clue what was real and what was fake. I had no clue who to trust. I certainly couldn't fucking trust myself. But I knew I couldn't walk away from Eve. I just couldn't. The idea of insisting we break up and walk out of that dorm room... I'd rather die.*

*So I said, "Okay."*

*And she threw herself around me sobbing happy tears. "Don't scare me like that again, Jake Spencer!" she said. "Don't you ever tell me you don't love me or that we aren't good for each other. It's a fucking lie!"*

*But I did scare her again. I left her. And I can barely live with myself for that.*

I'd gone over that night in my head a thousand times in the years since. It was the first night I'd taken a stand in my life. I'd believed in us so strongly from so early on, but it hadn't been enough. I'd analyzed that choice from every angle, wondering if there was a flaw in me. Why had I chosen my relationship with Jake to take a stand on? It was interesting to realize Jake's side. I don't think I'd ever really and truly understood how confused he was. It wasn't in my toolkit to understand brainwashing made a person incapable of discerning reality from fantasy.

I sat in the middle of my giant bed with the journal open to the last page. The bed was neatly made, the room was tidy, there was complete silence. I knew Jake would be home any minute.

I finally heard the sound of the Bronco pulling up outside. The doors slamming and Jake's footsteps on the stairs, "Hey darlin', I'm home!"

He sounded so happy.

I folded my hands in my lap and quietly waited to ruin his night.

## Chapter 19

The minute he walked into my room his eyes fell on the journal and he took a deep breath, his eyes steeling against the emotions that immediately boiled up inside him.

"Hey," he said tightly, throwing his bag on the ground near the dresser. "I wondered if you were going to read that while I was gone." He kicked off his shoes and loosened his tie, unbuttoning his cuffs and emptying his pockets onto the dresser. "I take it you have some questions."

I took a deep breath and dove right in. "I am in awe of you, Jake Spencer."

He snapped around surprised, his green eyes flashing in his handsome face. "Excuse me?"

"You lived in a bathroom for a month? He made

you live on nothing but rice for three weeks? You had no real friends. He beat you like a dog, used you as a punching bag during his drunken rages, blamed you for everything that went wrong. He brainwashed you. And yet here you are . . ."

All the color left Jake's face and he stood completely motionless, one hand leaned on the dresser. I suspect it was holding him up because he looked completely lost for a moment.

I kept going, "You should be broken. Anyone else would have folded under abuse like that, Jake. The fact that you are alive right now is remarkable. You could have turned to drugs or alcohol or any number of things to help you survive—but you didn't. And instead you somehow found a way to get away from it, put it in your past, and become this remarkable person. You amaze me."

He still didn't move, just a statue standing across the room from me. After a moment he finally took a deep breath and eased back into the dresser, his eyes focusing on mine. "I didn't have a choice."

I smiled. "No, you did. You just didn't accept defeat as a viable option. It takes an enormous amount of courage to change your life. And you didn't just try Jake—you *conquered*. You are amazing, and I don't just mean your work or your body. I mean you as a person. You're happy, you're positive and hopeful. It's like the past doesn't exist."

He shook his head, crossing his arms over his chest. "It doesn't, not anymore. It's like a fairytale or a nightmare, I guess. I know it was my life, but I've dealt with it and it doesn't matter anymore."

"No?"

He grimaced. "Look Eve, the way I see it, it was a different person who lived that life. By dealing with it all and moving past it, I can honestly say it has nothing to do with the man standing in front of you. All that matters is now and where we go from here. I know what I want my life to look like. I want to create good things in this world to help replace all the bad things I know are out there. I think a part of me believes if I do enough, then the bad will start to suffocate."

"How did you do it? He had you so fucked in the head . . . how did you learn to socialize and . . . I don't know, *function*?"

He laughed and rubbed his hands together, massaging his hands alternately as he spoke, "You know how I was. Sometimes I was fine, I got it, I faked it, it was good enough for college. But once I snapped and left . . . I had to actually put in the work. It was like going to college all over again, except it wasn't for math and English, it was for manners and conversation. I got lessons from my therapist and practiced. It took years to get it right. What you learned as a child and practiced as a teen, I learned over the last ten years. I can honestly say I really didn't know how to make friends, sit down and hang out, be a good employee. Shit like that was all fake up until my therapist actually put me on a regimen."

I had the journal laid open to the entry where Jake

talked about graduation night. He strode across the room, all male confidence and completely different from the boy he talked about on these pages, and stretched out across the bed. He picked up the journal and looked over the page in question.

"Everything changed that night," he murmured. "I had been standing with one foot in each reality up until that point. I was too afraid to walk completely away from my dad. But when he started in on me, and you were there watching . . . well, I had to make a choice. I had to pick a life. I had to either be the kid my dad trained me to be, live in his world and let him treat me like shit. Or I needed to take a stand. I needed to walk away and never look back." He closed the book and tossed it to the side. "Eve, you made that choice easy. What life was my dad offering me? I had just spent four years with you, seeing a whole different world. I knew it was out there. I think he knew it, too. That once I started fighting back I wasn't going to stop until he let me go. That was why it was so bad. There was no way I was letting him anywhere near you, and he wasn't willing to let me go."

I wiggled down on the bed until I was looking up at him from my back. He smiled sadly and ran his hand down my cheek, cupping my face. I still wished I could just take away all his pain—absorb it somehow so all he had left inside was goodness. "I love you, Jake."

"And I'm grateful for that every day." He dipped down and gently kissed me. "The past doesn't exist, only here and now."

I let him roll on top of me, his hips rocking into mine as I spread my legs and wrapped my arms around his neck. He was so sure the past didn't matter anymore.

I, however, was not convinced.

\* \* \*

IT WAS A WORK NIGHT, but we didn't care. We couldn't stop talking. We talked through sex, which was slow and sexy, but made even slower by every pause to talk. Then we moved to the shower and talked as we washed each other clean.

Jake stopped and stared at me. "What?" I asked. He was looking past me, thinking about something that was making him smile.

"I'm not a talker," he said scrunching up his brow and shaking his head in confusion. "I mean, I *talk*. But I don't just sit around talking about the universe . . . unless I'm with you." He chuckled as he pulled a white t-shirt over his head and a pair of boxer briefs over his ass. "When we get like this, I feel like I could just talk all night. It's so . . . *weird*."

I laughed but I knew exactly what he meant. This was the 'best friends' side of us. There was no one else I'd rather sit around talking about the universe with. We could talk about nothing or everything. I just wanted to hear him talk.

I reached into the same drawer and pulled out an identical white t-shirt. Jake basically lived here: he had a dresser full of clothes, a sizeable section of my closet, he slept here every night. And it wasn't as if we hadn't lived together in the past. Jake and I lived together for nearly three years in college. Something was holding me back. There was something specific that felt like a wall between Jake and forever.

"What about your father?" I asked.

Jake was still standing right beside me. He was frozen—the muscles in his body all stiffening. "He's not an issue, we've talked about this babe."

I raised my eyebrow and gave him a skeptical stare. "Seriously?"

His lips turned down in a grimace, "He is not an issue," he repeated.

"He's still alive and living in the same house with your mom. He's an issue, Jake."

"He is not an issue because I say he isn't an issue. He will never in any way be a part of my life ever again. I have a private investigator on my payroll whose sole job—his one and only responsibility— is to keep tabs on my father."

*Whoa.* Talk about a news flash. "What if he just shows up?"

"I will send him away," Jake said firmly.

"When was the last time you spoke with him?" I asked, needing to know these answers. Yes, it was Jake's life and Jake's demons, but they affected my life completely.

"Graduation night."

That couldn't be healthy. "You haven't spoken to

him since, yet you claim he won't bother you?"

"He's been appropriately warned. I have no intention of ever speaking to him ever again."

I swallowed, the panic growing inside me. "But what if he does. We live miles apart. There is a very good chance . . ."

Jake stared at me, but he wasn't looking at me, he was looking through me. "If he does, it will be fine, Eve. *I* will be fine." His eyes finally focused back on me. He was doing that thing where he looked into my soul. I could feel him inside me, connecting with me on a completely different level.

But my mind was running wild with a thousand scenarios that did not end in *fine*. I knew somewhere in the back of my head I was worried Jake Sr. would pop up one day, as angry and horrible as ever, and ruin everything. One bad night with Jake's father had changed the course of a decade. I didn't want to take a chance on him ruining anything else in our lives. "When I told you about Sebastian I lost you for a couple of weeks," I finally said.

Jake looked confused for a moment and I expected him to agree with me. But that wasn't what happened. "That was my first real world test, and I am ashamed to say I did not perform to my expectations." He cocked his head and smiled at me, brushing my damp hair back behind my ear. The gentle contact of his fingertips tingled against my skin. "I have all the tools and I know how to use them, but Sebastian was the first time I'd had to actually do it. I couldn't get my tools out fast enough and my insecurities got a chance to take over. I fell back on bad habits to survive." His eyes focused on me and their intensity sent a shiver through me. "I've evaluated what happened and now that I've lived through it, it will not happen again. I won't let it happen again."

"Not even with your father? Don't you think that's expecting a bit much out of yourself?"

He shook his head and cupped my chin, moving his body closer to mine so that we were almost touching. "No, I really do believe I'll be fine if I'm ever forced to see my father and I'll tell you why . . ." he paused, waiting for my nod. "I have you. And I'm not saying that to put any responsibility or pressure on you. It's a simple fact. You make me stronger. I think Sebastian was a bigger mountain for me to climb than my father for that specific reason. Jake Sr. doesn't have the power to crush my world anymore. I took that away from him. He's just a shitty asshole who ruined the first thirty years of my life because he couldn't deal with his own problems. He means nothing to me anymore. Despite him, I have everything I ever wanted and I worked hard for it. Even if it were all stripped away from me tomorrow, I know I have that power within me to recreate it. But if I didn't have *you* to share it with, it wouldn't have meaning. You give my world meaning, Eve. My father is an afterthought—he's something I can deal with. But anything that might take you away from me—those are the things that can hurt me."

His hand on my face and the depth of his eyes were a footnote to the overwhelming weight of his words on my heart. For as strong and confident as Jake was, there was one thing that could destroy it all.

And that thing was me.

"I would never let that happen to you, Jake," I whispered. "I'm yours, you're stuck with me, I'd rather die than let anything come between us again. I will fight for you, just like you fight for me." I needed him to understand.

He wove his hands up into my damp hair, the clean scent of our body wash overwhelming me and the spicy undercurrent of Jake making me dizzy. Or maybe it was just how much I loved him.

He ran his nose along mine, the tingle of his skin taking my breath away. Then he kissed my forehead and pressed his against mine. "I know." His voice was deep and rough, I could hear the real fear behind his words. "But there are so many things we can't control, Eve. Those things scare the hell out of me."

I tightened my hold on Jake. I didn't want to let him go... he was right. I really wished I had something comforting to say to him. I would have liked to have heard it myself.

## Chapter 20

It was Friday night and Jake's company was involved in a big project with the Channelside Entertainment District and all the initial plans were being unveiled. Everyone involved was going from the architects to the investors, and that meant Jake and his partner Greg. It was black tie and I was very much looking forward to seeing Jake in a tux. His tux was at his apartment so he'd gone there to get dressed, giving Jennie and I a chance to be girly.

"You two seem to be doing well," Jennie asked casually, handing me a glass of champagne. "Are you going to let the poor man move in?"

Ah, the ever sticky subject of our living situation. "Yes. Tonight was the final straw. It's ridiculous that he had to go to an apartment he's never in to get a tux."

Jennie smiled triumphantly, "Good. Living together is nice, by the way."

I could tell by the dreamy look on my friend's face. I didn't need an explanation. "I'm really happy for you two crazy kids."

Jennie smiled some more but I saw a flicker of something in her expression.

"What?"

She took a quick sip of her champagne, "Oh, it's nothing."

"Bullshit."

Jennie laughed. "You are going to a very nice affair, Eve. You might want to clean that mouth up."

"Spill. The. Beans." I insisted. My language was just fine, my best friend on the other hand, was not.

"Max came to see me at work today."

I lowered myself onto the bed, "And what happened?"

She shrugged. "He told me he thought he might love me and to give him a chance."

My mouth fell open, "You have got to be kidding me."

She shook her head and she looked so sad. "Do you know how long I've waited for him to say that? And even then he still couldn't say it. It was still 'I think'. *I think*. You know what Eve? *I* think I stopped loving anything about that man right then. I don't know what I thought I loved about him, but it's gone now. I can't possibly love someone who doesn't know what they want. I want what you have with Jake—absolute certainty. And I have that with Andrew. I know he loves me unconditionally and I love him more than I ever thought I could love a man."

The conviction on her face made it clear it was exactly how she felt. Her eyes flicked up to mine, "But you know what? I'm glad he came to see me today. I think I would have always wondered in the back of my mind . . . *what if*? Now when Andrew asks me to marry him, I will know with every fiber of my being that I am ready to give him all of me forever. No doubts."

I was happy for Jennie, but her words suddenly made me keenly aware of Jake. Was I ready to give him all of me forever? That was a pretty bold statement.

"You look fantastic, Eve. Finish getting ready, I didn't mean to stop you."

I'd picked out a soft and simple black strapless dress. It accentuated my shoulders that Jake loved so much. The front wrapped together in a delicate fold before falling and clinging to every inch of my body on the way down to the floor. I felt like a goddess in it.

My makeup was dark. Dark smokey eyes, my skin was powdered until it was flawless, and my lips were a deep shade of red. I'd styled my hair straight with a soft wave, parted on the side, and the short side pinned seductively back over my ear with a glittering pin. But my favorite part was the jewelry. I'd managed to find a bracelet to match the sun necklace Jake gave me. I'd barely taken the necklace off since that night, so I was glad to find more ways to add it to my wardrobe.

I knew I looked good, but I was dying to see Jake's reaction. I wanted his jaw to drop.

I was well rewarded for my efforts.

At exactly six o'clock he opened my front door and called up for me. Jennie squealed with as much excitement as I did. She hid in the corner to watch as I slowly descended the stairs.

Jake was checking a message on his phone, so he didn't look up until I was half way down. It gave me a chance to check him out. He looked good. His black tux was fitted to his broad shoulders and trim waist. He looked like pure, hot sex.

And he was all mine.

His eyes caught my legs first as they peeked out with each step. He froze, his fist locking around his phone, as his eyes traveled up. By the time his eyes reached mine they were a smoldering, brilliant green. His jaw wasn't hanging open, but it was locked shut and I could see the muscle straining to keep it there.

I walked right into his arms and he pulled me close, growling in my ear, "You look amazing." Then he spun me around, slamming my back up against the front door, and ground against me with his hip and his very firm erection. "You might look too good. Shall I fuck you first?"

I grinned, completely pleased with myself, and coyly looked up at him through my lashes. "Jennie is watching us from upstairs . . ."

He growled again. "I don't care." Then he raised his voice, "Jennie can close her eyes if she doesn't want to see this!"

To his delight, Jennie yelled back, "You're gross!

Glad you liked her dress, though!" And we heard the stomp of her feet as she very obviously walked away.

I swallowed hard, trying to control my breathing as Jake inched my skirt up, finally reaching underneath and running his fingertips along the edge of my panties. I sucked in a breath and leaned my head back against the door. He was teasing me in one of my most sensitive spots.

"That's right, darlin'. You look so good I could eat you."

And then he plunged two of his fingers inside me. I cried out, panting from the pleasure he was giving me with just a few quick strokes. Then he eased his fingers back out, let my skirt fall back to the floor, and stuck his glistening fingers in his mouth, sucking hard. "You taste amazing . . . as always." His free hand grabbed me around the nape of my neck, folding his fingers behind me. "You stay that way all night and I'll fuck you in the bathroom, in the car, and all night long in our bed."

I grinned and groaned in pleasure at his promise.

Jake had fun on the way to the party, his hand gently stroking further and further up my leg between gears, until he found my panties again. But by then we were there. I think he was enjoying drawing out the teasing. He knew how much I enjoyed it, plus that way I was on the edge of orgasm at all times. It made his job easier. Knowing he'd promised to fuck me in the bathroom had me grinning as we walked into the busy party. I think we enjoyed having sex as much where we shouldn't as we did where we should. At least we'd gotten it under control, saving our wild sides for special occasions . . . like tonight.

But everything changed in an instant. The moment my eyes fell on Sebastian.

The moment I saw him, I knew we had to leave.

"Babe, I don't feel so good. Can we go?"

His face immediately fell with worry and he clutched me to his side. "Of course. What's wrong?"

I just shook my head and tried to forcibly drag him from the room before it was too late.

It was too late.

Jake's partner was on him in a heartbeat. "Jake! Finally! Hello Eve."

Jake paused to shake Greg's hand. "I'm sorry, but Eve's not feeling well, we're leaving."

"Oh no, what's wrong?"

I shook my head and held up my free hand, the other still firmly wrapped around Jake for support. "My stomach just isn't right. Maybe I ate something?"

He turned and shouted at a waiter. "I need a water over here!"

It drew the attention of everyone around us. To Jake's credit, he knew how that would make me feel and pulled me closer to his side, tucking my head against his shoulder. "I think I'll just get her out of here . . ."

But it was too late. Sebastian caught my eye, his jaw going slack. He crossed the room in three strides. "I thought that was you, Eve. My God," he leaned in and kissed me on the cheek, a move I wished I could

277

have stopped. "I haven't seen you in forever. You look fantastic." Then his eyes raked over Jake with a dubious glint.

At that point I stopped trying to leave and stopped fighting Jake and Greg. I smiled weakly at my ex. "It's good to see you, too." Then I looked up at Jake. He could see the lie in my eyes and had a million questions in his. Questions I was about to answer with a simple introduction. "Sebastian Monroe, I'd like you to finally meet Jake Spencer."

The minute I said Sebastian's name, Jake's arm tightened around me and he straightened just a little bit. I felt his mood shift completely into the cold zone and I could have sworn I smelled testosterone. It was coming off of both men like a perfume.

To both their credit they played it off well. Sebastian extended his hand with a warm, practiced smile. "Well, well, well. It is good to finally meet the man I've heard all about."

Jake smiled back. "Same here. Eve has told me all about you."

They gave each other a good once over, it seemed understood between them what they were doing: assessing the competition. Not that there was an actual competition taking place. I was with Jake. Period.

Jake cleared his throat. "And this is my partner, Greg Hamilton."

Sebastian smiled at Greg politely. "Yes, we've already met. I'm the main architect on the project. But I didn't realize you were the 'Spencer' of Spencer and

Hamilton."

Greg looked completely confused so I decided to help him out. "Sebastian and I used to date a couple of years back."

A look of complete realization dawned on his face and he shot a sympathetic look at Jake. "Small world."

Sebastian ignored Jake and focused entirely on me. A move I was quite sure was deliberate. "How is your family, Eve? I see June is enjoying Yale. She's up to what? Her third major now?"

I laughed uncomfortably. This was getting awkward fast. "Fourth actually. I keep telling her she doesn't have to actually change it until she's sure, but I think she enjoys the drama."

Sebastian laughed so smoothly. I'd forgotten how smooth he was. Everything about him, as a matter of fact. I think that may have been why I was never completely attracted to him. I liked the rough around the edges, scruffy, casual element of danger too much. Sebastian simply didn't have it. "And Cassandra just had baby two?"

I nodded again, feeling Jake's mood plummeting beside me. "Yes, William."

He smiled politely, "Well, please pass along my congratulations when you talk to her."

"I will."

Sebastian smiled at both Greg, then Jake, before returning to me. "I am so glad to have run into you, Eve. I'm sure I'll be seeing you throughout the evening, enjoy the party. Gentlemen."

## Chapter 21

The moment Sebastian's back was turned, Jake gave Greg a look that said he'd better get the hell out of the way. Which he did—fast.

Then he trained his burning gaze on me. "So that was *the* Sebastian," he said through clenched teeth. Jake's anger and jealousy was palpable. And his grip on my arm was nearly painful.

"Yes, are you okay?"

His eyes flashed with fury. "Of course I'm fine, why wouldn't I be?"

Then he did something I never would have expected, Jake shook his head like he was shaking away everything that happened since we walked through the door. It was an act. A very good act, but an act just the same. Jake had put up a front, he was handsome and polite when interacting with me, but underneath he was hurting.

"Please don't do this."

He stared at me long and hard, to the point I thought he might actually listen to me, but then he shook his head and sighed. "I have to be here tonight and I'm not getting through it unless I pretend all of this didn't just happen. I promise to talk later."

If he hadn't looked so completely sincere right then I might have dragged him home and made him talk. But he really did look like he just wanted to get through the evening. "All right."

He pulled a fake smile onto his lips and gently took my arm, tucking it into his elbow. "Would you like a drink before we get started?"

"Absolutely."

Jake actually chuckled and patted my hand before taking a deep breath and walking me across the room to the bar. It was a good sign that underneath he was upset, but fine.

The evening took off from there. We socialized our pants off. Unfortunately any hope I'd had of a tryst of some kind seemed to have been dashed by Sebastian. Jake was stiff and as far from romantic as I could imagine. Normally he'd be whispering naughty things in my ear or allowing his hand to graze my ass or breast when people weren't looking. We'd be giving each other bedroom eyes and sexy smiles.

Not tonight. We were all business.

It hurt to see us like that. It was wrong for so many

reasons. It wasn't *us*. We weren't the 'all business' kind of couple. We were the couple that at the very least was caught making out in the corner. We were the couple that couldn't stop holding hands because we couldn't bear the idea of being separated.

Instead Jake was holding me possessively, as if I might run off. He seemed to have a hand on me at all times. My elbow, my hip, my hand . . . all tightly held against him.

I was so disappointed and it was starting to show. I couldn't keep faking the smiles and forcing the conversations.

Thankfully Greg saved the day.

"Eve, do you have any idea how hard Jake worked for Tom?" Greg asked, tossing back an appetizer and grinning. Greg was blond and a little rough around the edges, but one of those guys you warmed up to immediately.

I shook my head smiling up at Jake. "No, he doesn't tell me much about himself when he talks about being over there."

"Well," Greg leaned in toward me, "the kid would work every minute of every day if we let him. He didn't have an off switch. Three other companies tried to woo him away, even though they knew he was Tom's nephew."

I squeezed Jake's arm and he actually smiled. He shrugged his shoulders. "Gotta learn somehow."

Greg snorted. "I knew right away I wanted to work with him if he ever decided to come back. All he had to do was say the word."

"And it's been everything you hoped for?" Jake asked half joking.

"And more. You're gonna make me rich all over again, Jake. I love you man."

Apparently Greg had a funny streak.

"What does he actually do at work, Greg? He's always in these fantastic suits." I stepped back and put my hand to my chin like I was judging him in a fashion show.

Greg smacked Jake on the back. "He's our cover model. I send him in to land the projects we might not get. They take one look at Mr. Handsome with his rough voice, listen to his brilliant presentation, and beg *us* to work for them. You should know, Eve," he winked at me. Greg was as bad as Jake. They were both cocky bastards.

But I couldn't deny that was pretty much how Jake's presentation went for me. "True, true. I was pretty much a home run, though. That wasn't fair."

"Seriously Eve," Greg took me by the elbow and leaned in to my ear, "the student has become the master. He oversees all our engineers, takes every single one of them under his wing and turns them into beautiful little butterflies. Well, that is when we can get him out of his workshop."

Jake stood tall and straight, swirling his whiskey in one hand while watching Greg and I talk about him, only his eyes moving as he studied us. "All right, that's about enough. I can't leave the two of you alone together, ever. I have a feeling some sort of conspiracy might be unleashed on me."

Greg laughed. "You'll never see it comin'. Am I right, Eve?"

I nodded emphatically. I was up for planning a conspiracy against Jake anytime. Especially if it involved Greg's wicked sense of humor.

He walked off toward the bar and for the first time all night Jake actually pulled me against him. I melted, savoring the moment in case it disappeared as fast as it arrived. His hand wandered up to my hair and he kissed my forehead before pressing his own to the spot he'd just kissed. "I'm sorry."

I looked up at him through my lashes. "For what, exactly?"

He squeezed his eyes shut and sighed. "Everything. Being an ass, not having any fun... this wasn't how tonight was supposed to go. You are in this sexy dress and here I a—"

I ran my thumb along the smooth skin of his freshly shaven cheek. "Flirt with me for the rest of the night and all will be forgiven."

His fingers traced along the skin of my neck, taking my breath away. "You wore the necklace?"

"It's my favorite piece of jewelry. This amazing guy gave it to me and I can't seem to take it off."

His arm came around me and he roughly pulled me up off the floor, kissing me hard. I sighed into the kiss as relief flooded me. This was my Jake.

"So it's true, Jake Spencer and Eve Daniels really

are the hottest couple in Tampa."

I turned to find Tanner Stevens smiling up at us. Tanner was short, a mere five foot nine inches tall, red haired and a little round. And he'd been my favorite accountant with the Rays. That was, until he left three years ago to join a big investment firm.

"Tanner . . ." I smiled and patted Jake on the back letting him know I wanted down.

Tanner opened his arms and let me hug him. "I'm still single, Eve. You could always leave tall, dark, and handsome for short, red, and rich . . ."

I laughed and pinched his cheek. "You were always my favorite. Jake this is Tanner, he used to work with me."

I was infinitely relieved to see Jake's smile. "Nice to meet you."

Tanner placed his hands on his hips and eyed Jake. "He's not nearly as dreamy as you described him. I was expecting Superman and a cape or something, but this, this is just James Bond."

Tanner was incapable of saying anything straight. Everything had to be a joke or an over exaggeration.

"She's mentioned me?" Jake asked suddenly very curious.

Tanner snorted. "Of course she has. You were *Jake*. And I don't know if you two are aware of it, but you are the buzz of town. All I hear about is how hot the two of you are. Handsome and beautiful and having a great time. Count me jealous. And now that I've seen it in person, I'm sick to my stomach. If I didn't love my Evie so much I'd hate you."

I smiled. "But you do love me . . ."

He nodded and hugged me to him again. "Jake, you are a lucky man. Eve isn't just a pretty face—she's fucking brilliant. There was a reason she was my favorite and it had nothing to do with the juicy gossip she so wonderfully fed me on a daily basis."

"Please tell me more," Jake said with a raise of his eyebrow.

Tanner was so excited to talk. He was vibrating and animated, his hands moving with every word he said. "Every report was perfect, under budget, and brilliant. Did you know our approval ratings jumped twenty-five percent after she became Director? *Twenty-five* percent. That's huge. No one's ever made a leap like that!"

I shook my head. "But . . ."

He grinned at me and winked. "She's never dropped a point. Ever. Trust me, I still check in with my people."

It felt kind of nice to have someone singing my praises. I liked looking good at what I did to Jake. "If you ever need any help with your finances, Tanner is very talented when it comes to money."

Jake nodded. "I will keep that in mind." He held out his hand. "Do you mind if I take my brilliant girlfriend out for a dance?"

Tanner made some sort of noise I thought was supposed to sound like a yes, clapping his hands and shooing us away.

## Chapter 22

"A dance, huh?" I cocked my eyebrow and looked at him sideways. He had a glint in his eyes and I didn't see dancing in our future.

At least not that kind.

"Do you have any idea how hot it is to hear how amazing you are? To know that you're on *my* arm?"

I shook my head, my eyes locked onto his dark stare.

He paused, pulling me against him. "Hot." The muscles in my belly clenched and I started to throb. I wanted Jake—now.

"Bathroom?"

He nodded silently and smiled crookedly, pulling me down the hallway.

The minute we were inside he set down his half empty whiskey glass and locked the door. Then his hands were on either side of my head as he leaned into the door. "It is so fucking hot to know I have the woman everyone wishes they had."

I pulsed. I was so wet already and all he'd done was say amazing things about me. Of course there was also his proximity—his scent was intoxicating. His spicy natural scent mixed with his cologne was making me dizzy as he dipped his head down and gently brushed his lips along mine. I was a liquid mess as I pressed myself up against the door. I needed it to keep myself up.

"You look so beautiful tonight, Eve." He moved his soft lips over my jaw to my ear where I loved his kisses so much. My body kept throbbing, wanting more, but Jake was quite content to tease me, building up the desire inside me. I could barely catch my breath I was panting so hard.

He trailed his feather-light kisses down my throat and to the soft tops of my breasts. He paused and ran his fingers over them, his breath catching and hitching. "Fuck, Eve." His eyes were wild.

I frantically found my zipper. "Help me?"

His breath caught again as his hands slid my zipper down, softly caressing the skin beneath. "Like heaven, Eve. Your skin is like heaven. I can't see straight when I touch it."

I stepped out of my dress and he folded it carefully, placing it over the towel bar on the wall.

He actually shivered when he turned to look at me. "Dear God, woman. Are you trying to kill me?" I was braless, only wearing black lacey panties and black high heels.

I shook my head slowly. "I just know what my man likes."

I think he might have growled on his way back to me—his hands and his mouth tantalizing me as he moved from my mouth down my body, kneeling in front of me. He pulled my panties to the side, hooking them out of the way with his thumb, and dove between my legs. I called out as his fingers disappeared inside me. I hadn't expected such a sudden invasion, but I liked it. I liked his excitement. I liked feeling like us.

He teased me only for a moment before pulling his fingers back out and licking them, groaning. "Oh baby, I've been waiting all night for another taste of dessert."

I shuddered as his mouth moved over me, his tongue and his fingers teasing me, pulling me closer and closer to climax, my fingers weaving through his hair, my leg over his shoulder. "Jake," I rasped, "I want you. I want you inside me."

Jake shot to his feet, "Yes, ma'am."

I was suddenly alone and empty, my body pulsing and throbbing without his touch and all I wanted was him. I wanted us locked together when my body climaxed. His pants fell to the floor and his cock sprang free. Jake grabbed me and hauled me up onto the counter, my hands frantically moving down his buttons, looking for his skin beneath. I wanted to touch him, too.

And then he was inside me, I closed my eyes and sucked in a surprised breath. Even with as wet and ready as I was, his sudden invasion took my breath away. "Are you all right?" he breathed, his eyes rolling back and his jaw going slack.

"Hard. I want it hard, Jake."

His eyes flew open to meet mine. "Yes, ma'am." He gripped me around the hips and slammed into me again and this time I actually cried out. But I didn't care. It was probably bad that I didn't—anyone could be on the other side of the door. The only thing I cared about was what we were doing right then.

My hands ran up his naked torso, under his shirt, and gripped onto his shoulders as he took me on the counter. The feeling was overwhelming. Every thrust took my breath away and sent my heart rate skyrocketing.

"You're killing me, do you feel yourself?" he gasped.

I did, I knew exactly what he meant. My whole body was vibrating and contracting around him. I was so close to orgasm and yet not going over the edge. It had to be torture to feel me squeezing around his cock like that.

"Come on baby, let me hear you."

I'd been on the edge of release for so long, I had no idea what would tip me over, but I needed to figure it out. And then Jake slowed, releasing his grip on my hip and sliding up to my neck. His fingers wrapped around to the nape, and he tilted my head to look at him. "I'm here, baby. Look at me. This is just you and me." He moved slowly in and out. In and out. His thumb running back and forth across my cheek, and his green eyes burning into mine.

I came, my jaw falling open as my body shattered, and our eyes stayed locked. Jake was absolutely transfixed, watching me come until he couldn't hold back any longer, and then he came, too. Hard, powerful thrusts followed by a shudder and complete relaxation.

He folded me against him.

"Eve, that was . . . amazing. You were so beautiful."

Amazing. Yep, that was the word I would use, too... if I could remember how to talk. My brain was mush, my body was drained, and I was contemplating moving into this bathroom just so I wouldn't have to leave.

Jake chuckled, "That good, huh? I've fucked you into silence?"

"Yep." I finally managed a single syllable word.

His chest rumbled again and then his strong arms moved around so that he could look at me, "Darlin' I promise to take you straight home, but first I've got to get you dressed again."

I smiled and bit my lip. "No one's missing us. We can hide out a while longer."

He shook his head giving me a devilish look. "Well it is a damn fine thing I didn't try to fuck you in the hallway. This would have been a disaster."

"Oh, we would have gotten caught for sure. And with all these fancy people . . . we never would have lived it down."

"They'd be talking about it at parties years from

now: *Do you remember that one couple . . . the ones caught fucking?"*

We cleaned up quickly once I got my feet under me. Jake helped me back into my dress and after a few adjustments I felt we were as close as we could get to looking like we hadn't just had a wild romp in a bathroom.

Jake pulled me in for one last kiss. "You sure you don't want me to take you home? I could repeat my performance. In the shower perhaps?"

"No, I want to finish the night. It is a lovely party and there are lots of people we still haven't talked to. Besides, I think I might need a little bit to recover before we do that again."

Jake had a wicked grin. "I'll get you a water first."

"Wise," I agreed and opened the door.

Unfortunately there was someone waiting for us. He wasn't happy. And he was also my ex-boyfriend.

Sebastian was leaned up against the wall, a frown on his face, and his arms crossed over his chest. I immediately straightened up and stepped to the side as Jake followed me out. His surprise was as graceful as mine. "Sorry about that," Jake muttered, placing his hand on the small of my back and motioning for me to head down the hall ahead of him.

The only sound Sebastian made was the slamming of the bathroom door as we hurried down the hallway.

Awkward. That was awkward. As Jake got me some water I texted Jennie. It was one of those things you simply couldn't keep to yourself.

"Do we pretend that didn't just happen?" Jake asked with a look of mock horror on his face.

"What else would we do? Would you want an ex to come up to you and discuss the amazing sex they'd just had?"

Jake smirked, the pride glowing in his eyes and curling on his lips. "Amazing, eh?"

Cocky bastard. He knew it was amazing, he'd called it that himself. "I believe those were the words we tossed around, yes."

His arm snaked around my waist and he dipped his lips down to whisper in my ear. "It was fucking earth-shattering watching you come, Eve."

I melted against him and looked up at him through my lashes. "Glad I could rock your world."

Jake growled and nipped at my earlobe. "You *are* my world, darlin'."

Before I could enjoy his sweet words we were interrupted.

"Jake Spencer, I'm Lane Harris, one of the investors on the project."

Jake winked at me before turning to Lane and shaking his hand. "Nice to meet you Lane. How can I help you?"

"I was wondering if we could have a minute of your time?"

"Of course, Lane. May I introduce you to my date? This is my girlfriend Eve Daniels."

Lane smiled at me pleasantly. "It's nice to meet you Miss Daniels, I actually know your father."

I straightened up a little bit in Jake's arms at the mention of my father. "It's nice to meet you as well." I extended my hand and he delicately shook it, as was the usual custom of men at parties like this.

"You two are quite adorable together. I've heard a lot about you over the years, Miss Daniels. Joe is a very proud father and from what I've heard, it's all deserved. You've done a wonderful job with the Rays."

I was flattered. The last thing I expected tonight was to see so many people I knew from work. This was Jake's night and I had come with the intention of being his arm candy. But I was quickly realizing this was a small town and we were swimming with the big fish. Jake's circles and mine were quickly colliding.

"I appreciate that very much, Lane. And please call me Eve."

Lane lead us over to a group of three men. "Jake, Eve, may I introduce you to some of the other investors? This is Peter Salsburg and Jeff McComb. And of course I'm sure you've already met the architect, Mr. Sebastian Monroe."

We shook Peter and Jeff's hands and the usual nice to meet you's were exchanged, but Sebastian hung back. He was clearly in a foul mood, not that I would have expected any different, but he looked positively angry. His normally smooth exterior was ruffled, his shirt slightly out of place, his tie just a bit off center, his hair messy. On any other man—hell, on Jake—it would look normal and even a little sexy. But on Sebastian it looked wrong.

"Sebastian," I nodded in his direction, but couldn't bring myself to look him in the eye. It was just too weird.

"Eve," he replied, even his voice was rough. Sebastian was not doing well at all. "Jake, seems you've been busy this evening."

The temperature around us dropped. Jake and I understood the double meaning behind Sebastian's words, but the others were blissfully unaware of the strange conversation we were having.

"I have," Jake acknowledged, putting his arm back around my waist. It felt protective. I was glad, because the vibe I was getting from Sebastian was making me incredibly uncomfortable.

"So, now that we have both you and Sebastian here, we wanted to go over some details and bring up a few concerns we had for the designs."

I watched the two men I'd lived with, both brilliant and powerful, as they interacted with the investors in the project. All three investors were absolutely taken with Sebastian's designs and Jake's ingenuity. Both men handled the conversation brilliantly. Soothing the investors when they needed it, walking them through information when it was necessary. They were the very picture of professionalism.

But Jake was uncomfortable. I had the feeling his radar was going crazy, he was worried about Sebastian and that, in turn, made him worried about me. I noticed how he kept me opposite Sebastian, even moving his body to block his view when it seemed to lock on me.

Sebastian was completely unlike himself. He was short and clipped with his words, not nearly as smooth or eloquent as I knew he could be. The differences were subtle, but to me they were obvious.

"Thank you for your time, gentlemen. We look forward to seeing what you do with this," Lane said shaking everyone's hands once again.

And leaving the three of us alone together.

The uncomfortable silence made my skin crawl and the only thing I wanted to do was go home just like Jake had suggested when we left the bathroom. Why hadn't we just gone home then?

"Good night, Sebastian," Jake said turning me away.

"You had sex in a bathroom, Eve? With *him*?" The way he spat out the words, the condescending drip they had, that was what turned us around. Anything less and Jake and I would have happily walked away from Sebastian's game. But he baited us and we took it.

I froze and Jake tensed.

"I want you to really think about what you're doing, Sebastian. Think before you speak," Jake said as he turned around. "You can't take back what you say."

Sebastian was brooding, but defiant. He obviously didn't like being chastised by Jake. "It was simply a question."

"That wasn't just a question. That was a carefully placed insult. And I don't like it when anyone insults me or my girlfriend." The testosterone cloud was blooming again.

I stepped out from under Jake's arm. "Please don't do this, Sebastian. Not here."

Jake jerked. "Not ever."

But Sebastian was on a mission. Whatever his goal was, he wasn't going to be moved. "Are you going to answer me?"

I shook my head. "No I'm not going to answer you. You know the answer to both questions."

"The Eve I knew wouldn't reduce herself to such rude behavior."

*Oh no he didn't.* "Excuse me? The Eve you knew? Maybe you didn't know me at all. Did *that* bright idea ever occur to you?" I took a step toward him and my finger came out, pointing at him and waving, "We never had passion like that. You never needed me so desperately you had to have me wherever we were. *That* is why I'm with *him*."

Sebastian's mouth fell open and he laughed, but it was from disbelief. I was fairly certain Sebastian couldn't even imagine feeling that strongly about anyone. "He abandoned you."

He looked Jake up and down like he couldn't stand the sight of him. It kind of made me want to forget where we were or that I had any manners at all. Because at the moment we were keeping things pretty quiet. There were only a couple of sideways glances at our threesome.

But what I really wanted to do was beat the crap out of my ex. And that, I was pretty sure, would get us some attention.

"Are you insane?" I hissed. "My relationship with Jake is none of your damn business."

"I'm not so sure. I care about you Eve and right now you're not thinking clearly. I think you might need to hear some sense."

What did that mean? What the hell was he talking about?

"You are about to cross that line, Sebastian," Jake warned.

Sebastian glared at Jake. "You want to talk about lines, Jake? How about the one you crossed when you left your girlfriend?"

I was pretty impressed by Jake—he wasn't letting anything get to him. He was the picture of cool confidence. Sebastian would use anything he could get his hands on right now, so Jake wasn't giving him anything.

Me on the other hand, I wasn't so smooth. I didn't have it in me to stand there quietly and listen. "If you have something to say, just say it and stop playing games."

"I'm worried about you, Eve." He said it so simply and calmly I almost believed he was really worried about me and not his bruised ego. Somewhere inside I knew all of this was coming from that. He was hurt. Our relationship hadn't worked out, but clearly he'd wanted it to, maybe even expected for us to get back together one day. It was why he was still connected to my friends and family. Sebastian had never let go of the idea we would be together.

It probably wasn't because he loved me, not in the way I viewed love. I was pretty sure, especially looking back, that Sebastian was in love with the idea of me. I was the woman he wanted on his arm, the family he wanted to marry into, the external trappings of success he thought would make him happy. But he'd never really known me and never loved me the way I wanted to be loved.

"Eve, he can't be good for you. He left you and he broke your heart. Do you remember how you were? Because I do. We were friends before we dated, and I knew you even before that. You were miserable. *He* made you miserable. And now you're back with him—the man who destroyed you. What does that say about you?"

I hadn't expected him to go there, so it took me by surprise. I'd expected to hear all about how Jake had ruined my life before and he would do it again. The whole 'people don't change' line.

I didn't expect him to turn the tables on me.

"Me?" I tried the idea out on my lips. I wasn't sure how I felt about it.

"Yes, you." He squinted at me like I was a puzzle he was trying to solve. "You followed Jake until he left you even though you knew he was bad for you. He was a mess and yet... you wouldn't let him go. Then you waited. And waited. I don't call the bullshit halfhearted dating you did between Jake and me, dating. And then there was me. You were never really *with* me. No mat-

ter how hard I tried, there was always a brick wall between you and me. You never let me see inside."

He was seething with anger and saying a lot of
things. I was trying to keep up with him, but he just
kept coming at me with more. "What are you so afraid
of Eve? What do you have hidden inside you don't want
someone good like me to see? I think you like being
with Jake because he's safe. He is so screwed up that
the attention will never be on you and you can keep
hiding all your secrets behind that wall of yours—and
no one will ever notice."

My jaw fell open but no words came out. I had no
ready response for that. What Sebastian was saying... it
had never occurred to me before. I was so incredibly
fixated on the things being done to me, on the things
on the outside that I'd never really looked in. I had no
response to Sebastian's questions because I had no answers.

"Eve, don't listen to him," Jake warned. "He's
messing with your head."

"Sebastian... I want you to leave now," I said quietly. "I'm sorry we surprised you tonight. I know that
wasn't fun. But we never meant to hurt you. What
you're doing right now . . . you're trying to hurt me and
confuse me on purpose. So if you don't walk out of here
in the next thirty seconds I'm gonna kick your ass. And
the problem with that is my wonderful, passionate,
will-do-anything-for-me boyfriend here, will also have
to kick your ass. And seeing as I don't think any of us
really want that, I'm gonna need you to drag yourself

out of here." My voice got louder and firmer with every word.

I got a little satisfaction out of the shock on his face. Not a lot—that wouldn't have been very nice of me—but I did get some.

He looked at Jake then he turned to me. "Good luck. I hope you found what you were looking for."

And then he was gone and Jake was dragging me away from the party.

The minute we were in the hallway he released my arm. He stood over me, his size so much larger than mine I felt the difference. "Don't do it, Eve. I know this whole night has been one giant mind fuck, but don't do it." I didn't miss the warning tone to his voice.

"Don't do what, exactly?"

He looked me square in the eye with his jaw thrust out. He was breathing hard. "Don't shut down, don't get lost inside your head with all those thoughts and questions. It seems like a lot, but it isn't babe. It isn't."

"How is this," I waved my hands frantically around, "*not* a lot?"

He grabbed me. "Do you love me? That is all you need to know. Everything else is just bullshit."

But I wasn't so sure. I wanted love to be that simple, but I'd already seen how *not* simple it really was. My hopes, Jake's dreams, our confidence and personalities—all of it was tied to that love. And there was nothing simple about that.

I needed to think. I needed fresh air and quiet. I needed to be by myself for a while.

Jake must have seen the look in my eye, the need to flee, because his went wide. "No. You are not leaving me right now. We are talking. We are talking through this together." He was in a full panic and his grip on my arms only tightened.

"Let me go, Jake." I said softly. I was really surprised by how eerily calm I sounded.

"Not if you are going to walk away from me."

"You can't keep me here, babe. And I know you well enough to know that you wouldn't want to keep me here against my will."

The look of pain that crossed his face very nearly stopped me right there. I was hurting him. I knew this in the back of my mind somewhere. I knew he was terrified he was losing me. But I couldn't stop. I knew what I needed right then . . . and it wasn't Jake. If I couldn't clear my head and find a way through all the thoughts swirling through my mind on my own, I was going to go mad.

It was something I needed to work through by myself.

"Jake, let me go." I repeated and this time he complied.

I reached up and stroked his cheek. "I love you." I kissed him softly on the lips, looking deeply into his eyes.

Then I turned and left.

I didn't look back. I knew if I did I'd see how much I'd just hurt Jake, and that was something I couldn't handle.

## Chapter 23

*I* don't know what brought me there, it wasn't the smartest thing I'd ever done, that was for sure. But somehow after I left Jake, my feet took on a mind of their own. The next thing I knew I was in my car and headed out toward a part of town I hadn't dared step into for a very, very long time.

The streets were just a bit narrower, the houses crammed together with barely any yard between. The Vernacular homes were shotgun style: a front porch with columns and the house laid out in a row of rooms from front to back. These neighborhoods were older, rougher, and the languages spoken varied wildly.

This was where Jake grew up.

My Nissan GT-R stood out like a sore thumb and I knew the minute I pulled up outside their house they'd know it was me. I didn't know why I was there. Even as I pulled down his street, I was still wondering what I thought I was going to find.

There were no answers here.

And yet, I stopped outside their house anyway.

I fumbled around in my glove box for one of my cans of pepper spray. Not the pretty pink can that came in a leather case, but the nice one that came in a slick black design made to be worn on your belt. It had two high-powered shots inside.

My feet were in charge—my brain having taken a vacation—and I was out of the car, leaning against the passenger side as I gazed up at the house.

Jake's childhood home needed a paint job, but it was neat and tidy. Plants and flowers were growing from pots lined up on the porch above and below. There were even a few rusty tools lain out as lawn ornaments. The front was presentable; it always had been, just like Jake's family.

It was a façade. A fake front put on to make it seem like they fit in, like they were good enough. But once you went past the front room everything changed. The rest of the house was a cluttered mess that bordered on hoarding. The backyard was stuffed with junk, overgrown and disgusting. And the people who lived inside were angry and spiteful at the world. They wouldn't know a good deed if it saved their lives.

Jake said his parents were out of the picture, that he wanted nothing to do with them ever again. I was so close to my family I found it difficult to fathom cutting the people who raised me out of my life. How did you do that? What did that look like? Would Jake simply block out his childhood all together or choose to only remember key moments? What if he was wrong and hadn't moved past all of this, but was instead just wishing he had?

I needed to know the foundation Jake and I were standing on was strong.

I wanted to believe life would be easy once Jake and I trusted each other, but I was realizing life would never be easy. There would always be something else. If we were going to have a life together, if Jake and I were going to rely on each other, I needed to know we were strong enough to handle anything life could throw at us.

Whether it was my insecurities or Jake's demons. Whether it was accidents or tragedies—life was going to keep throwing us curve balls. Jake said he knew his past was behind him, that his father couldn't ever hurt him again.

But *I* didn't know that.

Everything that had ever hurt Jake was inside that house and I needed to know it couldn't come back to haunt us.

Just as I predicted, the front door opened and Jake's mother walked out. I didn't need to announce my arrival any more than pulling up out front. And of course the asshole inside sent his wife out to do the dirty work for him.

Always had.

"What are you doing here?" she hissed.

She never did have any manners, but at least we

weren't wasting any time either. "I see we're skipping right past the pleasantries and going straight for *get off my porch.*"

She stood at the top of the stairs, her hair up in some sort of messy bun, her face as contorted and wrinkled as I remembered, and she was wearing a housecoat. She looked as hard as the life she'd led. "Well now that you mention it, would you?"

I remained casually leaned up against my car. "I'm on the curb. I haven't stepped one foot on your porch. This is public property out here and you can't make me leave."

She stood and stared at me for a minute. I was pretty sure she was trying to figure out how to get rid of me as fast as she could, but her curiosity was killing her. She wanted to know why I was there dressed up and staring at her house.

"It's been a long time since you were here."

"Yes it has."

She stepped down to the bottom step, bringing her close enough that she didn't have to shout at me. "Have you heard from him?"

At first the shaky sound of her voice made my heart ache for the mother who had lost her son, but then I remembered everything she'd done to him and everything she'd allowed to happen to him. She hadn't lost Jake; she'd run him away.

"Yes."

She straightened and her hand moved to her chest. "How is he?"

"Amazing, no thanks to you."

Her chin lifted in defiance. "You always did think you were better than us."

"I am better than you, Lydia. And it has nothing to do with money."

Her eyes lit up and she walked all the way up to the chain-link fence separating her property from the street. "Jake needed a firm hand. That boy was wild. If we hadn't done what we did he would have been out of control. We did what we had to do."

I laughed and looked up at the night sky. There were a few dots twinkling above us, but most were blotted out by the city lights and a sea of clouds rolling in from the bay. "You really believe that, don't you? Did you talk yourself into that crap or did your useless husband do that for you?"

"You are a self-righteous bitch."

I finally took a step away from the car, my arms folded over my chest with the pepper spray tucked out of sight. "He is a wonderful man with a great soul and the two of you tried to beat it out of him. You tried to turn him into a useless angry piece of shit. But you know what? It didn't work. He was always better than you—smarter, sweeter, and with a good heart. He got into college despite you because he was so smart. And the day he set foot on that campus, away from you, was the day you finally lost him. Once he saw a world outside of this hell, he knew he could claw his way free."

She laughed at me this time, the kind that made my blood run cold. "You're still in love with him, aren't you? Oh, baby girl that makes me sad. You've waited all this time for a man who'll never love you back. He can't. You know why? Because he's his father's son. If you stick around long enough, you'll see him crack just like his daddy." She smiled, but it wasn't because she was happy. This woman had been ruined by a life she'd never had the courage to take control of. "He'll hit you and hurt you. He'll break your heart a thousand times. But you'll never leave him because he's your world. He's your everything."

Damn, she was good. She knew my weaknesses as well as I did, and she'd hit them all. Were they lucky guesses or were we really that similar? If Jake hadn't left, would we have turned into his parents? Would I have stayed at his side no matter what and let him hit me? Would I have let him strip away everything good?

I didn't think I would have. I was mesmerized by him and had been madly in love with him, but I couldn't imagine a world where I became Lydia or Jake became his father.

"You're not entirely wrong." I gave her a small victory, hoping it would give me some ground to work with. "He is my everything. And I do still love him. But you are wrong about the rest. If he was just like your husband then he never would have left in the first place. He would have stayed here and let you control him. He is different." *Jake would never, ever hurt me the way Jake Sr. hurt you.* I knew that in every fiber of my being.

The front door swung open again and my eyes fell

on the dark shadow of Jake Sr. He was visibly older than the last time I saw him. His hair was graying and balding on top. His eyes were piercing and harsh, but his body was the biggest change. He was slighter, stooped, and unsure. Years of alcohol, drugs, and cigarettes were taking their toll and I had to wonder just how badly diseased and damaged he was.

Jake Sr. was a shadow of his former self.

"Get out of here." His voice hadn't changed in the slightest. It still sent a shiver of warning down my spine. He had the kind of voice that made you want to run, it sounded like pure evil.

"She's seen Jake." Lydia rasped over her shoulder, never taking her eyes off me.

"I'm sure that bitch has. Now that our boy went and got himself a shitload of money I bet she made sure to track him down and use him some more. What, Eve? You didn't get enough sex out of him in college? You didn't put enough delusions of grandeur in his head? Now that he's gone and done what you wanted, you looking for more?"

"I never made Jake anything he wasn't." I was surprised by how sure I sounded. Inside I was losing it. I wanted to rip Jake's parents in two.

Jake Sr. laughed, walking down the steps to join his wife. "What are you doing here, Eve? Did you come to flaunt your fancy car and designer dress? Haven't you gotten your kicks in for the day? Decided to go hit up some poor people and make them look at you? You always were an attention whore." He shook his head and spit into the grass.

Why did I come here? I hated these people. I hated everything they'd ever done. I didn't want to stir the pot or cause any trouble, but I thought I needed to get back to the source. There were questions Jake and I couldn't seem to answer and since all our troubles seemed to start and end here, this house seemed a logical place to look.

"Do you regret what happened graduation night?" I asked.

The crackle of thunder and the deep roll of bass that followed caught our attention and I turned my head to look toward the bay. Lightning was streaking through the clouds. A late thunderstorm was brewing.

When I turned back, Jake Sr. was outside the gate. I could reach out and touch him. Even in his diminished state he made my blood run cold and my skin prickle. I wasn't sure how he had moved so fast. "You mean when I tried to bring Jake back down where he belonged?"

"He doesn't belong here. He's meant for more."

Jake Sr. just shook his head. "You'll never understand."

I stared at him, desperately trying to figure out what he meant, but I felt like we were speaking two different languages and we'd never, ever understand each other.

"Try me."

"You'd put a lot of ideas in his head. Filled it with all kinds of nonsense about seeing the world, having powerful jobs, and being happy. But you see, I know different. Life is hard, Eve. Especially for those of us who don't have money to fix our problems. We have to rely on ourselves, and my son was forgetting that. What good was it going to do him to walk out into your world and get crushed?"

"You know, I think you actually believe yourself. I think you've sold yourself that line of bullshit so many times you've forgotten it's a bunch of crap."

Jake Sr. just stared at me, his clouded eyes barely keeping track of me. It was late and he was drunk.

"Here's what I think really happened that night. You saw how great he was. You saw how smart he was. You knew he was going to be everything that you never were. People were going to respect him and want to be him. You saw how much power your useless son was about to have and you got jealous. You couldn't let him be better than you. So you lost it. You went nuts and you tried to put Jake back in the hole you'd forced him to live in his whole life. Only it didn't work out so well for you. Jake had grown up and gotten a backbone. He fought back. But instead of letting that ruin him, instead of becoming you, he left. He learned and he grew. And he became all of those things you were so afraid of him being."

Jake Sr. stared at me for a long minute, he didn't move or say anything. I wasn't even sure he was breathing. Until suddenly he spoke. "You need to leave. I have respected my son's wishes, but a man can only be pushed so far before he is forced to take matters back into his own hands." He lunged toward me, not to touch me, just to scare me.

I flinched, which was the worst possible thing to do in front of a man like Jake Sr. Men like him thrived on intimidation. They got their power and sense of confidence by taking it from others. He smiled and leaned in closer. "I must say, my son did have good taste, though."

He reached out and grabbed my arm just as a car came peeling down the street. Jake Sr. jumped back in surprise and I showed him my pepper spray. "Do not ever touch me again."

His eyes flicked from the spray to the car that squealed to a stop behind mine. I recognized it immediately: it was Greg's bright red Porsche.

The passenger door flew open and Jake unfolded himself, stepping out onto the sidewalk. I didn't know how he'd found me, but he was clearly pissed on a level I couldn't comprehend.

Jake Sr. barely had time to sneer before Jake landed the first punch, knocking his father backward into the fence. "Get in the car, Eve." He pointed at my car. Then he turned back to his father, "Do not touch Eve ever again. You do and I'll kill you. Period."

Everything about Jake was pure rolling masculine energy. He was mad, but that wasn't the predominant emotion coming from him. He was in full protection mode. He was protecting me.

Greg walked around to close Jake's door and he looked about as happy as the rest of us. He locked eyes with me and nodded reassuringly. "He's got this," he murmured. For some reason Greg's quiet confidence in Jake made me feel a sense of relief. Greg knew this side of Jake better than I did and he was the one who had driven Jake here. If he thought Jake was fine, then he was fine.

I turned and grabbed the passenger door handle, hoping like hell Jake was planning on driving us out of here. There wasn't a chance I was leaving him here no matter what Greg thought.

"Jake . . ." Lydia moaned. "Can't you do anything right?"

"No, apparently I can't Mother. I'm pretty sure I will never make you happy."

Lydia stared at her son.

Jake Sr. stood all the way up. "Your girlfriend has already said all that needed saying. You can take all your fancy cars and leave us be."

Jake shook his head and rubbed his face. He looked so different standing here in front of this house all these years later. The boy I'd come to pick up here never looked right. He always looked just a little off, his eyes always a little closed and sad, his body always hunched against the world. The man standing in front of me now was tall and strong, he looked damn good in the tux he was wearing, and he smiled all the time.

"We're done. After we leave, we're done. I want you to forget you ever had a son and I will forget you were ever my parents."

"She's not your blood," Jake Sr. said cocking his

head toward me.

"That's where you're wrong. She's more family to me than you ever were."

He and his father stared at each other while the thunder rolled across the sky. "Goodbye," he said simply, shaking his head and turning toward me. He scowled the moment he saw I wasn't in the car. "Get in the car, *now*."

I nodded and sat back, pulling the door closed once I saw Jake move around the back of the car. Only when he was safely inside with me did I dare to take a breath. Jake Sr. glared at us and I could feel the hate through the darkly tinted windows.

The throaty engine flared to life and Jake revved the engine before peeling away.

I didn't dare say a word until we were back on the highway. Jake was silent as he shifted hard through the gears and wove down the interstate. He was so tense every move he made was precise and measured.

"How did you know where I was?"

"Private investigator called me the minute you pulled up."

*Oh, right.* He had his father under constant surveillance. "I'm sorry. I didn't mean for you to come down there."

He didn't reply. He was brooding.

We exited the highway and shot down the quiet streets toward my house.

"Jake . . ."

He shook his head. "No. I can't, not right now." He

was vibrating with tension. Jake was pissed. I just didn't know for which reason. At this point I'd racked up a nice little list.

*Leaving when he needed to talk.*

*Leaving when I needed to talk and get out of my head.*

*Going to his parent's house.*

Or there was everything I said to his dad.

Of course he could also be pissed I'd accidentally forced him to see a man he never wanted to see again.

Yeah, I was on a fucking roll.

I sat back in my seat and quietly waited for him to take me home.

The black night turned into a wicked storm, but not the kind that actually rained like it did in the heart of summer. This was the kind that seemed to be everywhere—the wind and lightning lighting up the sky, surrounding everything as far as the eye could see—while not actually raining.

He didn't kill the engine when we stopped outside my house. We sat there for a long time, his hands on the steering wheel, gripping and squeezing while mine were folded tightly in my lap.

"What the hell were you thinking?" he finally asked. His voice rough with emotion.

Ah, the question of the night. It may not have been my most brilliant move, but I had gotten what I needed, so there was something in that. "It all comes back to them."

He closed his eyes. "You could have gotten hurt."

I shook my head and reached out for the smooth skin of his cheek. He let me touch him, which was a good sign. "I wouldn't have let that happen and I wouldn't have gone there if I wasn't sure I could keep myself safe."

He opened his eyes and looked at me. "There are never any guarantees in that house, Eve. It was stupid to go there."

I nodded, it didn't matter how sure I was, he was right, too. When it came to people like his parents there were too many variables. "I'm sorry I worried you."

He shook his head and took my hand, folding it between his two larger ones. "When I got that call I thought I was going to die. I made him repeat himself three times. 'Eve is at your parent's house'. It just didn't compute. And then my heart stopped." He reached up and cupped my face, his thumb stroking my cheek. "I have never been so scared in my life."

How badly I wanted to protect this man from anything that might hurt him. And his protective need to save me from the same thing was clear on his face. The way his eyes looked wild and focused at the same time, the way his muscles were tight and ready for action, the shallow way he was breathing—it was all for me.

I reached out and ran the back of my fingers over his cheek, then dipped my finger into the space where his dimple would be. "Kiss me."

His eyes lit up and his hands grabbed for my face, threading through my hair. He crushed his lips to mine. I ran my hands up his biceps, grabbing him at the shoulders. The next thing I knew, he was lifting me up and over the console and settling me on his lap. He didn't say anything, just watched me with those burning green eyes of his, as he did his very best to make me feel good, to erase everything that was hurting us.

His fingers kept tangling in my hair, but it was nice. One minute he was gently stroking, the next tangling and tugging. His tongue plunged deep into my throat. We were kissing like animals, there was nothing gentle or teasing about anything we were doing. I bit his lip and his earlobe between kisses. My skirt went up and my top went down as I continued to grind against his firm erection. And then I was undoing his belt and fly, digging inside for my prize. With a little help he sprang free, then with one finger, Jake pulled my lacey panties to the side, and with the other tilted my chin so that I was looking right into his burning eyes.

I slowly rocked against him, taking him in inch by inch, until he was fully inside. He didn't let go of my chin. When my eyes closed, he pulled down, forcing them back open again. He wanted to see me, wanted to know what I was feeling.

It was incredibly intense sex. Not fast and hard, but slow and deliberate. His thrusts were powerful and individual. With one hand on my hip and one on my chin, he had complete control of me, forcing me to keep my attention on him while gently coaxing me to do what he wanted by changing the pressure of his fingers against my skin.

His breathing was becoming ragged as he held back, waiting for my orgasm to come first. But that wasn't what I wanted. I wanted to feel in control of something, and right now, that meant Jake's pleasure. I took great pride in doing everything I knew he couldn't resist, from the focus of my eyes on him, to the squeeze of my muscles, to my little moans of pleasure.

He lasted about thirty seconds.

The moment I felt the first pulse of release, I let go of my own, and we came together, grinding against each other, moaning and groaning, until finally we were done.

I rested my forehead on his shoulder and relaxed for the first time in hours.

"Well, I think I'm good for the night now," Jake chuckled, maneuvering the top of my dress back over my breasts.

"I'm gonna need an hour in the shower," I agreed. And not just to get clean. I needed to loosen up my poor muscles.

But in all seriousness, I wouldn't have it any other way. The bottom line was that I loved the man I was straddling in the front seat of my car. I loved the way we were together, and how desperately we needed each other. And I loved how carefully he loved me in return.

Nothing about our relationship was a game. We were both painfully aware of how easily we could lose everything.

"Taking care of the one you love . . . that's what you and I do," I whispered, looking deep into his gorgeous green eyes. "Sometimes that means one of us is stronger. I lean on you when I'm weak and you take care of me. But I hold you up, too. It's a give and take. I haven't lost myself to you, not this time around. I love you so much and I will do anything to keep you safe and healthy, even if it means sacrificing a lot of myself in the process, but I'm not lost to you. I'm still me . . . and I think you're still you."

His thumbs stroked my cheeks and he kissed me. "Did you find the answers you were looking for?"

"Yes." I was confident in that. There were no more lingering doubts. I wasn't going to be second-guessing anything from our past. I knew everything I needed to know now.

He nodded back, "Okay then. Where do we go from here?"

I smiled because I knew exactly where we went from here, but I was still a little nervous about saying it. "You could move in with me."

## Chapter 24

*J*ake had officially moved in with me after that night and kept his promise of a romantic vacation in the Bahamas. Our little plane had just taxied onto the runway and I was already feeling more relaxed.

Jake leaned over to look out the window and I caught sight of a gold chain tucked under his shirt.

I reached out to touch it but he caught my hand and pulled it up for a kiss. Jake wasn't the kind to wear jewelry and he clearly didn't want me to ask about it. I fingered the gold sun hanging from my own neck. Jake had worn that, maybe he did wear jewelry—at least when it meant something to him.

Maybe it was another one of his mysterious projects. He'd been working on a few more demons from his past in light of what happened the night of the party. He'd gone to some therapy sessions, worked in his workshop, and finally opened a box of mementos his mother had sent him many years ago.

That had been an interesting night. His mother had a twisted sense of history. We'd thrown most of it out and fucked the pain away for the rest of the night.

But overall, things had been fantastic. Jake paid off the rest of his lease and officially moved his things into my house. We redecorated the bedroom, but decided to keep the bed. We liked that big, sturdy bed. He'd also taken over Jennie's old room as his home office.

And as for me, I'd finally let go of everything I'd been afraid of. Fear was my enemy and it was holding me back. I think I'd come to find a little fear was healthy, but too much paralyzed me. I never wanted to be paralyzed again.

So I'd started looking forward to the future, wondering where it was taking us. Jake's company was growing by leaps and bounds and my job was as secure as they come. We were happy in our house and with our friends. We'd started making lists. Our travel list looked a little different than the one we made in college, but I was looking forward to it just the same. It felt like the world was at our feet.

But I'd been wrong that night in the car when I thought all of our major hurdles had been crossed. There was one more. One we couldn't prepare for and there was no way to predict how things would go. All we could do was suck it up, find our courage, and plunge into the deep end.

If Jake had been nervous, he'd never let it show.

I, on the other hand, had been a mess.

It was just all too familiar. Driving up my parent's driveway in the Orange Beast, I felt like I was a teenager bringing her boyfriend home.

They'd been kind to us, at least. When we got there it was just June home for the weekend and my mom busy in her art studio. Dad was nowhere to be found. So while June and Jake goofed off, I went in search of my father.

I was frantic to find him at that point because I just wanted to get it all over with. This discord between the man I loved, and the family I loved, was driving me crazy.

I found him in his "man room."

I should point out that it was raining outside. Monsoon raining. It had started about five minutes after we arrived and looked like it wouldn't be stopping until sometime the next day.

This is important in understanding what I found when I walked in to the man room.

I found my dad standing on his pool table.

My dad loved his pool table and the last place I would have ever expected to find him was *standing* on his precious pool table.

And not only that, but there were golf balls (not pool balls) on the green surface, a putter in his hand, a pipe hanging from his lip, and a mostly empty glass of scotch on the corner.

"What are you doing?" I asked incredulously.

Maybe retirement was making him into one of those crazy, eccentric, old men I'd heard about. Not that he was an old man yet.

He glanced up from his ball and grinned at me, speaking through his teeth with the pipe firmly lodged in place, "Daughter! You made it before the rain, good."

"What are you doing?" I asked slowly, closing the door and leaning against the frame.

"Putting," he replied like *I* was the crazy one.

"On the pool table?"

"It's going to rain all afternoon. What else am I supposed to do?"

"*Not* putt on the pool table?"

He scoffed, "Losers say crap like that. Speaking of losers . . ."

"Don't start Dad. I am not in charge of the players."

He pulled out his pipe and started waving it around as he spoke. "No, I'm talking about your boss. You tell Josh to stop sending me all those damn emails. Do I look like someone you email? Tell his ass—" Dad hopped down and walked toward me. "Quote me, tell him this exactly, *Pick up the damn phone and call me like a real human being.* If he emails me again I'm driving up there just to beat him up with his laptop."

"Dad."

He shrugged his wide shoulders, still strong even years after leaving the field. He had a baseball player's body through and through. "What? Quote me, Eve. I mean it."

I shook my head and rolled my eyes. He was an old fashioned guy from another era. And worse yet, he didn't have to keep up with electronics, so he didn't.

"Are you going to be difficult the whole weekend?"

He locked eyes with me. He was holding his breath. He was really struggling with his feelings toward Jake. I understood it intellectually, I was his daughter and Jake had hurt me. It was his job to make sure that didn't happen again.

It was hard because we all loved Jake. It was hard to separate out all the things we were feeling.

"No. I just want you to be happy."

I forced a smile onto my face. We talked for a few minutes, moving to his big, comfy, brown leather couch. He picked my brain about the team, I asked him about Mom. Dad and I had always been closer. I think it was because our personalities were similar. It didn't take many words to say what needed saying and we were both just fine with silence when we were done.

The door opened and Jake strode in. He really did look a little like a kid again: eyes bright, energy high as he crossed the room looking to shake my dad's hand.

"Mr. Daniels, it is good to see you again, thank you for allowing me to visit this weekend."

My dad rolled his eyes and shook his hand. "Fine, you were right, Eve. I can't keep this up all weekend." He crossed his arms over his chest and glared at Jake. "I'm gonna go ahead and get it all out right now if that's all right with you?"

Jake slid his hands into his shorts pockets and nodded. "Give it to me."

Dad nodded. "You hurt her again, I'll kill you myself. I won't ask questions, I won't see straight. I'm just gonna kill you, dump your body in the gulf, and pretend you never existed. We clear?"

Jake nodded slowly, but before he could reply, Dad went on. "You need help, you ask for it. We're your family, and we take care of our own. That includes you."

Jake froze and a little color drained out of his face. I think he was a little shocked to hear a statement that bold from my father, of all people. "Yes, sir," he said quietly.

My dad rolled his eyes again and sighed, "Stop that 'sir' crap, too. It's Joe."

Jake nodded again. "All right, Joe."

"Scotch?"

Jake chuckled and followed my dad to the bar. "Sounds good to me." Then he turned and winked at me. That was when I knew for sure things were going to be fine between Jake and my father.

And now we were on vacation with everything right in our world. It felt so good I was a little afraid to enjoy it. But then again, we'd worked pretty hard to get where we were. So I decided to throw caution to the wind and just enjoy every second of my time with Jake.

The taxi ride across the island was bumpy and I enjoyed snuggling into Jake for comfort. We were only an hour's plane flight away from home and yet everything felt different. The tropical air had a different scent, it was more floral, less citrus. And the people vibrated at a different frequency. Their speech was staccato, fast and loud. Everything seemed to move at that higher frequency.

Our hotel, the British Colonial Hilton, was the same one we'd stayed at last time. It was a little quieter and a bit more romantic than the colossal Atlantis we looked at across the water. We'd stayed there in the past, too. It was fun there, always something new to do.

But we were here to relax.

Mostly, anyway. There was a snorkeling expedition, or two, or three . . .

But the rest of the time we relaxed on the beach, letting wandering waiters bring us delicious cocktails and hamburgers. Jake took me back to the Graycliff and we enjoyed a dinner on the porch. He bought a ridiculous number of cigars. He'd brought a small humidor with him just for that purchase.

And now we were back on the beach, our bellies full, our skin tan, and the moonlight reflecting off of everything around us.

I was starting to wonder if Jake's suggestion we take our money and run off to live on an island was a brilliant idea. If this was my one life with Jake, I didn't want to waste another second of it. Things like work and traffic seemed so pointless when there was sand between your toes.

He pulled me into his arms, my eyes catching on that gold chain again. He never wore it when we were swimming or on the beach. And he always seemed to have it tucked away out of sight. I didn't even know where he was hiding it in the hotel room.

"Darlin', I'm so glad we're back here. This trip has been amazing." His lips brushed against mine and his kisses took my breath away. It didn't seem possible he could still make me weak in the knees, but he did.

"I don't want to leave," I confessed.

He smiled his wicked smile. "We don't have to, you know. Offer still stands to find us a nice little house on a nice little island. We could raise some adorable water babies, have a lot of sex on the beach . . ."

I laughed and shook my head. "You're such a cocky bastard." It always came back to sex with Jake.

But he stopped joking, suddenly becoming very serious. So serious I stopped.

I couldn't breathe when he looked at me like that.

Then, while looking deep into my eyes he whispered, "Marry me."

I felt those two little words in every molecule of my body.

*Marry me.*

He pulled me closer, his arms wrapped tightly around me. "Will you do me the honor of being my wife? I want to give you everything I have. All of me is already yours forever, you know that, but I want to give you my name." His beautiful eyes sparkled with so much promise. "I want us to officially be a family, you and me, forever."

*His name.*

It was one of those moments where the world around us just stopped. For a few minutes nothing mattered but Jake and there was nothing I wanted more than to be his wife. "Oh, yes . . ." I whispered.

He smiled, looking at me ever so mischievously, and reached into his shirt for the gold chain.

On it was a ring.

He'd been wearing an engagement ring our entire fucking vacation.

"You had that this whole time? What have you been waiting for?" My voice was so high it didn't sound like me.

He bounced his eyebrows and his dimple showed up as his grin widened.

"The perfect moment."

"Why is this the perfect moment?" I asked wondering what hadn't been so perfect about just about any other second of every day since we got here.

Why had he been holding out on me?

He slid the chain over his head, unclasping it and sliding the ring down until it fell into the palm of his hand. "Sometimes, my love, waiting is worth it." He shoved the chain into his pants pocket and took my left hand in his. "Ten years ago I wasn't ready to be the man you deserved. I was a fool but I couldn't help falling in love with you. I will never be able to tell you how much I appreciate that you waited for me. And what we have now . . ." He shook his head and his eyes were bright. "The future we can build from here is so much more than it ever would have been. Sometimes," he got down on one knee, "waiting is so, so worth it."

He looked up at me and his eyes were shining, but his smile was wicked. He was the most handsome man I'd ever seen. It reminded me so much of the night I fell in love with him.

Maybe it was always that smile of his. I think it might be how I always think of Jake: wicked and sure, with a dimple put there just for me. He was exciting and safe and he was all mine.

"Eve Maria Daniels. Will you marry me?"

He slid the ring onto my finger. It fit perfectly. The diamond glinted back at me in the moonlight, set in a beautiful antique gold filigree. I stared at the ring on my finger and all that it meant. Finally, after all of these years, Jake and I were going to get married.

We were going to be husband and wife.

"Yes . . ." I whispered because that was all I could do. I didn't want to be a crier, but really, this was too special not to. I let the stupid tears do their thing.

Jake closed his eyes and squeezed my hand, pulling it to his lips. He tenderly kissed it, sending a shiver up my arm. Then he stood and pulled me into one of the dirtiest kisses I could ever remember. His tongue reached places I didn't know he could go and still feel good. His hands roamed, eventually finding their way up to my hair. And when I didn't think I could kiss him another moment without passing out, Jake pulled back and pressed our foreheads together.

"Damn, I love you."

"I love you, too," I replied. The crying was done, I

was grinning like a fool now.

Then he scooped me up. I squealed and he carried me back up to the hotel. In the lobby he waved over the concierge. "She said yes!"

The man nodded quickly, clapping his hands and ordering someone off toward who knew where. Obviously Jake had set up a plan for my positive response. The concierge ran to the elevator, pressing the button for us and holding the doors when they slid open. "Congratulations! Congratulations Mr. and soon-to-be Mrs. Spencer. Enjoy the rest of your evening."

"Mrs. Spencer," he whispered in my ear. It sent another one of those delicious shivers down my spine and straight between my legs. I knew what we were going to do once we got to our room and by the look in my fiancé's eyes, it was going to be wild and fun.

"I can't wait, Mr. Spencer. Can we have a fast wedding?"

He snorted, "Whatever Mrs. Spencer wants, Mrs. Spencer gets."

"Then let's elope. Let's go straight to Vegas."

Jake shook his head. "Nope. You may have fast, but not that fast. Mrs. Spencer is going to have a ridiculous wedding. You will wear a hot and expensive white dress, I will wear a fantastic tux, your sisters will stand by your side, your dad will walk you down the aisle, and we will eat a ridiculous amount of food before we dance until our feet fall off. Then I'm taking you on the honeymoon of your dreams and I'll fuck you in every way possible. I can't compromise on any of the above, darlin'. I'm sorry."

I was giggling uncontrollably by the time he was done. He was adorable in the best way possible. I was having a wedding. I was marrying Jake. And we were both happy.

The elevator door slid open and Jake took me to our door, which was open and waiting. A bellman was inside with a cart. A bucket with a bottle of champagne was on top.

Jake laid me out on the bed and I heard our door shut. My fiancé started to undress. His eyes were heated and locked onto mine as he slowly worked his way down the buttons.

"I get to call you my fiancée now. Much better than girlfriend, I hate that word." He wrinkled up his nose as he undid his cuffs.

"I'm yours now, what are you going to do to me?" I grinned with delight.

He tossed his shirt onto the chair and I took in all his muscular deliciousness. "I'm going to make you scream my name." He smiled and popped the cork, pouring two glasses.

The matter of fact way he just said that mixed with the very sexual pop of the cork and filling of the glasses . . . I trembled with anticipation.

Jake slid his hand all the way up my leg, pulling my dress up along with it. "You have some damn fine legs, Eve. I'd like to see them wrapped around me in about sixty seconds."

My breath caught as I pictured my bare legs

wrapped around Jake's tight waist. "I think I could be okay with that."

He handed me my glass. "Drink up, I'll also need to see your breasts smashed up against my chest."

The very thought of my body pressed up against his with my breasts the only thing keeping our bodies apart made me shiver. I was wet. I knew I was because I could feel the throbbing. My body wanted what he was promising.

His eyes heated as he watched me heaving. "Are you done?"

I gulped down another sip and shoved my glass back at him. "I'll finish it later," I breathed.

His eyebrows danced as he set both half-empty glasses down on the tray. Then his hand wandered up my leg again, but this time he didn't stop. He wandered all the way until his finger was inside me. His touch only made me want more.

After a moment of teasing he eased back out and stood, removing his pants, and watching me intently the whole time. By the time his cock sprang free, I was naked and waiting.

He slowly lowered his warm and heavy body onto mine. "Are you ready for this, Eve?" he asked, his voice rough and deep and full of double meanings.

I ran my hands along his jaw and up into his hair. "I've never been more ready than I am right now."

~~~~~~~~~~~

Thank you for reading Jake and Eve's story! If you enjoyed it, sign up for my newsletter. Subscribers get information on upcoming releases first!
If you have a moment, please leave an honest review where you bought this book. Reviews help authors be found by new readers.

Want more Jake and Eve? Turn the page to read a sneak peek at Reflected in the Rain!

THE STORM INSIDE SERIES
The Storm Inside - Jake & Eve Book 1
Reflected in the Rain - Jake & Eve Book 2
Never Let Go - Jake & Eve Book 3
When Lightning Strikes - Greg and Marie's story
Summer Heat - June's Story Coming Soon!

**More from Alexis Anne**

**The Storm Inside**
**Reflected in the Rain**
**When Lightning Strikes**
**Never Let Go**
**Tease**
**Stripped**
**Tempt**
**Burn**
**5 Dirty Sins**

**Box Sets:**
**The Storm Inside Box Set**
**Tease & Stripped Double Box Set**

# *Acknowledgements*

This book...you guys. This book is my life and my death. It is my pride and joy, and everything that makes me wince. Basically, it has my heart in it, so I love it and hate it equally (and at any given moment.) It's been on a wild ride of its own from the moment of its inception all the way through today. It's the wild ride that keeps on going, and for that I am eternally grateful. I owe so much to so many.

First off, I need to thank The Sexy Editor who not only read this book a billion times, but continues to calm me down. He brings me coffee in the mornings so I don't have to get out of bed. That means I get to start writing the moment my eyes open. He also generously volunteers to think through intense scenes before I write them. (You know which scenes I'm talking about!)

Mary Chris Escobar and Julia Kelly are my First Draught ladies and I'm absolutely positive I wouldn't be writing today without their love and support. You should check out our show. We're hilarious (and you can only imagine what we say when the camera is off!)

Jennifer Southard and LeElla Scott were my friends in high school, and to this day they both encourage me to keep writing. This book wouldn't exist without their support.

To all the platforms that have given The Storm Inside a chance, thank you. A little writer in this giant pond is lost without the support of the retailers and reading platforms.

And of course, to the fans, especially everyone in Coffee, Whiskey, and All Things Frisky. Writing is hard, but when you have fans asking for more, it gets a whole lot easier. Thank you!

*xoxo*
*Alexis*

## -BE A FRISKY FRIEND-

I'd love to have you join my Facebook reader group! Click on the link of search "Coffee, Whiskey, and all Things Frisky" on Facebook.

# About the Author

Alexis Anne is the author of the steamy *The Storm Inside* series and the sexy *Tease* serials. A recovering archaeologist, she loves writing stories about passionate people overcoming mistakes and finding where they belong (amidst some equally passionate sexy-times). Her heroines are smart, her heroes are strong, and her stories are always close to her own life experiences. She lives in Florida with The Sexy Editor, their two super heroes, and a dog who would be much happier in the snow (although he seems okay with the beach).

www.AlexisAnneBooks.com
alexisannebooks@gmail.com

Please visit me online!

Facebook: /AlexisAnneBooks
Instagram: @AlexisAnneAuthor
Twitter: @AlexisAnneBooks
Tumblr: @AlexisAnneAuthor

www.ingramcontent.com/pod-product-compliance
Lightning Source LLC
Chambersburg PA
CBHW030409180626
46812CB00005B/1984